SEDUCED BY THE SEA LORD

LORDS OF ATLANTIS

USA TODAY BESTSELLING AUTHOR

STARLA NIGHT

Copyright © 2017
All rights reserved

All product and company names are trademarks™ or registered® trademarks of their respective holders. Use of them does not imply any affiliation with or endorsement by them.

Cover by Earthly Charms
Edited by Linda Edits

For inquiries:

Starla Night
starla@starlanight.com
https://starlanight.com

SPECIAL THANKS

to Kara Lockhart, Angela McCallister, Nadine Mutas, Margo Bond Collins, and Andrea R. Collins for your insight, guidance, and assistance. You took this book from surface-level to the deep ocean.

and to A and Mr. E, for everything.

And special thanks to my newsletter subscribers! They enjoy bonus stories plus a steamy prequel novella, *Sea Lord's Castaway*. It takes place twenty years before the entire series, so there are no spoilers. It's just fun! Get it free at http://smarturl.it/StarlaNewsletter.

ONE

A dead body.

That was what had fouled her anchor chain.

Lucy broke the surface, spat out her snorkel, and rubbed fog from her mask. On the horizon, the setting sun lit the ocean on orange fire as it sank beneath the waves. Lucy barely had any time to dive, and now a dead body tangled her chain.

This was her third trip to the isolated atoll off Cancun in the Gulf of Mexico.

And it was officially cursed.

Her first trip, she'd discovered the largest Sea Opal in the world. Her second trip, she'd gotten engaged to her now ex-husband, who then made off with her Sea Opal.

On this third trip, Lucy was going to prove herself. Her good friend Mel had double-mortgaged her family house to fund the expedition.

Lucy was seriously worried about losing Mel's house.

Only ten minutes ago, she had waded into the trawler's waterlogged engine room for what was going to be her final Facebook Live expedition broadcast.

"Mel, as you can see, the leak's gotten worse. I'm heading back to port tonight. I should probably leave right now, but I can squeeze in one last dive. Something's out there. Something big." Lucy had squared her shoulders, made the victory sign, and grinned. "Let's see what I can haul up."

She'd signed off, gone to the deck to don her gear, and noticed the issue in her anchor chain. As if she didn't have enough problems with the trawler. Instead of putting on her scuba equipment, she'd snapped on the mask, snorkel, and plastic fins to do a quick review.

Then she'd found the body.

She could pretend she'd never seen him and search for her Sea Opal. But...she just couldn't. He had relatives. Friends. Maybe he even had kids.

They deserved closure.

Lucy replaced her mask, chomped her snorkel, and dove.

Her magenta plastic fins propelled her quickly below the thermocline into colder water, and her ears squeezed. She moved her jaw. Her ears popped.

The anchor chain clotheslined the man's midsection. His arms and legs hung off either side, horizontal in the current.

She grabbed his huge, muscled biceps.

His skin was slick, like trying to grab a fish. Her hand slid from his body.

Ew.

She grabbed his biceps with both hands and yanked.

His body rotated around the anchor chain. She tried again, and her lungs reminded her that she needed to breathe. He inched over the chain like an underwater pole vaulter scraping his thighs and knees. At his ankles, the chain hooked his feet.

His feet looked strangely giant from this perspective. Flattened out like wide scoops. She tugged, but he just was not going anywhere.

Her lungs convulsed.

Air!

Lucy raced for the surface. Her lips cleared the water. She spat her snorkel and gasped.

Could she haul him up with the anchor? Winding the chain would raise him closer to the surface, but it was sure to dislodge him. And by the time she donned her scuba gear, he might have already floated away.

The sun disappeared below the horizon.

Soon it would be too dark to see.

Lucy dove again.

The body hung from the anchor chain by one weirdly flat foot. She kicked too hard, overexerting herself as she reached out for him...and her lungs clenched.

Air!

She pivoted for the surface, broke out of the water, and clung to the bobbing ladder on her rusty trawler, gasping as she gathered her strength.

Maybe she couldn't save his body.

She wasn't the same person who had visited this atoll the other two times. She used to compete in triathlons, and now, she was fat. Old injection sites scarred her belly. She could hardly swim ten feet.

"Why would I want to stay married to you? Look at yourself. You're a failure as a woman and a failure as a human being."

Lucy sniffed and cleared her mask. Her problems weren't going anywhere. *Focus on the goal.*

She couldn't fight the current down to the man. She was already tired and overexerted, and crying didn't make her any stronger. How could she reach him?

By using the tools she already had.

Lucy located the anchor chain, took a deep breath, and followed it under the waves. Hand over hand, she guided herself down, resting on the chain instead of fighting the current.

This time, she wasn't coming up alone. No matter what.

The body was gone!

She hooked the chain with her legs and looked around.

There!

He drifted away, facedown, into the depths. She was about to lose him forever.

Lucy let go of the chain and kicked hard. Her lungs gave a warning. She reached his feet. Something was wrong. They were flat like fins. Ugh, were they disintegrating? Gross.

She grabbed an ankle joint. Hopefully, he'd stay together—yes, his ankle was firm, although slippery.

Lucy rotated for the surface and dragged him by the ankle.

He was heavy, awkward, and waterlogged.

Her lungs convulsed.

Almost there. The surface glimmered. Almost...

Air now!

She spat her snorkel and gasped.

Seawater hit the back of her throat.

Ack.

The surface broke around her like shattered glass.

She gagged up seawater. Her body trembled. A hundred years later, her throat finally cleared, and she could breathe. She swam against the current, dragging the man by his ankle, and grabbed the ladder.

He bobbed facedown in the mild waves.

Success!

Of course, it wasn't really a success. At the end of the day, which was literally right now, her expedition was still ruined, and this man was still dead.

Aside from his foot disfigurement, his body was in decent shape. He hadn't been in the water long.

She pulled him closer, skimming over the bulk of his impossibly broad, muscular back to reach his head. Intricate tribal tattoos shimmered like gold leaf on his bluish skin. Long white slashes raked his powerful shoulders. Propeller blades? The wounds were raw and deep, but no longer bleeding.

How bad was the front?

She steeled herself and rolled him over.

His face wasn't gross. Just sad.

Dark, scholarly brows, high cheeks like a haughty noble, an aquiline nose, and the firm chin of a man who was used to being obeyed. And more iridescent tattoos swirled across his cheekbones, above his forehead to the hairline, and under his jaw.

He seemed like more than a warrior, although he clearly had the brawn to back up his ideas. He'd been a man on a quest. A lone visionary.

More deep wounds raked his chest. She traced the gashes across his massive pectorals with her wrinkled fingertips. His body was the same temperature as the water.

Once, he had been handsome. Now, he was gone.

There were a hundred thousand ways to die at sea. Around Cancun, the most frequent cause was stupidity, such as leaning too far off the side of a cruise ship to capture the perfect selfie or throwing back a fifth of tequila before climbing on a JetSki.

But, with these deep claw marks, was he actually the victim of a deadly jungle panther, or—

Wait. What was that she felt? She rested her palm on the center of his chest.

Thub-thub. Thub-thub. Thub-thub.

Was that...a heartbeat?

Impossible. He had been submerged. And facedown. No—

The man spasmed.

Water splashed her mask.

Lucy shrieked.

His eyes fluttered open and struggled to focus.

He was still alive!

She gasped. "Are you okay?"

He focused on her. Aquamarine irises, like the ocean, were threaded with flecks of gold, impossible and gorgeous. And...didn't she know him? Somehow... Awareness flooded her veins, streaking her hot and cold and hot again. Unnatural recognition shuddered into her very soul.

His mouth opened and closed.

The man moaned and slipped into unconsciousness again.

Her heart pounded louder than a steel drum band.

The man was alive.

Get him out, drain the water from his lungs, warm him up, and get him to a hospital.

She wrapped the man in a secure net and winched him onto the trawler deck, then hung him upside down. Water poured out his mouth. He coughed raggedly.

She lowered him to the deck, freed him from the net,

and checked his vitals. Labored breathing, but his heart was strong, and his skin had already started warming.

He would survive.

The first stars twinkled in the beautiful indigo sky.

He was much heavier above the water.

Lucy dragged him down the stairs and through the living area to the cabins. A powerlifting routine would have seriously helped her for this moment. Huffing and puffing, she brute-forced him onto the guest bunk.

Under the bare bulb, his skin was as pale blue as the water around Cozumel. Its color made the gold tattoos even more unreal. They swirled around his crushing biceps, across his well-defined six-pack, below his masculine waist, and even around his...oh.

A massive blue cock hung between his bulging thighs. Gold tattoos spiraled around the thick shaft to the tip.

Maybe he hadn't lost his clothes to the current. Maybe he walked around nude. Anyone would be proud of that endowment.

She covered him with cotton blankets to warm him and to preserve his modesty. Just in case.

His chest rose and fell. Tendrils of dark hair accented his determined brow. She smoothed the silken threads.

How had he ended up here?

He clenched a ball of seaweed in his hand. She tugged at the strings. He moaned and gripped harder.

Fine. Keep it.

Lucy rested on her heels. She trembled from exhaustion. Her expedition was screwed, but she had saved a man's life. She'd figure out something in Cancun. Now, she was cold and ravenous.

She tossed on a swim cover, raised the anchor, and set her course for the mainland.

TWO

orun opened his eyes.

He was dry and in some kind of wood box. A loud rumble masked his surroundings, coating his senses in a thick layer of impenetrable silt. High-pitched, buzzing lights washed out the interior. Air wafted across his skin.

Where was he?

He jerked upright.

His head bashed a low overhang with a resounding *gong*.

He fell back. The gong reverberated in his skull, and a second *thunk* sounded below his resting platform.

Oof.

He lay still until the throb in his head receded and reason returned.

The mer would never transport him through the air. He must have been captured by humans.

How lucky.

He rose more carefully, ducked out from under the low overhang, and rested his human feet on the floor. He was on a boat, wrapped in some sort of cloth. Perhaps he was in one of their wooden sleeping places. What was it called? A bunk?

A woman appeared in the doorway. "Hello?"

Praise the Life Tree.

Her soul light shone in her chest brighter than any he'd ever seen. Brighter than any of the beautiful women who swam around the shores of Cancun. Brighter even than the sun.

She was his soul mate.

His chest lifted. Finally! After days of searching, after a desperate fight for his life, after defying his city and the rules of the mer, his quest was over. He'd found her.

His one.

"You're awake." His soul mate's lips pursed. "Are you okay?"

Her voice was quiet and musical, like all humans', and her words were created by an alluring movement of her lips in concert with her tongue. They crossed the air to his ears and tickled. Huh. So different from his normal method of communication, but one he had trained for his entire life.

Her chin lowered. "You are okay, aren't you?"

He forced his lips into position. "Yes."

"Oh, good." She sighed and smiled. "Welcome back to the land of the living. I just dragged you out of the ocean."

"I am today's catch."

She blinked. "Ha! I guess you are. How's your throat?"

He touched his neck. "It is raw." The vibration on his throat when he spoke tickled his fingers strangely.

"You took in a lot of seawater." She stepped into the small room.

Her body was perfect. Soft and delectably round, with dark eyes and hair the color of fine wood. Large breasts and generous hips teased him beneath her thin white covering. Pink algae colored her toes and fingernails. No, not algae. What had he researched? A colored lacquer called "nail polish." What a playful human decoration.

"And something chewed you up pretty badly." Her brows pulled together in gentle concern. "Oh, that's funny. I thought the wounds were a lot deeper."

He brushed the shallow scabs. "I heal quickly."

"I'll say." She shook her head, and her damp hair rustled against her white covering. "Only half an hour ago, I would have sworn that you'd ended up on the wrong side of an outboard motor. Now, you look like you tangled with a mildly irritated house cat."

"Is it a problem?"

"Only for me. And my mental capacity." She rubbed her forehead and emitted a shallow huff. "So much has gone wrong recently, and just now, I thought...Well, if I can't trust my own judgment, what can I trust?"

Her soul light dimmed.

No. The brilliance of his destined mate must never fade. His nearness should only ever make her shine bright.

"You can trust me," he said.

She snorted. A smile broke across her sweet face, and her soul brightened. "I don't even know your name."

"I am Torun, honored warlord of Sireno."

"A warlord? Wow." She moved another step closer, placing herself within arm's reach. "I've never heard of Sireno."

"It is far."

"Right. Okay. I'm Lucy. Lucy Shaw Edwards—" Her light dipped. "Uh, I mean, just Lucy Shaw."

Hmm.

A warrior's soul never faded or blazed in quick succession as Lucy's did. She seemed to move from one extreme to the other with minimal suffering.

How?

The sacred island brides, like the warriors, had always controlled their soul lights—so far as Torun could remember. It had been a long, long time since he'd seen a sacred island bride.

Was it because she was a mainland woman?

The Sireno elders said mainland women would never acclimate to the ways of the mer. But this woman, Lucy, *was* his mate. He knew it.

Unless... His senses *were* muted by the air and the rumbling noise...

"Lucy."

She focused on him.

He took her hand and stroked her strong scuffed and scratched fingers. "You are not afraid of the water?"

"Only when it comes pouring in from a crack in the hull." She stared at their joined hands.

"But you would be unafraid to live beneath the sea?"

"Oh, yeah, if I could score a spot as a submersible pilot, like for one of the oceanographic institutes, I'd be set. That's living the dream."

He understood about half of those words. "Living under the sea is your dream?"

"Sure, I'd love it." She traced the iridescent gold honor markings on his knuckles with a gentle index finger. "These tattoos are amazing."

"They tell my history."

"How did you make this color?"

"It is natural." He captured her wandering fingers. "Are you seeking a male to join with?"

Heat flushed across her skin, turning her cheeks a delicate pink, and her lips parted. "Join with?"

"Together. Here. You and I joining as one." He brought her fingers to his mouth. She tasted like the sea.

She closed her eyes and sucked in a breath. "Mm."

The quiet moan was more than enough answer. Her unspoken desires flowed into his awareness. Arousal pounded in her heartbeat, desire strengthened her hands grasping his, hunger sounded in the hitch of her breath. She needed a male.

She needed him.

He drew her arms around his shoulders. "On behalf of the mer of Sireno, I claim you for my bride."

Her eyelashes fluttered. "What?"

He sought her lips.

She resisted and then melted.

His.

Lucy was soft as floating seaweed, yet firm as a slippery fish. Her lips tasted hot and sweet, a flavor he had never known, but which curled deep in his belly and gave him a hard tug. He tilted her head to fully mesh their mouths.

With a hungry, feminine moan, she yielded.

He delved deep, discovering her shape, stroking neat teeth and dark crevices. She yielded to his insistent thrusting and then matched his demand, tangling him with her tongue. Waves of heat rolled off her body. She gasped for breath as if coming up for air, then dove back into his unyielding seduction.

Lucy was his bride. No other warrior would ever kiss her mouth. "You are mine."

Her soul flared even brighter. She accepted his claim in her soul.

Yes.

He took her mouth again.

She sank into his domination.

Lucy was his.

Torun curved an arm around her generous hips and lifted her onto the bunk.

He would claim his bride!

THREE

One moment, Lucy was leaving the galley to investigate a noise in the guest bunk, and the next moment, she was deliciously crushed by the most virile wall of masculinity ever to wash up on her trawler.

Torun tasted like sea salt and heat. His powerful biceps clenched with strength before lifting her as though she weighed no more than a twig.

This was crazy.

She tore her mouth free. "What are you doing?"

"Claiming you." His aquamarine eyes glowed with ferocious possession. He repeated in a deep tone that sent pleased shivers up her spine, "You are mine."

His? She was his?

A hard, gorgeous warrior took one look at her, Lucy, and was so swept away by passion that he had to have her this instant?

He consumed her hesitation once more with his kiss.

His embrace was passionate and demanding. Waves of

heat welled up in her cold, empty body like an unstoppable ocean tide.

This, finally, was what she had needed for so, so long.

And yet, he was gentle.

His iron forearm pillowed her head, and his huge hand clasped her hip, pressing her securely to the narrow bunk. All his weight balanced on his elbow, sheltering her, and that wasn't easy to do. She'd had her share of uncomfortable bunk encounters over the years.

But he was also fierce.

His tongue pulsed into her mouth. His firm cock pressed deliciously against her upper thigh.

He *was* claiming her. Right now.

And she...

She was going to let him.

A sweet, pounding ache twisted between her legs. Her center slickened with readiness. This powerful wall of male was claiming her for his own. Every cell in her body screamed *yes, more, now*.

On cue, the engine shuddered and began to squeal.

Low oil.

She jerked back.

Her warrior stared down at her with powerful intensity. "Do not withdraw from our joining."

"No, I love it."

He lowered his head to continue.

She put her hand on his mouth. "Stay right here."

"But—"

Another shriek sent a shudder through the hull.

"Don't move." She bolted from the bunk. "I'll be right back."

"Lucy!"

She raced through the tiny galley and splashed into the waterlogged engine room.

Her old dive shop boss had called this trawler—once a gorgeous Selene 43, now a salvage with *Missy B* on its patched hull—an opportunity. It had some character, like a slow oil leak.

Of course, speed was relative.

She ripped the seal from another carton of her bulk Costco oil purchase and poured the whole quart into its well. *Glug, glug, glug.* The engine smoothed from that of an unbalanced washing machine to a rough growl.

Crisis momentarily delayed.

Seawater seeped into the hold from an actual hull leak. Which, by the way, was *not* character or opportunity. It was a full, actual ocean emergency. She ought to have returned to Cancun the instant she'd discovered it, but how would she and Mel afford another tank of fuel?

Please just work a little bit longer. There's a real opportunity in the guest bunk, waiting for me.

But she had to check the bailing capacity of the backup generator. If it failed, she'd end up on the bottom of the sea. Lucy sucked in her gut and squeezed around the tight corner.

Her white tankini top caught on a sharp edge and tore.

Aw.

Her fat, pale, needle-scarred belly flopped out.

She stopped and pushed the two pieces of fabric together as if her six-dollar tankini could heal itself like Torun somehow had.

But Torun hadn't really healed. She'd just misjudged his injuries.

Like she'd misjudged everything else.

Lucy let go and exhaled. Her belly made an unfortunate shelf on the generator.

What was she doing?

Only a short time ago, she'd been running high-class expeditions for Van Cartier Cosmetics, the company that had bought her Sea Opal. They'd hired her and her ex-husband, Blake, to search for more of the precious gems. Van Cartier Cosmetics was located in Florida, and Blake had insisted they search the Keys before expanding elsewhere, but Lucy had always wanted to return to Cancun. There was more by this atoll, hidden beneath the surface, than she could see. She just knew it.

But Blake had disagreed, and after the divorce, he'd managed to keep the great job with pristine boats and paid company housing. Lucy had been tossed out.

And now...

Seriously, what was she doing? She was too big, too desperate, and too busy driving a zombie trawler *actively sinking* to think about a one-night stand with a half-drowned stranger.

Even in her wild single days when she'd been a broke dive master at the Cancun dive shop, Lucy had never slept with a guy five minutes after meeting him. What if he was a jerk? Or dangerous? Or *married*?

Something was wrong with her.

She exhaled heavily and focused on the backup generator.

"Lucy?" Torun's large shadow filled the engine room door.

"I'm here."

"I cannot sense you."

"Be right there." She squeezed out from behind the backup generator, capped the empty bottle of oil, and tossed it back in the mildewed Costco box. "Don't worry. We should still be able to limp into port—"

He pitched forward

"Whoa!" She caught him, setting her feet to support the heavy mass of hard muscle. "It's okay. I've got you."

"Forgive me." His head rested against her chest. "I am not ready to walk as a human."

Human?

English was definitely not his first language. His tribal accent was so unique. Lucy could listen to his seductive bass all night long.

"You've been through a lot." She helped him stagger into the galley and collapse in the dining booth. The bench sagged under his weight.

He relaxed, fully comfortable revealing his gloriously powerful gold-swirled cock.

Oh.

Yes.

Kissing him had been mind-meltingly delicious. How would his hot, hard cock feel thrusting deep into her slippery wet pussy? The question made her quiver.

Oh.

No.

She'd just had a whole conversation with herself about her judgment, and here she was, moments later, fantasizing about bad choices again. Her mind was going. She was seriously losing it.

Lucy retrieved the blanket, tucked it around him—for *her* sake—and brought him a bottle of water. "You're probably weak from low blood sugar. Let me check our position. Then I'll get you something to eat."

He grunted.

Lucy raced up to the cockpit.

The one system that had been easy to repair was radar, and since it was going on midnight, all sorts of marine hazards had to be avoided.

The route was clear.

Down the hatch again, she banged the unresponsive kettle against the dented wall.

Its light blinked on.

Good kettle.

She let it boil on the counter, ripped open two packages of Swiss Miss, and poured the powder into plastic mugs. Her dad always made hot cocoa on their voyages. She continued the tradition, swirling boiled water into the mixes and completing the meal with peanut butter chocolate chip Clif Bars.

A gourmet cook she was not.

She checked the radar, and then served the meal and sat across from him. His water bottle was untouched.

Torun eyed the dinged mug with a frown. "This is...?"

"Cocoa." She blew across her steaming mug. "It's got some quick sugar to pick you up. Oh, and drink that bottled water. You're probably dehydrated."

He jabbed a finger in his cocoa. "It is hot!"

"Right, you should let it—"

"No, Lucy. Do not consume that heated water!" He knocked the mug from her hand. Hot cocoa splashed the stained deck. Her mug bounced.

"Hey! My cocoa." She scooted across the bench and stood to clean up.

"Wait. It is still dangerous." He caught her arm. His grip was like steel. "You will injure yourself."

Whoa. His hand spanned her whole biceps.

She shivered with his touch.

He could grip her hips just as hard as she bounced on his cock...

No. Stop it.

She coughed and focused on his words. "Come on. I've kept myself alive for thirty-five years. I'm not *that* hopeless."

"You must always take care around heated water." He released her more calmly. "That is why we avoid foreign currents, and if we must take them, we always watch for the slightest shimmer. The warning is too easy to miss. Heated water can boil you to a painful death."

"I have no idea what you mean about currents, but I assure you that I haven't given myself a pizza burn in, oh, at least a week." She mopped up the spill and started the kettle again. "Anyway, one hot cocoa isn't going to kill you."

"Is it not?" He stared at his mug. "It steams like an undersea vent."

Huh. His tribe must be amazing free divers, and Sireno must be located next to an undersea volcano.

"Here." She cracked the cap and handed him the water bottle. "Drink this. It'll clear your mind."

He tentatively took the bottle, tested the liquid with his tongue, and frowned. "What is it?"

"Water."

"It tastes strange."

"Yeah, the minerals are probably different than you're used to. It's safe, though. I bought it sterilized."

"What is the meaning, 'sterilized'?"

"It's not going to give you Montezuma's revenge." She carried a new cup of steaming cocoa back to her seat, ignored his skeptical look, and blew the steam again. "There are no bugs."

"Does this, then, have bugs?" He indicated the cocoa.

"No." She snorted. "I used bottled water. I don't want to make myself sick."

"It is a muddy color."

"Have you never had cocoa before? That's funny because it's, you know, from Mexico. Where exactly is Sireno?"

"The Ixotlana Plains."

"Where's that?"

He pointed at the stained floor. "Ten songs."

What did that even mean? South of Cancun? Really south. "Cocoa is liquid chocolate. Try it."

He cautiously dipped his blunt index finger in the liquid, then more deeply. Satisfied it was cool, he gripped the mug with both hands and, shaking with concentration, brought it to his lips. He tilted it with his whole body. Did his tribe not have cups? His knuckles whitened. He lowered the mug, sweating with the effort, and then swallowed and rubbed his tongue across the roof of his mouth.

"Well?"

He took another determined sip. "It is a sweet *xocoatl*. No spice, yet invigorating. No bitterness, yet it awakens the senses. It is good."

She laughed. "Whew. Glad to hear it."

Nothing beat a mug of hot cocoa after a long, cold workout. It always brought tingling warmth into her limbs.

His answering laugh rumbled low in his chest.

Nothing beat his laugh for causing delicious, chocolate-like tingles in her body. Yum and double yum.

"So, you're a warlord from Sireno." It was funny to trade introductions after being flat on his bunk making out, but it answered the first of her many questions. "How'd you end up out here? Do you know what caused all your injuries?"

"My warriors."

"Your own people turned on you? I'm so sorry."

"Do not be. Watching my warriors use the skills I taught them to nearly capture me was perhaps one of my proudest moments as a trainer."

"Oh. So it was a training accident?"

"No, it was no accident. They tried their hardest to defeat me."

"Why?"

"They wished to prevent me from seeking my bride." He set aside the mug and drew her hand to his mouth and pressed a devoted kiss to her palm. "But they could not stop destiny. Their attack led me to you, Lucy."

Her heart quickened.

What would it be like to marry a tribal warlord? Would she enjoy long days of ruling over warriors, adventuring in the jungle, and fishing in the restless seas? Or endless nights of sensual pleasures, sweet promises murmured after midnight, and sleeping deep in his intricately tattooed arms?

"Accept my claim and join with me." Torun placed a tingling kiss higher on her sensitized wrist. "We will go to Sireno and share our vows before the Life Tree. Come, my bride."

Energy pulsed through her body. Her muscles twitched with readiness.

This was what she'd always wanted. What she'd been seeking her whole life. She was so ready to surge out of her seat, accept his proposal, and quit the expedition...

Thereby losing Mel's house.

Because of a stranger she'd just met.

And a future she could barely imagine.

Right.

"It's not that I don't want to." She extricated her hand. A heavy, dark pressure settled on her torso as if she'd shouldered three oxygen tanks and ten fully-loaded weight belts. It matched the frown on Torun's face. "And I really shouldn't want to. It's crazy. What you're asking is absolutely, wonderfully insane. I don't know why I'm so weirdly tempted."

"You are tempted because we are soul mates." Torun gazed at her with total devotion. "Your soul resonates only with mine. Mine resonates only with yours. Why do you not sense this as I do?"

"Well, I think I do. Weirdly." She rubbed her chest, even though she really ought to be knocking herself on the head for her strange thoughts. "I don't want another doomed rebound relationship. Even though the others didn't make me feel a fraction of the temptation you have, I'm sure once my head cools off, I'd tell you the same thing I told them: I'm never getting married again."

FOUR

"So I can't be your bride." Lucy curled her fingers, so recently in his grasp, around her mug. "Sorry."

But she had to be.

This *was* destiny.

She had rescued him. Her soul resonated with his.

And just now, when she rejected him, her soul darkened to match the night.

Torun slid around the booth until his leg rested flush against hers and cupped her firm jaw. "You are mine."

Her soul brightened. Her lips quirked to the side. "I wish."

"Yes? Good." His thumb stroked the softness of her cheek. "Then accept my claim."

Her lashes fluttered. A sweet, needy moan emerged from her lips.

He tipped her head back to accept his kiss.

"Mm. Wait, no." She pushed his face back and straightened, frowning. "I keep thinking one thing and then find myself doing the opposite."

"Because joining is our destiny."

"Yeah, that's the part where I'm not convinced." She opened the crinkly wrapper and handed him a thick bar. "Eat. You need the calories. And I need to think."

He obeyed, chewing the dense wedge of strangely flavored sustenance.

She felt their connection. Her soul light flared brighter with his touch. What more convincing did she need?

Ah. Of course.

He must give her his mating jewel. Then she would realize he was her mate.

Torun patted his bare waist.

Claiming a mainland bride was against the rules of the mer, and so his elders had sent an entire unit to stop him. But only the best two warriors had managed to track him to the correct shore and corner him in a fight.

Torun had tricked them into tight quarters against a reef, then pivoted to steal Malem's trident. Malem had successfully resisted, and Torun had wasted precious moments grappling with him. Prince Jolan had used his distraction to slice into the seaweed pouch tied around Torun's waist, spilling all but one of his mating jewels, then his blade had bitten deep into Torun's shoulder blades.

Torun had arched in pain.

Malem had stopped fighting him out of concern. "Warlord Torun, do you yield?"

Both their hands had still gripped Malem's trident.

Prince Jolan had floated back at a safe distance. "Yield, Warlord Torun."

Torun gathered his strength. "I...will..."

Malem's grip had loosened.

"...*never* yield!" Torun had finally wrested Malem's trident away.

Both warriors had jolted in surprise.

He'd whirled and struck Jolan's brow with the solid base. The turquoise prince's eyes had rolled back into his head. He had collapsed.

"No!" Malem had gathered Prince Jolan's vulnerable body to his purple-tattooed chest. "You will pay for striking your prince. The entire city will turn against you. I will destroy your Life Tree seed with my bare hands!"

Torun had swum away with Malem's trident and one single mating jewel in his pouch.

But his warriors had performed well. Torun's blood had flowed heavily into the current, and he'd had to evade opportunistic surface predators before weakness had stolen over his body. He must have lost consciousness and drifted on the currents. That must have been when he'd dropped Malem's trident and the last mating jewel.

Destiny, surely the work of the Life Tree, had washed him across Lucy's path.

But it had also stolen his mating gemstone.

How bitter.

But there was a place he could get more. Very near, in fact.

He scooted around the booth and rose, the human cloth slung low on his hips.

She watched him. "Where are you going?"

"I will bring you my offering."

"Offering?"

"So that you will know our joining is destiny."

"Huh? Oh! Wait." She jumped up and hooked his elbow. "No, no. It's not you. I'm divorced."

He tilted his head. That word had no meaning.

"Do you have divorce in your tribe? It means I had a husband, and he's long gone."

She had a husband.

The blood in Torun's veins turned to ice. He stepped back. "You have a husband."

"Had. Past tense."

Cold clawed into Torun's spine. If a warrior touched another's bride, even to save her life, her husband was justified in taking his revenge, cutting off the flesh that had touched, making sure he was banished from his city or executed.

His hands had touched Lucy's skin; his arms had embraced her soft body; his lips had pressed against hers. She was *his*. And yet, she belonged to another male?

"It didn't work out." She clung more tightly to his elbow, the one that he really enjoyed holding her with and would be sad to lose to a vengeful husband. "I couldn't give Blake what he wanted. He left me for a woman who could."

Lucy's husband had chosen another woman?

Torun pivoted to face her. "How could your husband do such a thing?"

"Oh, I've asked myself that a thousand times, but—"

"Were you truly his bride? Did you not share vows?"

"We did, but..."

"But what?"

"Well, things change. You think you're marrying one person, and then you find out they're someone else."

"That is why your souls must resonate." He pressed his hand to her glowing chest. "Do you not feel this connection? A warrior never abandons his mate. Near or far, our bond is forever."

She swallowed. "Yeah...well, I used to think stuff like that, but now...I don't even know if 'forever' exists anymore."

"Until death, then."

She took a shaky breath. "Yeah. Um...I better go check

the radar." She squeezed past him and climbed the stairs. The fabric that had been tied around his waist fell off and pooled at his feet.

Humans were different.

Yes.

Humans were very different. Lucy's past relationships had been with humans. They had not shared vows before a Life Tree. That was why their souls resonated now. Lucy's past did not matter.

Lucy belonged to *him*.

At the top of the stairs, well lit by the lights on the deck, she paused and stretched. Her bountiful breasts swelled the white covering. Her dark hair tumbled over her generous curves. She was a goddess. A perfect female. Everything he had ever wanted and more.

She glanced back. "You're naked and staring."

"You are female."

She snorted and dropped her arms, adjusting her covering. "You noticed, huh?"

"Yes."

Her breasts were a good size for filling his hands, and her body was soft and perfect for squeezing. Her pleasure-filled moans sounded sweeter than any ocean song.

Her shoulders hunched. "Okay. Seriously. What are you looking at?"

"Your body."

"Ugh. Don't judge by what you see right—"

"It is beautiful."

She hesitated. "Why would you say that?"

"Because it is true." He would plunge his cock deep into her liquid channel, thrusting over and over, inexhaustible at her command. And when she surged from pleasure and begged him to release, he would fill her fertile womb with his male seed.

Her hungry eyes trailed down his nude body to his hardening cock and lingered.

He flexed.

Her eyes glazed, and her tongue touched her lip.

Lucy suddenly blinked and shook her head. Stepping back, she pivoted away from the stairs. "You should have seen me five years ago."

"I see you now." He climbed the stairs, hunting her, and drew her into his arms. His ready cock pressed against her soft thigh. "You are my bride."

She moaned. "It's crazy how unbelievably tempted I am to say yes."

"Say yes."

"No." She stroked his taut pectoral. "Look. I have to get this boat back to dock and repaired. And then I owe kind of a lot of people kind of a lot of money. And then after that... well, maybe I could come and visit you in Sireno."

"No one visits Sireno."

"Okay, well, maybe you could come and visit me."

"That is—"

"Nobody is making life-changing decisions at midnight in a zombie trawler. We'll dock and figure everything out tomorrow on dry land."

Dry land?

Uh-oh. "We have no need for the mainland."

"Well, it doesn't matter, because we've almost arrived." She eased out of his arms.

Could this rattling actually be the ship's engine? Was this rocking the sensation of movement across the *surface* of the ocean? Could he be slipping further from his goal to take his bride back to Sireno now that he had finally found her?

The ocean moved under their hull, and the night sky lightened with a distant city.

Dread seeped into his stomach.

The mainland.

She walked to a booth, leaned over a board full of blinking lights, and clicked round pebbles.

"Anchor," he ordered. "Now."

"We're in the middle of a shipping lane." She picked up a glowing rectangular device and studied it, swiping her finger across it and pausing intently. "A new expedition backer? Wow…"

"We must return to the atoll."

"We've got to dock before the ship sinks." She set down the rectangular device, unfolded another long cloth, and secured it around his waist. "There. Try to keep this towel on, okay? I don't have any shorts that will fit you."

"You must not go to the mainland."

"Why?" She rested a calming hand on his forearm. "Are you trembling? Oh my God. Are we in danger?"

"Yes."

"From what?"

"It is too complicated to explain. You must trust me."

"I would love to, but others are counting on me, and…" She looked down at her glowing instrument panel, out at the city lights, and then back at him. "Give me something to trust."

Curse it. He gritted his teeth. "I cannot reveal my existence to mainland humans."

Her brows lifted. "Did the government oppress your tribe and take your homeland?"

"No. They cannot take my homeland. We dwell too

deep beneath the surface of the ocean for any humans to reach."

She frowned.

"You are a mainland woman, Lucy, so I had wished to explain this after you accepted my claim. But you leave me no choice." He took her hands firmly, set his feet, and did his best to convince her without a mating gemstone. "I am a mer warrior, Lucy. You are my mate. After we pledge our devotion before the Life Tree of Sireno, you will prove to the council that a mainland female can join with a warrior just as well as any sacred island bride."

"I'm sorry. Life Tree? Sacred island bride?"

"You must descend to the bottom of the ocean and save my race. Join with me now and become my mer queen."

FIVE

"Mer?" Lucy repeated, feeling like an idiot. "As in mer...maid? Queen?"

His aquamarine gaze was so intent. In the dim light, the gold threads shone iridescent. "Embrace your destiny. Join with me."

Torun's words awoke something in Lucy's soul.

"Join with me and become my mer queen."

She longed to say yes. She longed to run her hands across this warrior's broad pectorals, down to his tapered waist, close her hands around his massive cock, and follow with her tongue. She longed to give him even temporary happiness and rediscover her own in the process.

But she couldn't.

Because that was *crazy talk.*

Torun had a shiny dark bruise on his forehead. It must have scrambled his brain. He'd also drunk gallons of salt water. And didn't dehydration cause hallucinations?

His earnest, chiseled face awaited her answer.

Hmm. She didn't have much experience with temporary insanity. Was she supposed to go along with the hallucination or try to return him to reality?

He'd been through a lot today.

Lucy touched his rough jaw. "I wish I could."

"Good. I grant your wish."

"I *wish*"—she emphasized, stroking her index finger along his powerfully masculine jaw, trying to ignore the answering pulse of desire in her body—"but I'm not the mermaid-queen type."

"You are." He squeezed her. "I have seen a thousand women on the shore. You are mine."

Oh.

Wow.

He had seen a thousand women and chosen her.

Stardust fell on her soul, twinkling with beauty and promise.

Why did her good intentions keep getting derailed? Why was she so tempted to forget her responsibilities and throw herself at this strange warrior?

Perhaps it was the way he towered over her, powerful and gorgeous, and begged her to join with him.

Well, since he *begged* her...

"Sorry," she repeated, more to herself than to him, "but I'm definitely not. And once a doctor checks you over, you'll know that too."

"On behalf of the mermen of Sireno, you must accept my claim."

Thinking he was a merman was a totally plausible hallucination. He had survived drowning.

"Mermen? So, there are more than one of you, huh?"

He nodded.

"And are you all men who are half fish?"

"We are not fish." He lifted his noble chin. "Nor are we men. We are marine warriors."

Uh-huh.

"Well." She pointedly cast her gaze from the top of his dark head to the bottom of his normal human feet. "You sure look like a man right now."

"I shift in the water."

Wait.

His feet had seemed oddly large and flat, like fins. And his skin had been oddly slippery as a fish. What about the tattoos? They were iridescent, almost like scales...

What if it wasn't a knock to the head? What if it wasn't a delusion from near drowning? What if he was telling the truth?

"We must go now to Sireno," Torun continued. "It lies ten songs from the atoll."

"Songs. I remember." This was nuts. "Songs of what?"

"Giant cave guardians."

"Okay. Sure. Giant cave guardians. Which are?"

"You call a cave guardian an octopus."

"I do? Sure I do. Every day," she said, shaking her head. This craziness was like a fractal expanding ever outward. "And they sing? Octopuses, I mean."

"Terribly."

"Of course they do." Lucy extricated herself from his arms and focused on the radar. Obviously, *she* was the one who had been drinking the seawater.

"Lucy, your shine is diminishing."

"Is it?" She tsked. "Funny how a girl can lose her shine when things don't go your way."

"Now your light is almost completely out. Mainland women flicker so strangely."

"Probably you're just catching me from a different

angle." She kept a steady hand on the steering wheel and a steadier eye on the instruments. "I look thinner from the front."

The mega-resorts of Cancun stained the night sky and washed out the stars.

Perhaps, when the swelling went down in his brain, he'd look her up. Thank her for dragging him onboard and saving his life. Maybe he'd even volunteer to join a future expedition. She could use another hand, so long as it was free.

Oh, his wide, sexy hands.

Sliding down her back, scooping her under the butt, squeezing...

Speaking of the expedition, she'd forgotten to document this event. She took her phone out of its undersea case, queued the live broadcast, and trained the camera on herself.

"Hi, Mel. Here's the prize I pulled out of the water." She turned the camera on Torun. "He insists he's a merman, and I'm supposed to be his bride."

"Mer queen," he corrected.

"Mer bride, mer queen, what's the difference?"

"A bride joins with her male and returns alone to the surface. A queen joins the city forever."

A shiver of awareness sizzled through her.

Lucy quelled it. "Well, that sounds important. You'll definitely need the right woman for the job."

"The right woman is you."

Heat flushed through her pores.

"You shine brighter than the sun." He stepped forward, totally ignoring the camera. "You must stand with me against the council and liberate our race. Why do you hesitate?"

She wanted it to be true.

Of course, she'd wanted a lot of things in her life. "Smile for Mel."

He looked deeply into the camera. The intensity lit by the dash lights would certainly give her old friend something to appreciate. He was gorgeous and absolutely bonkers.

"What is Mel?" he asked.

"An old friend. This is her boat we're standing on. Well, it's technically mine, but she bought it."

He frowned.

"Don't be sad. I wanted her to hear your message. You make revolution sound very attractive."

"Attractive? You do not believe me."

"I think you need a long rest." Lucy trained the camera on herself once more. "Sorry about the last dive. I got your email about a new backer, and I can't wait to see you too."

Lucy ended the broadcast and turned to Torun. "And we'll get you all the help you need."

"Lucy." Torun's deep bass voice tightened with a terrible urgency. "I do not have the offering you deserve. My pouch fell from my grip before I ever reached you. But—"

Pouch? "So that's what you were holding."

"I...what?"

"Some pouch. I thought it was seaweed. You were holding it so tight, I couldn't get it out of your hand." She led him down the stairs to the guest room and peered around the few bolted-down furnishings. "You had it in the bunk... There!" She pulled it out triumphantly. "Here you go."

He fell upon the pouch. His aquamarine eyes shone.

He fished something out. "Now, you will become my queen."

"Are you forgetting everything we just talked about?" Right. Head injury. "I guess that's pretty common, probably."

She turned on her heel and huffed back up to the cockpit. This close to Cancun, if she left the radar unattended too long, she was likely to broadside a cruise ship.

"Lucy." He followed her with a new intensity. "You will accept."

"Forget it."

"Look here."

"Give it up." She did not want to spend even one second staring into his gorgeous eyes and fantasizing about things she should not have. "There's not a single thing you could show me that would change my mind."

He lowered his palm to her level. In his grip rested a gigantic Sea Opal.

SIX

N o way.

Lucy almost dropped her cell phone. "That's a…"

"It is my offering," the crazy, sexy, *supposed* merman said. "Come to Sireno with me now."

The Sea Opal reflected the meager dashboard lights around the pilot booth, and it gleamed as though a thousand stars burned within its pearly white depths.

It was nearly twice as large as the one she'd found before.

Mexico was the place to find them! Not the Keys. Mexico wasn't exhausted yet, not by a long shot. Take that, stupid Blake! Lucy had been right!

Lucy licked her dry lips.

This jewel would get the collection agencies off her back, cancel her loans, pay off her credit cards, and show up her ex-husband, all in one. This was her redemption and triumph.

She reached out, her fingers trembling. "You found this?"

"It is the resin of our Life Tree."

"Are there more?"

"Many more." His deep voice rumbled with need. "Our Life Tree has not flowered in so long. It is dying. Our race is dying. Only you can save us, Lucy."

Only she could save them...

She took the Sea Opal.

It felt cool in her palm and heavy with promise.

Promise of hot nights, long showers, and delicious, lazy afternoons under the covers. With Torun. A warrior who needed his head examined.

If she dared to accept this... Well, he hadn't *said* he wanted children...

"I'm going to hell," she murmured, for even thinking about it.

"You are going with me." He drew her into his arms and cupped her neck. "By the covenant, I claim you for my bride."

His mouth descended, and she lost herself in his kiss.

This time, she didn't fight it.

At their touch, her body throbbed with need. Arousal ached, hunger for Torun heating her to the core.

His lips were cool and tasted of salt. His wide palms spanned her back, pressing her to his hard body. His proud cock made delicious promises against her thigh.

He teased her lips with his commanding tongue, and she opened to his mastery. He delved in, tasting her. Their tongues tangled.

She explored his broad back. Muscle upon muscle, thick and strong, made her insides quiver. No man had ever enticed her like he did. Not her ex, not anyone. Torun intoxicated her from the inside out. She clasped him like an anchor in a storm.

He stroked her mouth with his tongue, pumping desire within her. Wetness slicked her channel. She wanted him now, on the deck, plunging his hard cock into her pussy and rocking her with soul-shattering thrusts until her passion exploded into an orgasm.

He palmed her buttocks and ground her femininity against his cock.

Could he hear her wishes?

"Lucy. You are shining again." He smiled and pressed hungry kisses against her forehead, cheek, jaw, and sensitive neck. "You will be a powerful mother for our young fry."

Young fry? That was such a weird way of saying baby.

Oh, because mermen were fish. Like salmon fry.

Ohhh.

She slowed his hands and disentangled herself. "Okay. I, uh, and you..."

"Torun," he supplied.

"No, I know. Look." A wave of grief broke over her. *Deep breath. Let it out. Deep breath again. Let it out.* One of them had to be the adult. Lucy stepped back and faced him. "I can't be your queen."

"You must."

"But you said your race is dying. You need a woman who can give you children."

"That is also you."

"It's..." Her throat closed. *Crap.* She covered her eyes. Was she going to be okay? Yes. She cleared her throat and dropped her hands. "It's not. Sorry."

He set his feet, a proud tribal warrior. "You belong with me. Your hunger is heightened by my offering."

"Sea Opal," she corrected, her throat rough. "Funny you should mention it. They're ridiculously valuable. I'm not the only woman whose hunger will be heightened if you flash it around."

"I want you."

Desire tugged at her.

"Okay, listen." She tapped the jewel against his gorgeous, hard chest. "I can*not* be your bride."

"Queen."

"Whatever. But in exchange for showing me where you got this beautiful Sea Opal, I'll introduce you to every fertile young woman I know. It only takes six people to meet Kevin Bacon. I have hundreds of Facebook friends, so you'll definitely find your, uh, queen."

"I will give you more Sea Opals in Sireno."

"Take my offer or leave it."

"I will take your offer." He closed his hands around hers over the jewel. "I will also take you."

"Torun—"

"You wish to become my queen. So become her. It is within your power. Accept."

Torun's demand rang across the deck.

Lucy's heart swelled with his conviction. He was so proud, so determined, so certain of his desire for her.

But he didn't know who she was. Or, in this case, who she wasn't.

I'll never have kids. I'm sorry. No, really. I'm the one who's sorry.

And she didn't want to tell him.

It was an argument that she just couldn't handle right now. Even Lucy's close friends and family gave her well-intended but agonizing encouragement. *"Don't give up. It'll happen when you least expect it."*

Yeah. Sure.

She'd been in the "lucky" position of being able to put

her body through five cycles of treatments before her marriage wore out, but the roller coaster of hormones and injections and clocks and pills had only led to failure upon failure. Why? Science had no answer. She had a uterus, but it just…it didn't work. Or something.

Blake's voice intruded. *"You're a failure as a woman and a failure as a human being."*

Torun wouldn't say that.

But Lucy didn't have the bandwidth to argue with him. Not about this. And not when every other sense tempted her to ignore her problem, pretend that maybe it really *would* happen if it was with Torun, and give in.

Being the adult sucked.

Lucy gently pressed his chest, feeling his heartbeat radiate beneath his cool skin. "I'm not the woman you need."

He opened his gorgeous mouth to argue.

She stood on her toes and kissed his cheek, brushing her lips over his to silence him.

The powerful warrior focused on her. She held a magnet, and if she moved an inch, she would lose herself to crushing hunger.

Hunger for her old dream. For the new fantasy he was spinning.

Hunger for a family.

"Anchor us," he said softly. "I will take you to the Sea Opals, Lucy."

She wanted to. She wanted him. She wanted…things she couldn't have.

"It's late." She stroked his high cheekbone with her index finger. Rough, sensuous. Sexy. "I have a meeting with my expedition backers tomorrow. I'll show them your Sea Opal, and they'll find you another woman."

"I do not want another woman."

"You will. And when we find more Sea Opals like this one"—she clenched the gem—"I'll help your people repopulate their city, whether you're from an isolated fishing tribe, or whether you're actual gill-breathers living twenty thousand leagues under the sea."

He frowned. "You do not believe I am a merman."

"You took a sharp blow to the head."

"I could show you now, but..." He gazed at the lights of the mainland as though fighting a war between his duty and his need. Then he captured her in his arms. "We are destined to be together. Believe in me, Lucy."

She forced down the rising, fluttering, overwhelming rightness of nestling in his embrace. "Believing in you isn't so hard. Believing in *me* is the problem."

"I believe in you."

"Like I said." Lucy pulled away to navigate the entrance to the Cancun marina. "One of use needs a serious reality check. And right now, I'm not sure if it's you or if it's me."

SEVEN

His Lucy refused to recognize their destiny. She refused that night, on the sea, and the next day, on the land.

Probably because she had not grown up on the sacred island.

Torun watched her maneuver her rusty boat between the sleek white ships to the crowded main dock.

On the sacred island, she would have heard about his kind from her mother and grandmother. She would know it was her fate to live on the bottom of the ocean and give him a young fry.

As long as she carried his mating jewel, which she called a Sea Opal, in a special pouch at her hip, its siren song would call to her. She would believe in him, and her soul light would shine.

"You move this boat skillfully," he stated.

Her soul light burned brighter.

Then she dimmed and waved his comment away.

"I've been sailing these waters for years," she said. "My

dad had a charter business off the coast of Oregon, so when I grew up, I sailed through rocky shores every summer. This is nothing."

"Many others do not handle their boats as well."

She looked over his shoulder. The crew on larger vessels struggled, and smaller vessels got hung up on hidden snags. "Well, it can be deceptive if you don't know the area."

She eased into their docking place.

The engine squealed. They bumped the dock hard.

She winced. "Ugh. You praised me too soon. I'm out of practice."

He caught her in his arms. "You are wrong."

"I am so out of practice." She pushed against his arms, her cheeks reddening. With their skin contact, he felt her heart thump loudly in her chest. "Usually, I do better. I haven't had the chance to get out much."

"No, Lucy. I must praise you."

She stopped struggling. "Huh?"

"Praise makes your soul shine brightly."

She paused.

He luxuriated in her softness. Her gentle skin caressed his forearms, and her swelling curves pressed against his thighs.

"Something has beaten you down and caused your light to dim. But you deserve to shine, Lucy. You are more beautiful than any woman I have ever known."

Her dark eyes were glued to him, and her sweet tongue licked her lips. Then she shook herself. Her frown returned, and she pulled away.

"Since you're from an isolated, all-male tribe, I'm guessing I'm also the *only* woman you've ever known." He had told her more about his city last night, and now she was using that knowledge to dismiss him. "It's sweet of you to say it, though. I almost can't stand to turn you loose."

"I do not wish to be turned loose." He stroked her sinuous spine and pressed her against his rock-hardness. "I want you close. Naked with me. Making our young fry."

She sucked in a breath and pushed free. "No."

Doubts panged.

Every time she refused him, and every time her soul dimmed, the council's words of warning echoed.

"You cannot claim a modern bride."

No! He would not believe the council. She was his destiny.

Lucy was his.

He controlled his frustration. "Why do you refuse me?"

She stomped across the deck, echoing the anger he'd tried not to express. "It's for your own good."

"How could an action that dims your light ever be good?"

She glared at him from under a thick fringe of lashes.

Even her angry expressions enticed him. She burned like a fire, and all he wanted to do was throw himself onto the flames.

Lucy flinched as though she read his mind. She backed away, secured the trawler, and crossed a wooden plank to the dock. "Trust me, merman warrior."

"Marine warrior," he corrected her quietly as he followed her barefoot from the marina. One hand secured a towel to his waist. The other he clenched, ready to combat anyone who recognized his kind and attacked. "Or you may call us 'mer warriors.' *Merman* warrior is an old name for megalodon."

"Megalodon? The gigantic prehistoric shark? They're all extinct."

"We killed one in the Seven Cities War, but more are hiding in the blacknight waters of the abyss. When they rise, they are deadly."

Lucy had assured him that no one on the mainland would realize he was a merman. "They might stare because of your skin," she'd said, "and because I don't have a pair of shorts in your size, but wondering if you're secretly a fish is going to be the last thing on anyone's mind."

So to prevent being separated from her, he defied the council's threats and risked the ancient covenant.

Strangely, the more people packed together, the less anyone looked at him. The crowds hid his oddities. Growling engines in moving boxes called cars and buses jockeyed around narrow streets. Sizzling foods, smoking pits, and flames erupted from stationary carts. Humans lined up to exchange paper money for the foods.

Lucy passed one cart and waved a hand in front of her nose. "I love these tacos. They smell delicious."

What did she mean by the word smell? Was it the smoke that made a caustic tickle at the back of his throat? No difference existed in the air between one cart and the next or between the vehicles and the buildings.

Lucy selected clothes from a street vendor: long blue shorts, a tight shirt with a beach scene, and a pair of yellow flip-flops.

"Shirt, shoes, service," she said in approval.

Her approval filled his chest. He straightened and threw his shoulders back. Her eyes traced the contours of his muscles. Good. He possessed a shape his bride enjoyed, and that would help convince her to put aside her fears and join with him. He flexed to give her maximum pleasure.

She sucked in a long breath and then shook herself.

"Time to meet some eligible women." She held paper money out to the vendor.

Torun caught her hand before it touched the human male's. "You are mine."

She blinked at Torun.

"You touch only me. I touch only you."

Her mouth dropped open. "I'm just paying for your clothes." Her cheeks flushed hot. Her heart beat hard beneath his palm.

The street vendor watched them too carefully.

Torun pulled Lucy to his chest with a growl. "Do not touch other males."

"All right. Don't go overboard." She reached over Torun's shoulder and dropped the money onto the street vendor's palm from a distance. The vendor deposited different papers on the counter.

Lucy scooped them into her black embroidered pouch and led Torun back to the main street. "You should be careful. Women don't like the caveman treatment."

Caveman? Whatever that was, he would do it more. "You like it."

She twitched. "No, I don't."

"Your soul glowed when I ordered you to touch only me."

"Because...ah... Look, don't use me as an example of what mainland women are like. You'll never form a healthy relationship. I'm a little love-starved. Most women's ex-husbands didn't throw them out like trash." She turned to a building entrance.

He stopped her with an arm across the door. "I want only you."

Lucy's soul light burned bright. She liked his declaration.

"I want you," he repeated.

She slowly straightened and crossed her arms over her chest. Her hands trembled. "You want me, or you want a woman who will give you kids?"

"Yes," he said.

She shook her head, ducked under his arm, and continued into the restaurant. Hmm. He had missed something.

"You want 'kids' too," he said, using her unfamiliar word.

"That wasn't my question."

Air blasted down. The sensation of the space grew in his mind. Without a rumbling engine to muffle his sensations, the height of the ceiling, the distance to the glass and cement walls, the pulse of music in his chest, and the individual heartbeats of all the patrons sounded in his ears. The pops and sizzles of foods were loud in the kitchen.

But most interesting were the soul lights.

Men and women sat at tables and sipped drinks at the bar. Small stars shone in their chests. Some engaged in animated conversations, shining brightly. Others flared or faded when they fell quiet. Even the brightest soul did not shine as his Lucy did.

Modern humans had flickering souls, but none were as bright as his Lucy's.

Lucy squealed and raced to hug a large, vibrant woman. "Mel!"

Mel returned the solid hug. "Here's my expedition leader. Week one and you're already bringing home treasures."

"Oh, you have no idea." Lucy introduced Torun. "This is the man from my video. He's a warlord and a merman."

"A merman warrior!" Mel exclaimed.

"Mer warrior," Lucy corrected. "The other is a megalodon."

Mel held out her arms and walked to Torun. "So nice to meet you."

He stepped back. She followed, arms out, her step quickening. Was she herding him in some direction? He bumped into a table and stopped.

Mel put her arms around his torso.

He froze solid.

"Oh!" Lucy waved her hands. "He doesn't do touch."

"It's fine." The smaller woman squeezed his midsection. Her heart beat steadily in her chest, and her musical voice was soothing like a mother's. "I'm a hugger."

Lucy bit her lip.

Humans had different rules. Humans had different rules. Humans had different rules.

"It is fine," Torun assured Lucy. Although, was it? Sireno warriors never encountered more than one female at a time, so he made up a rule on the spot. "Lucy, you are my only bride."

Her soul brightened, and she flushed.

"Bride?" Mel pulled back, mouth agape. "Congratulations!"

"He just says that." Lucy dragged her friend away, her cheeks reddening and her soul dimming with the dismissal. "It's not what you think. Every woman's a bride. You're probably a bride."

"Not *my* bride," he clarified.

Mel lifted her brows. "Good thing. My husband would have choice words if I ended up as someone else's bride."

Husband?

Torun's gut clenched.

No. Human rules were different. Mel's husband would not demand justice.

If he did, Torun would take Lucy to Sireno now, over her objections, and ignore the consequences.

EIGHT

Lucy hugged her college friend again. "I'm so glad you're here. I thought you weren't coming until next week."

Mel squeezed back. Her woolly black hair cascaded down her back, and she beamed in a flowy, yellow maxi dress with sunny orange accents. "We had the timeshare, and you posted the craziest videos. Did you get that leak fixed?"

"My old boss from the dive shop, the one who sold me the zombie trawler, is supposed to be looking at it now."

"Great. I took the week off as soon as I found our new supporter, and we flew in this morning. Elyssa couldn't wait to meet you."

They sat at Mel's reserved table, Torun in the seat next to Lucy. They brushed elbows, and she pulled away. Lucy was too, too aware of him.

Mel lowered her voice. "The only thing is, she's kind of affiliated with Van Cartier Cosmetics."

Lucy's stomach dropped. "Wait. What?"

"Oh, there she is." Mel stood and waved.

Elyssa waved back cheerfully and crossed the restaurant. A long bohemian blouse and green capris hung stylishly on her thin frame, and a scarf tied back her dirty-blonde hair. She reached the empty chair, paused, and removed her fashionable sunglasses.

Mel introduced her. "Lucy, this is Elyssa Van Cartier, from Van Cartier Cosmetics."

Lucy rose and held out her hand. "Thanks for backing our expedition."

Elyssa smiled. Her slim fingers were accessorized with chunky amethyst and turquoise rings. "Thanks for having me."

"So, how are you related to the president of Van Cartier Cosmetics?"

"She's my aunt. By marriage."

"Elyssa works in HR," Mel said.

"The Florida office," Elyssa added.

"Oh, the one that fired me," Lucy said.

Elyssa didn't answer because she focused hard on pulling out the empty seat and sitting on it. She picked up the menu. "What are you having?"

Everyone read their menus silently.

What a graceful, slender, gorgeous woman. It was like looking at herself five years ago. Lucy clamped down on her jealousy while a waiter took their orders, then brought drinks and appetizers. Mel was the reason Lucy was on the water in a leaking boat instead of stuck in Florida, crying at the bus station, too poor for a ticket back to Oregon. She had to get over her anger. Elyssa was a Hail Mary last chance.

Lucy shifted the conversation back to Elyssa. "Your cousin is the vice president of Van Cartier Cosmetics, Aya?"

"That's right." Elyssa scooted in her chair. It hit the table. Their silverware rattled, and a fork fell on the carpet.

Lucy bit her tongue on her next question. *Is Aya really screwing my ex-husband?* She focused on the positive. "I appreciate your support."

"Sure." Elyssa dropped to the carpet and grabbed the fork. "Aya and I aren't as close as, um, before." Her head hit the table from underneath with a loud *thunk.*

"Honey, are you okay?" Mel asked.

"I have a hard head." Elyssa rose, rubbing her forehead, and resumed her seat. "Sea Opals are my passion. When I heard Mel was trying to raise the money for your expedition, I jumped in. You found the biggest one, after all."

Finally. Someone outside Lucy's immediately family believed in her.

Blake had convinced everyone that even though Lucy had found the gem, *he* had told her where to look. Somehow.

Lucy scooped up fresh pico de gallo and crunched the homemade corn chips. "Everyone else in Van Cartier Cosmetics is investing in my ex."

"Blake makes me uncomfortable." Elyssa leaned her elbows on the table. "Anyway, I know what it's like to have your credit stolen. You can succeed honestly without hurting anybody."

Aw. Lucy was about to tear up.

"And, after your last video, I'm intrigued." Elyssa checked out Torun's tall, hard body. Barely contained in colorful Bermuda shorts and a taut surfer tee, he was a visual meal any woman would enjoy. "Are you honestly a merman? You don't look like one."

"I am in the air world now." Torun shifted and cleared

his throat. "Did this video transmit to many humans? My people have worked hard to hide our existence."

"Not many," Lucy said. "And don't worry. Like I said before, no one will believe you."

His eyes darkened on her. "Only you must believe me."

Warmth spread through her veins. When he looked at her like that, it felt like they were the only two in the restaurant.

Elyssa's smile sparkled, reminding her they were not. "Do you believe him?"

"Of course, it's unbelievable."

He growled. "It is very believable."

Honestly, Lucy didn't want to believe him. A harmlessly delusional man with a set of abs she wanted to lick was much better than an actual merman who needed her to repopulate his undersea city. A delusional man could get therapy. An actual merman...well...

Elyssa was beautiful, young, and probably fertile. She loved Sea Opals. Elyssa could repopulate his city.

Torun might not see it right away. But eventually, he would realize, just as Blake had, that Lucy couldn't fulfill his needs. Then he would seek a woman elsewhere. Like the beautiful, young, sweet woman across the table from him.

And now Elyssa was flirting. "Lucy's right. If you want her to believe you're a merman, you'll have to prove it."

Torun glanced around the restaurant. "This is too exposed."

"Can't you just do a hand or something?"

Naked jealousy rammed up her spine. "Let's focus on our research. Don't get sidetracked by silly claims. This is a serious expedition."

Elyssa's smile fell. "Oh. Of course. Sorry."

"It's fine."

The waiter brought their meals.

Elyssa moved a napkin holder, and her elbow knocked a glass of ice water into her lap. She ran to the restroom, her face a bright red.

"Do you like Elyssa?" Mel leaned closer and asked under her breath. "I posted about your ordeal with the boat, and she contacted me. I about choked. We've been on a couple committees, but we hardly move in the same circles."

"She seems nice." Wow, could Lucy be any chillier? She was not reacting from jealousy. She was *not*. "I just have to wonder. She works in HR. Where was she when I got fired?"

"Probably at a college recruitment fair. She's not the hiring director, you know. The money she sent for the expedition isn't from Van Cartier Cosmetics."

What?

Mel lowered her voice and side-eyed the other patrons of the restaurant. "She's backing you from her own savings."

Lucy dropped her spoonful of melted cheese with a clank. "Seriously?"

"Her cousin's the vice president, and her aunt's the CEO, but Elyssa isn't in their inner circle. We double-mortgaged our house to fund you. But she..." Mel glanced up and closed her mouth. "Oh, you've been gone awhile."

"I got a phone call." Elyssa flopped in her seat, still plucking at her damp, water-stained shirt and capris. "Sorry, that was my bank. They were just double-checking on a few, um, recent expenditures. So, what's our plan?"

"Ask the expert," Mel said.

Both women looked at Lucy expectantly.

Her heart swelled three sizes. Her chest ached.

These women put their faith in her. They invested their

own money because they believed. Mel double-mortgaged her house. Elyssa didn't even know her and had invested a much larger sum. Lucy's jealousy was stupid. She would justify their faith.

Lucy leaned forward. "We're going to kick Blake's ass. I've already found a source for the Sea Opals. Torun's tribe collects them to gift during marriage proposals."

Their eyes widened.

She opened her pouch and showed them the Sea Opal. "Torun knows where to dive for more."

NINE

Lucy's friends were riveted by her exciting news, and Lucy's soul light brightened with regal command as she explained her plans to collect more of the Sea Opals and keep it a secret from evil credit-stealers such as her ex-husband.

"In exchange, I've agreed to find women for Torun's tribe," Lucy told them, forgetting the most important part—that she would become his bride. "The tribe is all male."

Mel grinned. "You have to create a dating site and name it Plenty of Fish."

"That's already taken," Lucy said.

"Oh, but it would be perfect! Sign them up," Mel said.

"We'd have to read their terms and conditions." Lucy's mouth twisted. "But let's be practical for a minute. This is all a little crazy. Isn't it?"

Mel pursed her lips. "Hmm. I guess. But I have faith you'll find someone with the technical skills to set up a tribe of good-looking mermen."

"What? No, I mean, the rest of it." Lucy raised her

brows. "Tell me I'm crazy for going back out on the ocean all alone."

Torun leaned forward. "You will not be alone, Lucy. You will be with me."

She swallowed. "Yeah..."

"Not to worry." Mel clinked her glass against Lucy's. "Praise me. I found you some unpaid interns."

"Good job! Who?"

Elyssa had never taken her eyes off the Sea Opal in Lucy's pouch. "May I?"

"Hmm? Oh, sure." Lucy handed over the gem.

Torun's belly flipped.

The Sea Opal passed to Elyssa, then Mel, and back to Elyssa again. He had given the jewel to Lucy, and she was, therefore, free to do with it as she liked. Even give it away to another in front of him.

But he did not like it.

Lucy kissed him. She refused his claim. She promised to stand up to his council. She planned for another woman to become his queen.

Had any warrior in a thousand years had to fight this confusion to claim his bride?

Then again, no other warrior had selected a modern bride. Torun would endure. His endurance would be rewarded in the end. It had to be.

The future of his race depended on it.

Elyssa turned Lucy's jewel over in her palm, her soul glowing as it resonated with the gemstone. "These stones are magical."

"They are mating jewels," he corrected. "Are you also seeking a husband?"

"If I found the right guy." Elyssa turned the sphere over

and over. "Did you know when certain people get close to them, these gems actually glow?"

"Yes. We call it resonance."

"We do too! I was volunteering in the lab when I noticed the change. It's just a tiny glow. You can't see it with your naked eye."

"All warriors can."

"Really! I wish one of them had been in the room to back us up." She sighed. "The company scientists didn't believe us, but when they measured the samples, we were right. And the people who resonated with the samples also experienced stronger effects from our Sea Opal-infused cosmetics, like smoother skin and better healing from sun damage."

"Yes, that is natural."

"Natural? I think it's amazing. These gemstones are so mysterious."

"There is no mystery. Sea Opals are the tears of our Life Tree. All warriors are connected to it in our blood. When we find another who has an affinity for the sea and is compatible with our Life Tree, their soul will brighten. That is why we offer the Sea Opals to our brides. In the gemstone's presence, a bride's soul will shine."

Elyssa turned the gem in her hand. "You can see people's souls?"

"Yes."

Being with Mel and Elyssa brightened Lucy. She laughed and talked a great deal, but her light was fragile. Worryingly fragile. Now, Lucy finished the conversation with Mel and saw him speaking with Elyssa. Her light dipped.

He held out his hand to Elyssa. "May I?"

Elyssa handed the Sea Opal to him.

He returned the jewel to Lucy. "This is my offering to you."

Lucy flushed as her soul flashed brilliantly in her chest. "Yes. We all know. She can have it."

"It is *yours*," he emphasized. "This Sea Opal resonates with *your* soul."

Lucy stopped objecting and returned the stone to her pouch.

Like compliments and reminding her of his claim, she needed the stone with her to shine. Until her soul regained its natural brilliance.

His tension eased.

Elyssa sighed again. "So that was a marriage proposal?"

"Yes," he said.

"No," Lucy said, too quickly, flushing brightly. "It's business."

"Normally, it is a marriage proposal," he amended. "Lucy is the most beautiful, powerful, resonant woman I have found."

Her friends stared.

She swallowed. "He's just saying things."

"Good things." Mel's smile glowed with warmth. "Go on. Tell me more about this proposal business."

"Our city sends the worthiest warrior to the surface to claim his sacred bride. Lucy is mine."

"And I'd love to accept, but I'm done with marriage." Lucy laughed nervously and toyed with the pouch at her waist. "I promised to help Torun stand up to his town council and meet the right woman. That's all this is."

She would love to become my bride. Heat pulsed under his skin. This was the second time she had uttered those words. Some barrier prevented her. He would uncover the barrier, remove it, and then claim her wholeheartedly as his queen.

"So." Mel rested her chin on her folded hands. "If Lucy said yes, would she become a mermaid?"

"Stop." Lucy lifted her pink watermelon *agua de sandía*. "He's supposed to convince you he's not crazy. Otherwise, one of us needs a psychiatrist."

"Honey, Torun thinks you're as great as I do." Mel straightened. "He sounds perfectly sane to me."

"Oh my God. Wait." Elyssa placed both palms flat on the table and scooted forward in her chair to the edge of her seat. "If a bride accepts, *does* she become a mermaid?"

Lucy turned on Elyssa. "Don't tell me you believe him now."

"You should want to know, Lucy," Elyssa said. "You could end up as a mermaid."

Lucy shook her head. "Elyssa—"

"It's for science. He knows about resonance." Elyssa gestured at her empty drink vessels, accidentally tipping one over. "And I've had three margaritas. Go on, merman. Explain."

Torun hesitated.

These females were all mainlanders, but Lucy trusted them. If she did not see a risk to his city, he did not either.

"A bride drinks the elixir of the Life Tree. And then, yes, her body transforms to accept the sea."

"What does that mean?" Elyssa asked. "Does her skin turn all swirly and gold, like yours?"

"The tattoos are not a natural condition. We add them as we acquire rank and honor."

"So, no wild colors. How do you breathe underwater?"

"Gills."

"Where?"

He indicated the small of his back. "Closest to the lungs."

Mel shook her head. "That would make it awkward to sleep. Roll over on the bed and suffocate yourself."

"You used to sleep with your face stuffed in a pillow," Lucy said.

"Only after all-nighters. Or those dive trips you used to lead."

"Or while training for triathlons."

"Well, sure." Mel patted her generous belly. "The pre-baby body. I'll get there again. Someday."

Elyssa looked at him as though she were still awaiting his answer.

"There are few beds underwater," he said. "No chairs either."

They all sobered, considering an undersea world with no beds or chairs.

"So, you don't have to surface to breathe, like a whale?" Elyssa persisted.

He shook his head.

"That would prevent the bends, I guess," Elyssa said. "Do you have a tail?"

"No."

"Not even in the water?" Elyssa's eyes narrowed thoughtfully. "How do you swim?"

"I move my body." He undulated, demonstrating.

Elyssa's gaze fixed on his feet.

His right foot stuck out from under the table near to her, and his gesture caused the foot to widen instinctively to a flat, cupped scoop. It strained the fabric straps of the flip-flop Lucy had just exchanged for paper money.

Curse it.

He must not damage Lucy's gift by inattention. He flexed his foot back to the narrower, land-walking shape.

Elyssa's gaze flew to his face.

The other women were joking and laughing to themselves and hadn't noticed his transformation.

Awe passed over Elyssa's features. "You really are a merman."

"Yes."

The light in her chest brightened, hot and warm as the island sun. "And there's more of you? An entire tribe seeking women to marry and transform into mermaids?"

"Yes, but they refuse brides who are not from the sacred islands. Only I disobey the council and choose a bride from the mainland."

Her light diminished. "Only you?"

How unsettling that these human souls were so volatile. Brighter than the sun one minute, darker than the deepest cave the next.

"The council fears if we break tradition and choose any bride, we will also leave Sireno for the abandoned city of Atlantis."

"Atlantis," she repeated. Her star brightened. "Of course."

"A young, strong lord spoke of raising the sunken city. It was once a gathering place for mer and humans. With a single lever, the city rose above and descended beneath the waves again. There, any mer could meet any human, and choose."

The others listened. Now that he had her attention, he spoke to Lucy.

"This young lord's words inspired me. He has inspired many to speak out, but only I have acted. His plan will reveal us to the modern world. Councils across the oceans fear the outcome."

A harsh punishment also awaited Torun if he did not soon prove that his action was right. A warrior who disregarded the will of his city's council faced castration or execution. Or, worse, dishonor.

"When will he raise Atlantis?" Elyssa made fists. Her cheeks burned as brightly as the light in her chest. "What can I do to help?"

"Kadir has been imprisoned in the deepest trench for his treason. A great many would have to rebel against their councils, free him, and then rebuild the ancient city."

Determination flared in her shimmering green eyes. "Maybe your marriage to Lucy will inspire others to free him."

Lucy sucked in a breath.

Warmth glowed in his own chest. Elyssa's words moved him. Could his rebellion give back hope to the young lord who had led Torun to his Lucy? Could it ripple beyond Sireno and inspire others to chase their mates?

"But," Lucy interjected, "I'm not going to be Torun's queen, so he'll have to find someone else."

"You're great together," Elyssa protested.

"Torun needs a woman who can give him children."

Elyssa tilted her head.

Mel rested her hand on Lucy's shoulder. "And?"

Lucy grimaced at her. "You know."

"I know that you got discouraged. You don't know for sure—"

"I know," Lucy snapped.

Mel rubbed her shoulder. "Well, miracles happen. Never say never, or you'll end up pregnant when you least expect it. Trust me."

"Yeah." Lucy's tone and distant look said she didn't believe the words.

Torun needed to ask her—

"Speak of the little devils." Mel rose and opened her arms. "Here they are!"

Two young fry hurried across the restaurant, calling for *mama*. They clustered around Mel. She hugged them close and kissed their small faces.

Everyone rose from the table.

Mel's mate pushed a wheeled vehicle; inside rested a chubby pink young fry who regarded the world with wide blue eyes. Her mate greeted Mel first with a kiss, as was proper, and then said hello to the rest of them.

Torun tensed, but the hand the male held out to him was warm and friendly, and their shake firm. Humans *were* different. This family lived by an honor code free of fear. Their young fry all shone with pure, blissful lights. They were secure in their mother's love.

His throat tightened.

Beside him, Lucy also stared at the close family. Her pain and longing burned him like volcanic undersea currents. This was the family he wished for. She clearly wished for it too. Her hand squeezed the pouch holding his Sea Opal.

He touched her fist. "I will give you young fry."

Her pain ebbed and then pushed back harder. She opened her mouth. No words emerged. Her lips tightened.

"Lucy, believe in me."

"I told you. The problem isn't you."

"Then there is no problem."

"Torun..." Lucy pulled away. "Later."

She would not run from him forever.

But she could run from him now. And she did so as she turned on her heel. "Our new team is waiting." Lucy bid her friends farewell and tugged him from the restaurant. "Let's go."

TEN

"*I will give you young fry.*"

Torun's earnest promise slapped her ears like a sneaker wave. Lucy hurried through the streets as though she could outrun it. "*I will give you young fry.*"

No, you won't.

The reply had been on her tongue. The words had almost come out. Only through force of will had she swallowed them back.

Mel had been an ordinary single woman like Lucy once. They'd met their husbands, gotten engaged, and married within a couple of years of each other. Then Mel glowed with pregnancy after pregnancy. She joked about her post-baby weight, but there was no doubt that her husband still desired her. He shouldered parental duties eagerly, and they both kept up their activities and careers. Children added a rosy wholeness to Mel's life, a huge fulfillment that Lucy craved more than oxygen.

She had so desperately wanted her own family. She'd imagined her husband's love growing as her body grew with their child.

But it didn't. Because her body couldn't.

And now that pain washed over her again, a riptide threatening to drag her under.

She had told Torun over and over she would not be his queen or give him children. He thought she was unwilling to give him babies, not incapable.

No one looking at her would believe she was such a failure of a human being, right? She had all the equipment, didn't she?

"Lucy." Torun's deep bass vibrated soothingly in her ear. Intimate, as if his words in the crazy heart of Cancun's tourist areas were only for her. "You are upset."

He sounded concerned. Like he was going to hold her again and make her heart swell with promises that she knew he couldn't keep.

She scrubbed her face to keep from doing something stupid, like reaching out for Torun and accepting that comfort. "I'm just late."

Lucy ducked into her old dive shop.

Her former boss was out on the trawler resurrecting the engine. As well he should! Selling her a zombie boat was a rotten way to repay their friendship. Lucy headed to the marina and used Elyssa's new credit card to pay for fees and gas.

Busyness kept her from dwelling on the real reason she avoided the burning aquamarine gaze of the so-called marine warrior.

Mel was supposed to have taken one look at Torun and thumped Lucy upside the head. *Are you crazy?* the Mel in her imagination demanded. *He says he's a what? And you want to take him out diving? Is this the expedition I double-mortgaged my house to finance?*

But instead, Mel had been completely in favor. When

Torun had been distracted meeting the rest of Mel's family, she'd pulled Lucy to the side for a woman-to-woman chat. "Skip the psychiatrist. You *must* take him back out with you."

"He knows the location of the Sea Opals," Elyssa had chimed in.

"And he's good for you. You haven't been this alive since you signed the divorce papers."

Lucy had put her hands on her hips. "You'll feel bad if he's an ax murderer."

Mel had laughed and patted Lucy. "Honey, I'd still put my money on you."

Elyssa had studied Torun skeptically like he actually might be an ax murderer.

"I'm kidding," Lucy had said. "But come on. Who goes around claiming to be a merman?"

"Maybe he's not lying. He did the foot thing."

"Foot thing?"

"Yeah, a thing." Elyssa had flexed her foot and nearly toppled over. She'd grabbed a chair for balance. "And he didn't drown, and he's sort of blue."

"He could be from a tribe of professional free divers who take silver supplements."

"I think he's real," Elyssa had said. "But whatever. If you trust him, I trust you. Let's video us together for posterity." She'd turned to grab her cell phone and knocked the saltshaker off the table.

Lucy had helped Elyssa clean up. The younger woman was sweet. Three margaritas had convinced her that Torun was the real deal. She was obviously a dreamer who also believed in crystals, tarot cards, and star signs. There were worse things to be.

So now Lucy was stuck with the gorgeous, crazy male

who made her long for things she couldn't have. She'd already grown too used to his presence. His delicious kiss, and his oceanic scent, and the promise of more to come. She'd already started to need him.

Her soul craved more, and her body pulsed with demands.

No! He had demands of his own, demands she couldn't meet. No matter how she wished she were different. Lucy had promised she would introduce him to a woman who could give him children. Beautiful, bouncy, blue-and-gold tribal children.

Her heart squeezed in half.

"Lucy!" Torun dragged her into his arms, stopping her in the middle of the busy dock. "Whatever you are thinking, change your thought. Right now."

She swallowed and curled her hands around his forearms. So strong, one arm wrapped around her chest and the other around her wide belly. So commanding. She closed her eyes to the curious pedestrians strolling around them.

"I'm just being dumb." She cleared her throat. "Sorry."

"You are not being dumb. You are being dangerous." His lips nuzzled her sensitive neck. "I have never seen your light so dim. Please. You are my bride. Take strength in our connection and let me care for you."

Unlike Blake, who'd dropped her as soon as she became a drag, Torun sensed her feelings and faced them head-on.

Lucy was stronger than her sadness. She was stronger than her depression, and she would get over the fallout from this odd crush who claimed to be an escaped creature of the sea.

She took another deep, settling breath.

"Good," he murmured and nibbled on her lobe. "Much better."

His nibble teased her with tingles. He offered himself to her fearlessly. Couldn't she accept a little taste?

No. That path led to shattered dreams. He needed a woman who could give him children. And if she stood in his sheltering arms for too long, taking strength from his immovable devotion, she *would* fall in love with him.

She squeezed him, silently thanking him, and pulled free. "Our crew is waiting. Come on."

The interns Mel had hired were already on board. Setting up solar panels to power his undersea mapping equipment, the cartography grad student waved over his shoulder. "I'm Cash. Nice to meet you."

"You too." Lucy put her hands on her hips. This expedition would get official scientific support. "Let me check on some repairs."

"Yeah, an old guy just left. He said something about replacing the bubblegum and duct tape."

Lucy started for the engine room to see the state of the repairs.

Torun frowned.

She paused. "What's wrong?"

"This man does not shine," Torun said in his cryptic, formal way. "He dislikes the water."

"You've got that right." Cash straightened. "The grad school clock is ticking. I don't have a lot of internship options."

Well, Mel had said as much. She'd played hero for finding the interns and then confessed that the interns had emailed her first.

"So long as you can do your job, you're welcome on my expedition."

"I got my bracelet and my anti-nausea pills. I'll survive."

Torun's frown deepened.

"We don't have a lot of options either," she told Torun quietly. "This is the data we need to find the Sea Opals."

"I know where to find—"

"I know you do, but this makes it official later." There would be documentation. No one could question her success. "And we can't afford to advertise your gem. If we sell one Sea Opal to upgrade our equipment, a thousand treasure hunters will swarm us and scoop up the rest."

Speaking of treasure hunters, she needed to remember Blake. He couldn't marry the Sea Opals away from her a second time. If he learned about her newest discovery, what would he try?

She didn't want to find out. The eager adventurer who'd proposed to her was nothing like the cold, hard businessman who'd slammed her with divorce.

Their final crew member, an oceanography intern named Gracie, hopped onto the trawler with her arms full of groceries. She was taking on Lucy's old role on dive trips, but Lucy had never looked that good. Tight shorts hugged her thin legs, and a tube top obscured her tiny bikini. White earbuds buzzed with almost audible music. Gracie looked Torun up and down and up again, craning her neck to see the top of his head.

He greeted her. "Gracie."

Gracie waved two fingers, nodded to Lucy and Cash, and disappeared below deck.

"She is quiet," he noted.

"She'll be our data analyst and my partner on the dives," Lucy said.

"Partner? I will be your diving partner."

"You don't have equipment."

He puffed out his chest. "I do not need equipment. I am a merman."

Cash lifted a brow. "Well, okay then."

"It's the name of his tribe." She headed for the hatch. "Don't worry. I have everything under control."

Cash muttered something about nuts.

Great. Even the unpaid intern was second-guessing her leadership.

Torun followed her down the stairs.

Gracie and Cash were bunking in the guest room, their things sprawled across the twin bunks. The engine room was dry, amazingly. A note from her old boss was duct-taped to a new Costco box of oil. She checked her levels, hoses, and the tackiness of the newly applied fiberglass. *Missy B* was a Frankenstein boat, but it would get her out and back again. She started the predeparture checklist in her head.

"Lucy." Torun followed her too closely. "Do not fear the water."

"I'm not fearful. Just respectful."

"I will keep you safe."

She stopped. The edge to his voice matched the dark lines creasing his eyes. He was seriously concerned for her. It was kind of nice having a large, powerful male devoted to easing her slightest fears. She could get way too used to that.

He touched her cheek. "I will bring you the Life Tree elixir. You will not drown."

Ah yes, the magic mermaid potion he was telling Elyssa about.

"Great." She eased away from her temptation and headed out of the engine room, counted supplies in the galley, and went up to the deck again. "The Life Tree grows in the center of your city. Isn't it guarded by your council?"

"It is possible to drink a diluted elixir. The brides of the sacred island drank it to transform for their journey. Once joined to their Sireno husbands, they drank the pure nectar of the Life Tree blossoms, and the ability to transform became permanent."

"So, where's the sacred island?"

"Far." He considered the marine charts she unfurled across the cockpit. "There is a closer location. A deep cave within the atoll where we met. Long ago, it was also a sacred island."

The same place where she found the first Sea Opal.

Wouldn't it be nice to drink a potion like Alice in Wonderland and gain magical mermaid powers? She'd never have to come up for air.

While fantasizing, she also wished to be a size ten again. Maybe this time with luxurious blonde hair.

"You think I am not serious," he said.

"I wish you were serious." She grabbed the steering wheel to pilot them out of Cancun. "It would save me a ton on oxygen tank refills."

ELEVEN

They motored out to the unnamed atoll where Lucy had found him.

Torun considered his problems.

Lucy did not trust in him. She was keeping a secret. Every time he brought up her future as queen mother of his young fry beneath the sea, she froze.

Could she be afraid of the water? She said no. But perhaps the council had been right.

Humans can never become queens. That era is over. They cannot give up the air. They are weak and fear the ocean.

Curse it, she had chosen his Sea Opal. She said she would like to join him as his queen. When they touched, her soul brightened. When she spoke of diving freely beneath the waves, her soul brightened. When she planned to stand up to his council, her soul brightened. She was born to be his queen.

And yet she froze and said she could not.

He had thought this mission would be simple. He would come to the surface, claim a bride, and prove her worth to the council at the Life Tree. He had not imagined it would take him so long to find his Lucy, that she would resist, or that days would pass on the surface.

He must melt her resistance and drown her in the pleasure of their connection. Her light should shine like the sun. She would have nothing more to fear.

They reached the old atoll as the sun disappeared and the sky turned pale. Lucy set the anchor and called an expedition meeting to plan out exploratory dives.

"Tomorrow, Gracie and I will start searching." She pointed at their current location on the sea map. "We'll do three dives depending on what we discover and how everyone feels."

"There is no need to search," Torun said yet again. "I will show you where to go."

Lucy patted his hand. "I know, but if I'm systematic, we won't miss anything."

"You will not miss anything. Once you drink the elixir, you will feel a Sea Opal's presence. It will resonate in your soul."

The interns stirred.

She did not answer.

Impatience gnawed at him, like waiting at the mouth of a trench, knowing a tasty sea bream floated on the other side. The goal was almost in sight.

Cash grimaced. "Are you sure this is where your husband found the Sea Opal?"

"*I* found it," Lucy snapped. "And Blake is my *ex*-husband. Why, do you have a problem?"

"From the surveying equipment we've been dragging behind us, there's nothing to separate this hunk of ocean floor from the rest."

"You must have missed something. Gracie and I will collect rock samples in the morning. Right, Gracie?"

Gracie stared at the map. Her earbuds buzzed with music.

Lucy turned to Torun. "How close are we to your city?"

"Ten songs," he reminded her.

"Right, songs. How far is that in nautical miles? Ten miles? A hundred?"

He shrugged. "Perhaps farther."

"Then why did I find a Sea Opal here before?"

"Currents," Torun said. "Many warriors once swam these waters. And luck."

"Luck is about right," Cash muttered.

Lucy threw up her hands. "Forget everything. I'm done. Expedition canceled."

"Great. Wake me when we hit Cozumel." Cash ambled to the railing and bent over the side.

Gracie went to the railing beside him and stroked his back.

Lucy's light flickered dangerously.

She stared at the maps.

Torun reached across the table and clasped Lucy's hand. "Dive with me tonight."

"Forget it." She coughed. "Didn't you hear? The expedition's canceled."

"You do not give up so easily."

"That proves you don't really know me."

"Lucy."

She pulled her hand away and rubbed her face. "I thought your city must be close because we've found two Sea Opals here."

"This was once a sacred island. Nothing above the water remains."

Lucy stared at the electric maps Cash had made. "So anchoring here is a waste of time."

"No, it is a fine place to anchor." He pointed at the atoll lit by the brilliant gold sunset. "By that outcropping, beneath the sea, is an entrance to a cave. Inside, you will drink the diluted elixir. Then we can go to Sireno."

"Which is possibly hundreds of miles from here."

"I can traverse the currents in a few surface days."

"You know where else is hundreds of miles from here?" Cash asked from the railing. "The Keys."

Lucy's light flared. She barked at the intern, "If you wanted to go to Florida so badly, you should've applied to Blake's expedition."

Cash's dim light darkened to black.

"It's not too late," Lucy continued angrily. "Van Cartier Cosmetics has great benefits. They even give you a company house. And so long as you don't get divorced and then fired, you won't get kicked out."

Gracie put a hand on Cash's arm. His shine returned to its dim level.

"I just meant Blake has higher-grade equipment," Cash said behind a clenched jaw. "If you want to show him up, you have to actually find a Sea Opal. Don't hire a ripped native dude with empty promises."

Lucy erupted to her feet. "Torun isn't making empty promises."

Cash stared at her. "Yeah?"

Torun rose more slowly. "They are very full promises."

The young man swallowed hard, pulled a bottle from his shorts pocket, and tapped out a small pill. "Uh-huh. Have you ever even seen a Sea Opal?"

"Yes, I have seen many such, although we do not call them by that name. We have trenches full."

"Trenches?" Cash swallowed the pill, grimaced, and eyed him. "I think you don't know what you're talking about."

Lucy crossed her arms. "Of course he knows."

"Got any proof?"

She studied Cash for a long time. "Are you going to stick with my expedition or turn tail and head home?"

He reddened. "I'm sticking. As much as I hate to say it."

"Are you committed?"

"I just told you—"

"Then here." Lucy took out her Sea Opal and shoved it at Cash. "See for yourself."

Cash's eyes widened.

Gracie dropped his arm.

The two crew members crowded around the jewel. Gracie's light shone in her chest, resonating, while Cash's remained dim and untouched.

"Is that really one?" Cash asked.

"Yes."

He reached out. "Let me scan it."

"No need." Lucy whipped it away and returned it to her pouch. "This is why Torun is my location consultant. When it gets light, we're going wherever he says. Any doubters are welcome to find themselves a new internship. I'll even write a letter of reference."

Cash and Gracie looked at each other.

The sky around them darkened to indigo. The small boat lights twinkled.

"See you in the daylight." Cash headed for the hatch.

Gracie trailed behind him, disappearing into the interior. Her low music buzzed.

Lucy stroked her pouch. Then, seemingly conscious of

her abruptness, she went to the rail and curled shaking hands around the metal.

Torun followed. "They dim your light. You should make them return to the mainland."

"It's too late to fire anyone. They're both desperate, and we're already here." Lucy sucked in a breath and gripped the railing harder. "They're not the only desperate ones."

Deep pain was etched in her short breaths.

She needed to be stroked beneath her clothing. Wet and slippery, swimming with him in the sea, she would be polished and shining and happy once again.

Torun touched her silken hair.

She leaned back into his touch. "Why are you here?"

"Because you are here." He stepped forward, hemming her in against the railing.

"That's no answer."

"It is the only answer that matters."

Her shoulder blades pressed his chest. Her biceps sloped down. He followed their gentle lines to her sensitive elbows and traced his curious fingers farther, to her delicate wrists. This was the form of his bride, and he wanted to memorize her with his hands, with his mouth, with his tongue.

But now, she needed comfort.

Spreading his thick hands across her delicate knuckles, he slid his fingers between hers. She let out a deep sigh and relaxed against him. Her soft buttocks pressed against his awakening arousal.

In the air, they couldn't commune. Yet, the heating surface of her skin passed some communication to him. Her heart quickened, inviting him closer.

He pressed his lips to the hollow behind her determined jaw and licked.

She shuddered.

Her skin tasted sweet and salty, an arousing flavor that flooded his cock with heat. He nuzzled into her soft, warm neck.

She tipped her head to give him better access. "We shouldn't do this."

"We both enjoy it."

"It can't go anywhere."

Her words clashed with her feelings. In the uncertain air, he couldn't ignore the contradiction. "Do you want to stop?"

She ground her buttocks into his aroused member and moaned. Her hot invitation wrapped around his cock like a wet hand and squeezed.

Torun trailed kisses down her neck. Her large breasts rubbed his forearms. The nipples pointed, erect, through the thin white cotton of her top. They cried out for his touch.

He worked his hand under her tank top and palmed her heated flesh.

She glowed. "Torun."

Turning in his arms, she lifted her hot mouth to his.

He plunged his tongue into her sweet offering and massaged her full breasts. Her nipples pearled beneath his fingers. She made an inarticulate noise. His cock pulsed with readiness.

Her small hands brushed his shorts and caressed his hard cock.

Need consumed him.

He had to strip her naked and plunge into her right now. Take her in the darkness, standing up, braced against the railing as her back arched and her pleasure-filled cries echoed across the water. Until she reached her fulfillment.

Until he spread his seed within her, entwining their souls for all of time.

Lucy tugged the cord loosening his waistband. The shorts fell to reveal his long, hard male rod, ready to please her. She stroked the masculine length. Her hand was cool. He pulsed with pleasure.

"Lucy." He touched his forehead to hers.

She stroked him again.

Pleasure radiated from her gentle exploration. "You are so beautiful."

Her soul light flared. Her lips curled. Naughty. "You're magnificent."

"For you."

She licked her fingers and curled around him. Two hands worked his pulsing cock. Heat blossomed across her skin.

Joining with her was right. Destined. Yielding to him took all her trust, and Torun would not let her faith be betrayed. He cupped her feminine mound.

She leaned into him with a welcome moan.

Yes.

He slid aside her bikini bottoms, explored her soft folds, learning and treasuring her shape, and stroked her wetness. He growled. "You are strong and determined."

Her moans came in short gasps. Her soul glowed brighter. The light pierced him with need.

"Torun. So good."

She buried her face against his pectorals.

He must reward her trust.

Her hands moved faster on his cock as though she shared the same wish. To increase his soul's glow as hers did in the life-growing ritual of joining as mates.

His pleasure rose to an unstoppable point. He growled

his claim. "You are mine. Heart of my heart. Mother of my young fry. Forever."

She stiffened. Her emotions changed as loudly as if she had cried in pain.

He froze. "Lucy?"

"Oh, sorry." She stroked his cock, but her fingers were awkward and forced. "Never mind. I'm into it. Just let yourself go."

He released her feminine heat.

"Torun?"

His cock went flaccid. He curled his hands around her wrist, gently slowing her movement.

Panic charged her features. "What's wrong?"

What was wrong? He cupped her face and stroked her cheek with his thumb. "You are in pain."

"What?"

"Did you not realize your own agony?"

"Oh, but I thought... Weren't you almost there?"

"I will go nowhere without you."

She pushed him back and stepped away. "Yes, you will."

He remained at the distance she had pushed him. His shorts bunched around his ankles like a bola. He pulled them up.

"Look, we don't have forever. I didn't tell you this because...well, but you have to know. Whether you're a merman or delusional or whatever. You just...you're so serious about me. It's not fair." She scrubbed her cheeks. Her eyes reddened, and her darkened soul showed her true agony. "I'll never be your queen. I'm sorry."

"You are mine." He rubbed one arm, and when she only looked away, he closed the distance and drew her shivering form into his embrace. Rubbing the bumpy skin, he sought to give her the warmth she claimed to need. "I am yours."

"No."

"Believe, Lucy."

"No!" She faced him with absolute agony. "The thing is, I can't give you children. I can't give *myself* children. If you want to save your race, you have to choose another bride."

TWELVE

The warrior she was coming dangerously close to loving tilted his head in confusion

Lucy sucked in a breath and fought the tingling of tears. She had dreaded this moment from the instant he'd begged her to mother his children on the Cancun marina. Now it was here, and she felt horrible.

"You do not wish for young fry?" he asked, cautiously frowning.

"I can't have them," she repeated. "It's biological. I can't have them, you know, inside me."

"You do not wish for young fry inside you?"

"No. I want them, but they won't..." Her throat closed. Why wasn't she over this already? She cleared her throat and tried again. "They won't grow."

"Young fry do not grow inside you because we have not joined together."

"No! Because I *can't* have kids."

"Not until we have joined."

"Even after! There's something wrong. It's impossible for me."

He frowned harder. "It is very possible for you. After we join, you will carry a young fry. That is how it happens."

"Not for everyone."

"Yes, Lucy. I will teach—"

"Torun!" Clearly, infertility was entirely new to his tribe. Lucy gripped her needle-scarred belly in her fists. "There's something *wrong* with me. My ex-husband and I tried for kids a thousand times."

His brows lightened. "With me, it will be different."

"With you, it won't be different. There was nothing wrong with him."

"Lucy, a husband whose memory dims your light as his does is abnormal. He must have had something wrong with him."

Well, okay. Fair enough. She appreciated Torun for saying so.

But that was beside the point.

"He could not possibly give you a young fry," Torun continued. "I brighten your light, and so I will help you experience this gift."

If only that were true.

She'd cried buckets of tears, and each one started with the fervent wish, *if only*.

Torun didn't understand. He stood there as if waiting for his pronouncement to ease her sadness.

She took a deep breath and tried again to explain.

"I went to doctors. I got injections. I spent all my savings, credit cards, money I didn't have. All to prove I don't have 'a conducive uterine environment for ovum implantation.'"

Her hands shook, and a helpless tear from her memories leaked out.

Sitting in the exam room with her hospital gown tied up

in the back, kicking her socked feet and trying on names—Willow? Scarlet? Blake Junior?—with her hands resting on her still-flat belly. The nurse coming in. The sympathy on her lined face not matching the happy news she was supposed to be giving Lucy. *"We reviewed your test results. It's not a baby."*

Two years later, trudging to open the mail in the front hallway, accidentally kicking over a potted cactus and being too exhausted to pick it up. Exhausted from treatments, exhausted from life. The top letter was the final decision from the insurance company to discontinue coverage on account of Lucy's change in employment status. The bottom letter was a notification of divorce proceedings from Blake's attorney.

But the thing that really made her cry that day was the cactus. She'd given it to Blake for their first anniversary because it was supposed to be unkillable. She hadn't notice until she leaned over to pick it up, but the cactus had fallen out of its pot because there was nothing inside. It was a husk rather than a plant. Perhaps it had never been alive.

"Lucy," Torun said urgently, jerking her free of the past and centering her on the rusty trawler in the dark, sea-scented night. "Let me give you young fry."

She swiped the tear away. Hadn't she promised herself she wouldn't cry? And here a big, stupid, gorgeous tribal warlord with sexy tattoos and muscles begged her to bear his children. She wanted to bear them. *Please, God, let me bear this hot male's children!* But she couldn't, and now she had to go through the same denial, acceptance, and grief all over again.

Lucy jabbed her index finger against his hard pectorals. "Stop trying to convince me, okay? We don't always get our dreams. Get used to disappointment. It's a fact of life."

He closed gentle hands over her trembling ones. Sincerity burned in his gaze. "You are strong enough to overcome any challenge."

"Not this one."

"Even this. Your sadness too will pass."

His words, like his warmth, were a balm on her soul.

"I lost my savings, my house, my car, my job, my size, and my dreams. Blake gave up on me. I gave up on myself." She sucked in a breath and let it out. "But maybe you're right. I can at least try to become the naïve, upbeat, thin woman I was before all this happened."

"That is impossible."

She choked on a sharp laugh. "Harsh! At least tell me I have a chance. I wasn't always this weepy, or weak, or fat."

He winced at each adjective as though she'd struck him with a dart, then said, "Are you finished injuring yourself?"

The lump in her throat squeezed. She cleared it. "I'm not sure."

"Lucy. Your culture is very focused on a body's size. Yes? A smaller size like Gracie's is more desired."

"Or Elyssa."

"Or that one." He held her in his warm hands and fixed his steady aquamarine eyes on hers. "Under the water, this body difference disappears. All women are radiant. Your soul sings and shines. It does not matter what you look like. Under the water, every woman is beautiful."

She swallowed hard.

"Now, you are feeling the pain of your old injury." He stroked her fingers with his, soothing and calming her with his touch. "But, Lucy, a bride who has drunk the elixir of the Life Tree has never failed to produce a young fry. In all the generations, there has never been a single failure."

She sniffed. "Trust me to be the first."

He stroked her cheek, palmed her head, and pressed her to his chest, drawing her into his embrace and rocking her softly. "These are the thoughts that dim your soul light."

Yeah. She closed her eyes and accepted his kind comfort. Yeah, they probably did.

The tired thoughts, the negative thoughts, the powerless thoughts, the defeated thoughts. Maybe he was right. She'd been battered for so long, it was impossible to recover on her own. She needed his helping hand, his undefeatable strength, to rise once more and become a bright, vibrant, determined woman.

She needed to reclaim her power.

"Believe in yourself," he softly echoed her thoughts. "Believe you can overcome any obstacle."

Of course, if she believed, the pain of slamming into that obstacle would hurt a hundred times worse. Skepticism was the thin shell that held her guts in place when she sobbed so hard she could barely breathe. It wasn't much. But it was better than nothing.

"Believe," he repeated firmly.

"Yeah. Okay." She scrubbed her face and stepped back. "Sorry. I'll drink your magic elixir and believe in myself tomorrow, if that's okay. Tonight, I'm kind of tired."

"Do not despair about your old injury. You will understand when you meet the Life Tree and become healed by it."

"Sure. Healed. Right."

He raised his brows. "Is a secret race of mermen living beneath your ocean really more believable than a healing tree?"

"I already said I didn't believe you."

"Elyssa does."

Jealousy shot through Lucy.

"Sorry I can't be more like her." She turned away and gripped the railing to stare into the dark, star-spattered night.

He stepped close her once more, his hands resting on either side of her on the railing, his hard body pressing against her soft derriere.

"You are tense."

"Gee, I wonder why."

He still didn't *get* that she couldn't have children.

Okay. Fine.

Let him have his delusions. Why not? She'd already promised to try his diluted elixir. When it didn't heal her, she could say, "I told you so." And that would be greatly satisfying for about five seconds before he had to leave her for a woman who was undamaged.

Oh, she was going to regret this.

A stronger, better woman would tell him firmly no. Giving in to temptation and flirting with the dream would only end in heartbreak. Hers. Also, just possibly, Torun's.

And for that, she couldn't forgive herself.

"I really am going to hell," she murmured.

He rumbled a low laugh. "If you are going there, I will join you."

"I believe you will."

The long length of his masculinity brushed against her buttocks.

Her heart pounded, and her body came to sudden awareness. His skillful fingers had been *inside her* minutes ago, bringing her right to the delicious edge of a hot orgasm. For a dying civilization of virgins, he had an excellent command of female desire.

Hey. Wait a minute.

"How come you are so good at getting me off?" she asked.

"Am I?" His deep voice purred with pride. "I listen."

"Just listening?"

"And taste. I can see the glow of your desire."

Her desire had a glow?

"It is easier to see in the water, but I am getting familiar with seeing it in the air."

His rough jaw brushed her cheek. It was a good sensation. A masculine, husband sensation.

An honest person would push him off, and an angel would force him to find another bride.

Lucy tipped her head to the side, making room to fit him closer.

She was dishonest. Hellward bound. And she was dragging Torun with her.

He murmured an order against her sensitive neck. "Come with me into the water."

"Right now?"

It would feel great to slip into the ocean depths with him. Naked, their slippery bodies pressed together, with nothing between them.

"Now, while the others sleep."

She could forget about her problems, forget that Torun's embrace was temporary, forget that she would wake up tomorrow still the same broken, fat woman who no one believed in. "So long as that's all you're asking."

He wrapped one powerful forearm around her waist and tightened, pressing her against his mounting arousal. His lips nibbled sizzling imprints on her trembling earlobes.

"We will swim to the deep cave, and you will drink the temporary elixir and transform into my bride."

THIRTEEN

Lucy's soul light darkened. "I told you, I'm tired. Let's talk about it tomorrow."

"Tomorrow might be too late."

She was so close to coming with him. Every hour they delayed, his council armored the citizens of Sireno against them. Lucy thought up new ways to injure herself and darken her soul light. She had to see her own beauty as he did. Accept his claim, gather her power.

"This delay is senseless."

"Senseless?" She pulled back. Her soul light brightened with her protective anger. "You want me to spelunk an uncharted cave system, at night, without telling anyone, and you don't even have scuba gear?" She shook her head. "You're crazy."

"I will keep you safe. The water is not dangerous."

"Oh sure, the *water's* not dangerous. Forgetting a turn in the dark, running out of oxygen, and dying is the problem." She walked away from him and tidied the deck.

"I will be there with you." He walked after her, holding

the items she picked up and handing them back for her to secure in their proper places. "You will not lose your way."

"I definitely won't lose my way because we're diving in the daylight like normal people."

"The sooner we reach the Life Tree, the sooner you can experience its healing."

She ignored him, pattering down to the galley.

Cash faced away in the lower bunk. Gracie lay on her upper bunk watching a flat-screen.

"Do not fear the water," Torun repeated.

"Of course I'm not afraid of the water."

"You are."

"I'm not afraid of the sky either, but you don't see me jumping out of a plane without a parachute."

He opened his mouth to argue.

She stopped him with a kiss.

Demanding and giving, yielding and strong. She yanked his attention from the delay and focused it entirely on her.

What was this sensation?

Her soul light did not change intensity, but *his* did. His chest swelled with her kiss. New thoughts slammed into him as his body reacted to Lucy's attention and poured heat into his throbbing cock.

Lucy chose him. Over and over again, she chose him. She pulled him from the water, she introduced him to her friends, she defended him to the interns. Now she kissed him. All those actions turned his craving for her body into his craving for something more.

He didn't know what it was, exactly. He would figure it out later. He was not just a warrior but also a thinker, and once she became his bride, he would have all the time he needed to explore this new desire.

She pulled back. Her cheeks reddened, and her lips darkened to a prettier shade.

"I'm trusting you enough to go into the water with you tomorrow." She licked her lips. "My last dive partner horribly betrayed me."

He tightened. "I am different."

"I know you are." Her gaze dropped to his broad chest and traced the honorable markings of his house and rank, and lower, to the still-loosened rim of his shorts. "That's why you're here. Don't push your luck."

When she spoke with such confidence, the brilliant, shining aura of a queen filled her.

His anxiety eased.

The council's fears were based on ancient misconceptions. Lucy was strong enough to overcome any challenge. Together, they would prove his grandfather wrong and save his city.

Lucy ducked into her own cabin and closed the door with finality

Torun passed the night on piled deck cushions. It was not as comfortable as sleeping in water, but the currents here were untrustworthy, and he didn't want to be caught unawares.

Splash!

Torun twitched and jerked upright.

What was that? ... It must have been nothing. He lay back and stared at the vast, starry sky.

Lucy had committed to enter the water with him tomorrow. Had he carefully considered all the risks?

Prince Jolan and Malem must have returned to Sireno. Jolan would have needed healing. The king might have been horrified by his injuries and finally turned against Torun, ordered his castle destroyed and him punished. The council would dispatch different, possibly more numerous, warriors to recapture him.

They could easily trace his disappearance to this region. Perhaps the warriors even knew he was aboard this vessel.

They might even be blocking the atoll cave...

No. The cave guardian was loyal. If a war party tried to hide and spring a trap, all Torun and Lucy would find was bone and blood.

Lucy would pass by the cave guardian unmolested with his Sea Opal. She would drink the elixir, journey with him to Sireno's Life Tree, and unite their bodies. Her soul would glow with the highest brilliance. Of course she would bear his young fry. Together, they would prove the council wrong. Modern mainland women could bear young fry and save the mer race.

That was the only possible outcome.

FOURTEEN

In the bright midmorning sun, Lucy tightened her dive weights around her torso, shouldered her tank, partially inflated her buoyancy-control vest, clamped the regulator with her teeth, and held her mask in place with the palm of one hand. She rolled backward into the water.

Turquoise ocean closed over her head.

Her breath whooshed in her ears, an astronaut entering a new world. Bubbles escaped to the shimmering surface.

Up above the surface, Cash appeared over the end of the boat. He waved.

Gracie stood behind him. She held the Sea Opal, looking not at Lucy's departure, but staring, mesmerized, into the gemstone's white depths.

A pang of separation stabbed Lucy.

Cash had convinced her that the risk of losing the Sea Opal beneath the waves overpowered her irrational need to keep it close to her heart. He was right. She'd immediately turned it over to Gracie for safekeeping. Now that it was gone, though, she desperately wished for it back.

Lucy rolled over. Somewhere in the depths below, she'd find Torun...

He hung upside down, watching her.

She kicked.

Her big plastic fins propelled her through the water. Keeping one eye on her altimeter and the other on her oxygen gauge, she swam down to his level.

The nude warrior tossed her a cocky grin.

He was unencumbered by gear. No oxygen tank, unless it was invisible, and no weights or BCD to control his buoyancy. Yet he floated, neutral, like it was the most natural state in the world.

Lucy flipped over and hung upside down too. She couldn't duplicate his smile. If her lips curled, she'd break the seal around her mask and regulator and spring a leak.

He floated closer.

The dappled shadows made hard, ridged patterns on his face and body.

Was he really a merman?

No. There had to be a trick. The world freediving record was seventeen minutes. Tribesmen who'd never been observed by an Olympic judge might last even longer.

She really should have gotten him examined by a doctor.

He made a purring noise in his chest and gestured to the deep. *Was she ready?*

She grabbed her grease pencil and wrote on her wrist-sized white slate. "Let's go."

He kissed the patch of skin on her cheek exposed between the rim of her mask and the edge of the regulator, then darted away.

Fast! Holy moly, he darted like a missile.

She struggled to keep him in sight, pumping her fins

hard. Wasn't she in terrible shape? The guys she used to dive with would never have let her live this down. She gasped, using up her oxygen way too fast, and pushed herself harder.

Torun paused, a dot in the distance, and zoomed to her side. He thrummed in apology, and, while she laboriously kicked, he hovered beside her without even seeming to paddle.

He'd claimed to have gills on his back, but she only saw tattoos and rippling muscles.

What augmentation allowed him to swim so careless and free?

Oh! He'd snuck on some gear after all: long, flat scuba fins just like her. Hers were magenta plastic, and his were the same tone as his skin, complete with gold tattoo swirls. Neat.

Other augmentations?

His arms hung loosely at his sides, just like hers. He navigated with his head like she did. He had so many taut muscles, making him both compact and efficient.

She, on the other hand, had loose, wimpy muscles, making her uncoordinated and weak.

His brows rose, and he made a questioning purr.

She wrote on her tablet. "Feeling fine. You?"

He purred again, more decisive, and darted lower.

Shadows filtered through the blue depths, darkening as they descended and bending shafts of sunlight in familiar refraction patterns. Roy G. Biv—the color spectrum—meant that red and orange and yellow faded out close to the surface, greens faded deeper down, and then everything appeared only blue, indigo, and finally violet before the light disappeared completely into the black depths.

At the laser-blue layer of water, the mouth of the cave yawned.

She recorded short videos. This deep, her phone couldn't connect to a satellite. They would post as soon as she ascended and her phone reacquired a signal.

How was her oxygen? Lucy checked her gauge. She probably could afford only a few minutes inside the cave. Descending was the easy part. She had to save enough air to ascend safely. Pausing extra minutes to breathe out the nitrogen pooled in her joints avoided the bends.

The last thing she needed was to rise too fast to the surface. An emergency evacuation to a hyperbaric chamber would cost thousands. Popping a lung as depth-compressed air suddenly super expanded could cost her life.

She respected the ocean the same way a skydiver respected his parachute, a pilot respected his jet, and a jockey respected his horse.

Lucy descended toward the cave entrance.

A strange ball rose from the depths. It appeared gray, then violet, and now blue.

Torun paused.

The ball passed the cave entrance and kept rising. Its size grew massive, and eight legs uncurled. Two gigantic eyes rotated around its bulbous head.

It was a mammoth octopus.

Wow.

Watching the gentle giant move was like seeing the sun rise for the first time. Its sheer girth was like a mountain vista so gorgeous, they made it into desktop wallpaper.

She fumbled for her cell phone and started recording.

It floated directly in front of them. Its plus-shaped irises traveled around and around its eyes. Curious? It seemed to be waiting for something.

Torun tapped his heart.

Yes, she was so thrilled her heart was about to explode. Lucy took one hand off the camera and tapped her chest. Her heart was beating a thousand times per minute.

He made a fist and cupped it in his other hand.

Huh? A fist?

She let go of the camera, which was attached to her wrist by a strong strap, and drew a question mark on her tablet.

He frowned and frisked her, diving into pockets and checking her gear.

What was he looking for? She offered him her altimeter, her undersea knife, her flashlight, and her spare grease pencil. The octopus watched them curiously. Torun shook his head and drew a black circle on her tablet. He tapped it.

Yes, the cave was beneath them. Its entrance looked just like the circle.

His brows drew down in frustration.

The behemoth floated closer.

She grabbed her camera again, mentally composing her Facebook Live commentary to overlay after the video posted. *Look at those curling tentacles!* Octopi were territorial. Perhaps this cave was its territory.

The gigantic octopus floated so close, she could reach out and touch it.

Then it touched her.

No way.

Gigantic tentacles curled around her body, stroking her skin thoughtfully. It regarded her with one giant eye and then the other.

Hello, *National Geographic!*

She held herself completely still. Yes, it could crush her like an elephant stomping on a grasshopper. But she felt unnaturally calm. This giant octopus's magnificence and gentle intelligence impressed her. It was almost like she could hear it telling her not to fear. That she was safe.

Its arms tapered to tips the size of her fist. One tickled her bare cheek, where minutes ago, Torun had kissed her. A white sucker lightly suctioned her skin and released.

This octopus was hereby dubbed Mr. Huggles.

Torun made a loud thrumming noise and darted forward. He pushed the tentacles off her and raised a fist.

Mr. Huggles snagged his ankle and swung him away.

Torun flew through the water and into the cave wall. He floated, as if stunned, and then rubbed his head.

Uh-oh.

She kicked toward Torun. Was he okay?

The octopus blocked her path.

Again, she didn't feel afraid. She stroked its slick, rubbery tentacles. The ultimate neoprene, it was perfectly suited for underwater. Arms wrapped around her, tangling her in a gentle, undulating hug.

Wow.

She didn't expect the octopus to understand written English, but all the same, she wrote on the tablet. "Sorry, I need to check on him."

The octopus watched her writing. One curious arm curled around her grease pencil and carried it away. Another tentacle tugged on her tablet, and a third stroked her hair.

Safe. Curious. Safe.

Torun shook his head, kicked over to them, and hummed loud and deep as a bellow.

The octopus twitched. Mr. Huggles caressed her, but with surreptitious glances at Torun, like a dog who knew it was disobeying its owner to eat the steak on the table.

Torun bellowed again and gestured for it to get lost.

The octopus released her and scooted into the depths. Several tentacles curled apologetically in Torun's direction. One clutched her grease pencil.

Amazing!

She turned the cell phone camera on herself. A bug-eyed selfie showed her hair in disarray. *What would the girls think of that?* She made the A-OK gesture and stopped the recording. It saved to her internal memory and turned off.

Torun smoothed her hair. Worried lines ringed his eyes. He checked her over, but she was fine. The only injury was sucker marks, red impressions, on his ankle. She touched him to make sure he was all right.

Hey. His fins were not only flesh tone, but also smooth and formfitting, as if they grew from his skin.

Her hard plastic fins were ridged. His fins were more like frog's feet, with the toes elongated and skin spread out between them in an accordion.

This was…advanced diving technology, right?

What the hell *was* Torun? A CIA tribesman with secret military undersea augmentations?

Her brain struggled.

Maybe she was narced. Nitrogen narcosis caused crazy hallucinations. She'd passed into the depths where her tank's pressure-condensed gasses acted like a drug, and even experienced divers made idiot mistakes.

Or maybe her once-in-a-lifetime encounter with the world's friendliest gigantic octopus made her thoughts swim wild. If the oceans could hide an octopus so big, why not a merman or five?

Oh God. What if she *was* narced and the only thing that showed up on video was empty ocean because the whole awesome octopus was in her head?

Yeah, that was the most likely explanation.

Her mysterious could-be merman beckoned her into the cave.

Well, she was here, wasn't she? Maybe her brain was playing tricks on her. Maybe she wanted his merman story to be true so badly, she tricked herself into seeing things that didn't exist.

Lucy clicked on her undersea flashlight. Time to find out where this new adventure led.

FIFTEEN

Torun's heart would not calm.

Lucy swam in front of him. Her electric light cast a meager glow swallowed by the large, winding cave neck. He replayed the scene outside the cave.

The deadly cave guardian rose from the depths. Lucy did *not* brandish the Sea Opal. The cave guardian stroked and tasted her fearlessness.

Why did she not show the gem? The cave guardian must have tasted the Sea Opal on her body. Otherwise...

Imagining his crushed, mangled bride gave a metallic taste to his nightmares.

Lucy tapped a device on her wrist and pointed to the surface. She wanted to rise.

He gestured for her to continue on. Half the cave complex remained.

She recovered her second grease pencil, cleaned her board, and wrote inscrutable symbols. He guessed the meaning from her body language. She worried about her air. Back on the trawler, she'd performed complex calculations with Gracie before wrapping herself in plastic-encased bubbles and entering the water.

"You are almost at the cavern," he assured her. "There is air for you to breathe. You will not need this portable supply once you have drunk the elixir and transformed."

Inside the air bubble in her face mask, her brows furrowed. She underlined symbols.

"Trust me." He stroked her cheek. Cool and smooth. "I promise, upon the honor of my castle, you will be well."

She clamped the black circular device in her mouth. Bubbles flurried out with every breath. They tickled.

This was why the cave guardian had played with her. Air-breathing humans were so interesting. And so ticklish.

He arced over her and drifted through the tunnel. "The sooner we arrive at the cavern, the sooner you will feel reassured."

"Waghlaghl," she said, attempting to speak normally.

The water medium terribly distorted her words. Still, wasn't she saying his name with disbelief?

"Come, Lucy." He floated at the edge of her flashlight. "Do not fear the water."

She wrinkled her nose, breaking the seal of her mask and losing bubbles. Seawater sloshed in.

Lucy sighed, pressed one edge of the mask, and blew even more bubbles. The air returned to the mask full and clear. She grimaced at him as though that were his fault and followed him deeper.

He had to convince her twice more to continue, and she whimpered with anxiety by the time they finally reached the open-air cavern.

Uncounted centuries ago, the seas had been lower, and this cavern had existed above the water. When the island broke and the seas rose again, this small bubble became trapped. Many atoll caves contained bubbles. Their isolation gave mer an opportunity to practice land walking and air breathing unseen.

Lucy floated to the ledge. She removed the black tube from her mouth. "This is amazing! I'm sorry I doubted you. Help me up."

He assisted her from the water. She unclipped the heavy belt of weights from her waist, wriggled out of her leaden air tank, and unsnapped her inflated vest. Beneath the surroundings of artificial air, she wore a skintight, short-sleeved dive suit in pink-and-blue stripes.

She ran a ticklish finger down his spine to his bare buttocks.

He swayed toward her. "Yes?"

She backed up a step, reddening. "Nothing. I mean, where are your gills, Mister Merman? I didn't see them underwater."

"You will see them after you transform."

"Right." Her flashlight strained to illuminate the distant ceiling. Her words echoed in the cavern. "So, where is the magic potion?"

"The elixir is this way." He led her across the rocky floor. His feet changed shape, returning to a compact human foot.

"This is a pretty good place to hide it. You don't have to worry about thieves breaking in." She stumbled after him. "Our return will have to be more direct. I'm on fumes. No dawdling with giant octopi on the way out."

"Yes, I hope the cave guardian is satisfied by your right to be here. She tasted you thoroughly."

"Tasted?"

"Cave guardians taste with their skin and their suckers.

She touched you all over, so she knows everything about you."

"Like my brand of sunscreen?"

"And what you ate, where you slept, and your likes and dislikes. You communicate many things through your skin. Taste is how cave guardians come to know us and each other."

"So a hug is like a hello. Oh! The octopus is a she? I was going to name her Mr. Huggles."

"I am sure you may name her as you wish. Her name is untranslatable for our tongue, certainly."

Lucy shivered.

"Are you afraid?"

"No. It's cold in here. Aren't you cold?"

"I do not feel cold."

"Hey." She focused her flashlight on an ancient column. A face and hands emerged from the shadows. "This almost looks like a carving."

"It was a church. A sacred church on a sacred island."

Her mouth opened. She touched the stone reverently, awed. "There was more than one?"

"So many, they were scattered across the sea. Our cities also used to be closer to the surface. In that ancient time, we had as many females as males."

She removed her hand and struggled to laugh. "You know, when I'm in a mystical place like this, I almost believe everything you say is literally true."

"It is."

"I mean, that it's not just a mistranslation by our language barrier, or culture or something." She climbed the worn steps to the dais.

"It is the truth." He stood before the weathered offering bowl. "Drink."

She peered into the depths. Her flashlight washed out the natural iridescence of a thousand years of liqueur steeped in the Life Tree Sea Opals. "This is the elixir?"

"Diluted. It will create a temporary transformation."

She hesitated.

"What is the problem?"

"I was imagining a future conversation with my doctor. As in, 'Well, Doctor, I was feeling fine until I followed a mysterious tribal warrior into an undersea cave and drank from a pool of stagnant water.'"

"It is not stagnant," he said.

"It's brackish." She disturbed the silt, revealing the mating jewels. Her jaw dropped. "Are those Sea Opals?"

"Yes."

"There's enough here for a hundred yachts! A thousand!"

"Please do not gather these." He stopped her from fumbling for her bag. "You may collect unclaimed gems in my city. These belong to the brides of the past."

She closed her bag as he asked and shivered again, harder. "Now I really have made the pool brackish."

"Turn off your light."

She did. Beneath the swirling silt, the pool shimmered with the pale opalescence of the still-potent jewels piled in its depths.

"Now do you see?"

She didn't answer.

A new, small light appeared. Her cell phone.

"There's no signal," she said to the camera, "and I can't see a darned thing, and also it's freezing, but I wanted some documentation of this"—she shot the pool with the phone flash—"in case someone has to recover my body. I am drinking this cold, brackish water from a pool filled with Sea

Opals so that I can gain the power of mermen and travel to Torun's undersea city, where he says there are 'many more' Sea Opals than here. Ready? Elyssa, Mel, here we go."

Lucy scooped up a handful of water and slurped it for her camera.

His belly tensed.

Although he had imagined a bride joining him like this a thousand times, now that the moment had arrived, Lucy's actions were both more practical and more worrying than he had imagined.

Would the temporary elixir work on her? Was there something special about the brides of the sacred island? Could this mainland woman from a country called Oregon also not transform?

Her soul must resonate with his to activate the Sea Opal-infused elixir. Would it do so? Had she bonded to Torun deeply enough?

Lucy was a special human. She possessed the capacity for great brightness, more than any other woman. Her soul had shone steadily since she left the trawler and entered the water, proving her connectedness to the ocean. She had flared brighter yet with her introduction to the cave guardian and had been allowed to pass.

She swished the liquid around in her mouth and swallowed. "Not bad. A little salty, which is what you'd expect, but also, there's another flavor. It's not sweet, not bitter. Maybe savory? A bit umami."

"How do you feel?" The words were tight in his throat.

"I don't know. Normal, I guess." She swirled her hand in the water. Iridescence twinkled. "How long does it take?"

He had never attended this ceremony. Brides completed the transformation before they entered the water. He barely remembered their arrivals, escorted by an honor guard into the city, from his youth.

"What signs should I look for?" she asked.

"You will be able to swim better and see without your flashlight. Come, let us test it in the water."

Her toe stubbed against an outcropping, and she swore. "Forget seeing without the flashlight."

"Try in the water, without the air bubble on your face."

She knelt on the ledge, set up her cell phone, and started another recording. "In the interest of science, here is the first test of the fabled mermaid elixir."

Lucy held her breath and dunked her face in the water.

He slipped in, darted beneath her, and looked up.

She had her eyes closed.

He tickled her nose and spoke to her under the water. The words vibrated in his chest. "You will never see anything that way."

She wrinkled her nose, eyes still closed, and lifted her head out. He bobbed to the surface beside her.

"I'll never see anything with my eyes open either." She wiped her face.

"Come all the way in."

"I should have brought my snorkel."

"Come." He rested his hands on her knees. "Remove your human coverings. Leave the surface world behind. Take a deep breath beneath the ocean and immerse yourself in your destiny."

She squinted. "And don't choke when 'my destiny' pours into my lungs?"

"Believe, Lucy. Your body changes at your will. You *must* will it."

Her soul diminished. She hugged herself. "You don't

always get what you want. It doesn't matter how badly you want it."

"Breathing underwater is as natural as losing yourself in your true love's kiss."

She stared across the pitch-black cave pool. Her fingers stroked his hair, slivering through his wet locks. She no longer shivered, and her skin had smoothed. Her fingers did not wrinkle.

"Maybe I'm overthinking it," she murmured and focused on him. "I'm afraid."

His gut clenched. "I thought you were not afraid of the water."

"I'm afraid of you."

Him? No, impossible. He misunderstood. "Me?"

She smoothed his cheek with her firm fingertips. Sadness touched her lips. "What will you do when I transform, we go to your city, and the Life Tree *doesn't* heal me?"

"The Life Tree is more powerful than you can imagine."

"What if it isn't?" She burned with the intensity of her question. "Will you leave me for another woman? Or will you stay with me no matter what happens?"

SIXTEEN

Her question, no matter how she phrased it, didn't seem to penetrate Torun's thick skull.

"Your soul light is so bright," he said. "You will surely be healed by the Life Tree."

"But what if I'm not?"

"Lucy."

"Promise me you'll stay."

"Of course."

"Don't just toss off an answer. Promise me you'll give us a shot even after you finally realize I really can't have kids."

"The Life Tree *will* heal you." His aquamarine eyes gleamed with intensity. "Have faith."

Faith was the one thing she couldn't give him.

She had wished for a baby for too long. Her chest trembled with her unanswered prayers. The agony from the past year threatened to well up like a tsunami and drown her in the self-destructive longing that had ended her marriage, hope, and career.

"You're a failure as a woman and a failure as a human being."

Lucy had always just assumed she would have children. People did all the time, and frequently by accident. It was so unfair. She wanted a baby a hundred thousand times more. She wanted it with her whole soul.

Science had failed her. Then her marriage had failed.

Unquenched desires had ripped her soul in half. How could she trust in a magical tree to stitch her back together again?

Torun waited for her in the water with complete faith.

Could she throw off all that pain and leap forward, blindly hopeful, all over again? Maybe this time, the fertility treatment would work. It was magical, after all. Maybe this time, the husband would stay. Maybe this time, she could have the family she'd always desired.

Maybe this time.

Her cell phone camera light turned off. The recording had timed out and stopped.

The blackness sank into her. She sat by herself, more alone than she had been since signing her divorce papers.

Lucy turned to start the recording again. The expedition recordings were for posterity. For science. Not for a weepy record of yet another failure.

Her hand hit the edge of the precariously balanced case. Her phone clattered off the ledge and disappeared into shadow.

"Darn." She quested for it with her hands in the darkness. "I forgot my flashlight by the Sea Opals."

Water sloshed, and Torun's form pulled her upright. He was a lighter shadow against pitch blackness.

"I will get this flashlight. Do not fill your head with any more fears or doubts. You are capable of great things. Focus."

Right. The reason she was here, in this cave, breathing

air was because she had trusted in him and quested after the—

His lips brushed hers. Cool and firm. Wet from the ocean. Filled with promises.

Desire sizzled through her veins and awakened an answering need in her center. She clung to his hard biceps. This was right. *He* was right.

Torun showed her a new world. All she had to do was open her eyes and accept it.

He pulled away. Hunger gleamed in his eyes.

She was no longer cold, and it was no longer quite so dark. His features almost glowed with his confidence in her.

"Have faith," he said again, and turned away.

She sat.

Hey, there was her cell phone! And it was recording, of all things. She switched it to battery supersaver mode and affixed it to her BCD. The next time she surfaced, the phone would awaken and search for an internet connection to post the videos on Facebook. Hopefully, they would post after she discovered mermaid superpowers, and not after she gave up on another stupid, gullible dream.

Well, that was probably what the comments would call her anyway. *You honestly believed he was a merman? And drinking brackish water would make you into a mermaid? Ha-ha! You got punked!*

Wait. Was that the only reason she held back? Because she worried about internet trolls calling her dumb?

That was like worrying whether the sun would rise tomorrow.

Trolls were going to troll. Haters were going to hate. Did Neil Armstrong hesitate to stand on the moon just because it had never been done before? Moon landings must have sounded science-fiction crazy in the early 1960s.

Remove your human coverings.

Lucy stripped off her tight dive suit and tankini, folded them beside the BCD, and knelt at the edge of the water. Her naked butt rested on her bare feet. The rock was wet and cold.

Have faith.

Torun needed a woman to continue his race. Eventually, he would understand the woman he needed wasn't Lucy. Should he promise to stay with her after that? No.

All Lucy could do was enjoy every minute with him until their last.

Once he tossed her aside, she would be left alone...with mermaid superpowers. Wow. Not a bad outcome for a professional diver. There were worse ways to come out of a relationship, that was for darn sure.

Plus, she already *had* one Sea Opal. No matter what happened after today, she would use the Sea Opal Gracie was safeguarding to pay off the expedition debt, refill Elyssa's savings, and un-double-mortgage Mel's house. She would start a dating site for Torun's tribe. If the tribe was a fraction as hot as he was, their profiles would get hits from loving, romantic, adventurous women by the boatload.

Concentrate on your Sea Opal...

Right.

Focus.

She eased into the water naked. Chilly ocean seeped into her cracks and bits. She wriggled. Her body felt funny and exposed and crazy and free. She closed her eyes, held her breath, and slipped beneath the surface.

Something brushed her nose.

She opened her eyes.

A white fish about the length of her index finger stared at her with first one eye, then the other. It glowed with an inner light, like an angel, and illuminated the water around it.

More fish joined in.

The undersea world was lit as bright as midday in downtown Cancun. Algae sparkled, and fish gleamed.

Even Lucy herself glowed.

Was this bioluminescence? She'd missed it because of her flashlight. Or was the elixir working?

Strange singing filled her ears.

A low *hum-hum* emerged from the small, white fishes. Higher pitched *whee-whee* came from the gently swaying anemones. Barnacles clacked and drummed like the bass line from *The Lion King* song "The Circle of Life."

She swam to a rock formation. Undersea slugs called nudibranchs inched across the rocks. They sang a *baba-dum* noise and wiggled their Technicolor feelers in her direction. They must have sensed her like she sensed them.

One off-kilter noise, a combination of gargling and strangling, disrupted the undersea harmony. Kind of like the tone-deaf seagull from Disney's *The Little Mermaid*, which she'd watched growing up about ten thousand times.

The awful song came from the mouth of the cave.

What could be out there? She swam to the neck.

Something crashed into the water, and movement whispered a gentle breeze across her body. She turned.

Torun dove deep. A powerful, dark energy emanated from his chest, hot like chocolate and spicy as cinnamon. His head whipped to her. He jackknifed and flicked his fins. He was coming, and he didn't stop. Crashing into her, he embraced and rolled her end over end.

Relief filled his deep, resonant voice. "You are here."

She laughed in surprise. Bubbles escaped her mouth, and she tasted sea salt.

Where else would she be?

"I did not find you on the surface. I became alarmed."

Well, he shouldn't worry. She wasn't going anywhere without him.

He held her close, stroking her. His limbs twined with hers. Need for him filled her veins with fire.

His mouth found hers. Heat streaked to her center, twisting with a pounding ache. His tongue teased her seam. She opened to him, inviting in his unstoppable confidence, his masculine force.

He responded, his tongue tangling with hers, bringing her to full, hungry awareness.

Lucy splayed her hands across his broad back.

His muscles rippled. Hard ridges flexed on his shoulder blades.

She pulled back and tried to say, "You have little fin-ridges."

It came out as, "Yaghlagh."

The words bubbled away. Water poured down her throat. Cold and heavy, it filled her nostrils and weighed down her lungs. She choked.

His voice penetrated her panic. "Do not try to speak. Not as you do in the air."

She was drowning. *Drowning!* She scrambled for the surface.

He caught her ankle and yanked her to him again, enclosing her struggles within his arms. "Shhh."

No, no. She jerked. She had to get to the surface. Air. Her instinct to run couldn't be controlled.

"Sure you can," he said, replying to her thoughts.

Air. She needed to breathe. Air.

He renewed his grip, his thighs tightening in a powerful

clench. "You are already breathing. I will hold you until you recognize it."

Was she?

Oh.

Yes, she had been underwater far too long to hold her breath, and even though her lungs felt heavy, she was still... well, not breathing, but not dying either. Lucy opened her mouth, releasing the last of the bubbles. Ocean cooled her belly, like drinking ice water on a hot day and noticing as it slid all the way down.

But how?

She contorted to touch the small of her back. Thick ridges, like the vents on an air conditioner, opened and closed like a fish's gills. Except it was her.

Magic.

The water felt natural, and she hung, weightless, perfectly balanced even without her BCD. How? It was like a dream of flying.

"Yes, and you will not crash to the ground," he agreed.

How could he understand the words she wasn't speaking aloud?

"You are saying them." He thrummed deep in his chest. "You communicate your meaning with gestures and vibrations."

No. That didn't make any sense.

"You are doing it right now. Do you not sense the vibrations? My words, how am I speaking them? My mouth is not open, and you do not hear them with your ears."

The truth smacked her head like an unsecured cabinet.

His eyes gleamed, gorgeous aquamarine with more intense gold threads, and his words hummed in his chest. The vibrations rumbled across her skin and then formed words deep inside, behind her sternum, in a sort of echo chamber.

She tried to create the same vibrations. "Like...magic."

"Now you are vibrating on purpose." His lips stretched wider. He kissed her deeply, and while his mouth covered hers, he continued communicating. "You have understood so much so fast. Truly you are meant to be one of us."

Yes. She rubbed against his hard, slippery body. Her nipples pearled against his bare chest. "I want to be with you."

They twirled together upside down.

"Will you join with me?" He nuzzled her gently. "Forsake the world of the air, and become a mer forever?"

If you keep me...

"Of course," he responded to her silent caveat—which was strange because she *knew* she hadn't vibrated it. "I will worship you as my queen."

"Okay," she vibrated, even though she knew he was asking for more. He didn't just want a queen. He wanted a queen who would have his children.

SEVENTEEN

Lucy's tentative promise nestled deep in Torun's heart.

Even more important than when she had accepted his Sea Opal, her promise to join him forever etched their fate in stone. She knew what his ocean world truly entailed. She promised to leave the air world behind.

"Come. We will go to my city."

She wiggled. "Let me grab my cell phone. How deep is your city?"

"It is on the bottom of the ocean."

"The bottom close to an atoll like this, or the bottom of a trench?"

"We are not near a trench. However, swimming directly up to the surface would take a long, long time."

"Probably deeper than the waterproof case is rated for." She relaxed into him. "I'll come back. We'll organize deep-sea cameras later to take pictures of a real mer city."

"You will have many chances." The council would have to relax their secrecy restrictions to woo modern women. Lucy would show others the beauty of their world.

He somehow sensed her unexpressed doubt, which was odd because he never heard unexpressed feelings from other warriors. *I hope so.*

"You will."

She smiled.

He twirled with her through the water. His body pulsed to fulfill their ancient destiny in this submerged church. She shone within his arms, nearly blinding.

But her doubts remained. She feared she could not give him young fry. She needed the healing song of the Life Tree to chase her last fears away.

He led her to the cave entrance.

She kicked furiously to keep up. "I can't make my feet into fins like yours."

"You must flex." He demonstrated, flicking back and forth between fin and foot.

She tried to mimic him. Her adorable features screwed up in concentration. "Do it slower."

Slower made the movement more difficult. Like focusing on breathing could cause choking in the lungs.

"You can't blame me for choking like that," she said, responding to a thought he hadn't meant to transmit to her. "It was my first time! Normally, breathing underwater is death, if not from actually drowning, then from the bacterial infection and pneumonia you get afterward. Oh!"

She flexed her foot in the right way. Her two smallest toes flattened, and her foot half expanded. She kicked, wheeling in a lopsided circle. "This is awesome!"

Her light shone so brightly, it made his heart ache.

But she couldn't get her other foot to relax into the correct shape, and her first one flexed back to a human foot when she wasn't paying attention. He put his hands on hers to stop her from being too violent with herself.

"It just won't go," she cried.

"You have mastered breathing and communicating underwater," he told her. "Forgive yourself if you must practice longer to achieve flight."

She blew a stream of water out of her mouth. Her bangs danced. "I'll get it."

"You will."

She brightened. His faith in her made hers stronger.

Again, his chest ached.

This precious woman captured him. His heart stretched to hold their love. He would protect her with his life.

He drew her arms around his neck. "Hold on to me. This first flight will be mine."

She nestled against his chest. "Don't drop me."

"Never."

He kicked powerfully. They rocketed from the cave, shooting past the occupied cave guardian, and wove through the atoll formations to the open sea.

"Whoohoo!" she cried, clinging tight.

He held her safe, suctioning her softness to his body.

This was how all mates were meant to travel. Once she grew her fins properly and adjusted to the permanent change, they would forever travel the seas together in their mated pair.

Such a wonderful future dazzled him.

"Hey, I meant to ask. What's that strange noise?" she asked. "It's behind us now. It's like singing, only really off-key."

"Probably Mr. Huggles," Torun said, adopting her name for the cave guardian. She would name many more things in their ocean, and he wanted her to feel proud of doing so. "Their songs are loud and terrible, especially after they have collected a new object."

"She did steal my grease pencil."

"It is now her new favorite possession, and she is announcing it to every other guardian."

She swallowed. "I'm kind of touched."

He squeezed her. Her empathy, like her kindness, resonated in her soul.

"I'm also sorry I made her sound worse."

"Do not be. Their awful song gives warning for miles. You can navigate half the ocean by using cave guardians as markers. It is as reliable as your GPS."

"Do we sound as awful to them?"

Did they? All living creatures sang. Even inanimate rocks possessed a song under the water. The mer must also have a soul sound.

"Don't assume it's beautiful," she said. "Or, at least, not to everybody. What if we sound like sandpaper or a diesel engine backfiring? Or squealing brakes, or nails on a chalkboard?"

"We sound like no such thing," he said. "We sound like solemn tones."

"Perhaps we toot."

She made him laugh. The absurdity of it all. Human women would turn mer warriors into philosophers.

"Or scientists," she said. "If we can measure animal and rock sounds, we can measure our own."

Again, she had picked up thoughts he was certain he had not projected. How odd.

"It's so bright," she said, changing topics and staring out across the wide undersea sky of the ocean. "I can see so far."

"More than before?"

"So much. I can see tiny plankton on the surface miles away. I can see Mr. Huggles hanging out behind us in her cave. Ocean currents move like clouds. It even feels like I can see *through* rocks to the other side."

All objects and creatures gave off a resonance. Some part of the resonance Lucy now experienced as song. Other parts of the resonance she experienced as light. Some as taste.

He had struggled at first to handle the opposite problem on land. He could see only so far, and he experienced air as a cold, empty, silent vacuum.

"Are you ready to go faster?" he asked.

"Faster? But we're already outpacing schools of fish."

"We are approaching a finger of the super-accelerated Sol Sud current. We have a long way to reach our city."

Her eyes opened wide. "Yes!"

"Hold tight." He arced into the current.

She laughed with joy.

Torun flew fast within the current at first to show off, then soared for the joy of doing so. How had it been long since he'd pushed himself to peak effort? Chasing mini-accelerated currents within the main one, he dove ever onward, ever down.

When he had been a young fry, his wise elders took him to safe fields near the city to learn his abilities. When he had grown older, he'd tested himself against dangerous creatures, pitting his life against their speed to overcome near-death experiences and survive.

Now he flew in his mating dance, pushing himself to ever greater bursts, astonishing and delighting his bride. Joy suffused her, and she opened her eyes to all around.

Soon they would reach his city, and he would enjoy her in the privacy of his castle. Thick walls would keep out danger and muffle their passion. He kicked harder.

They traveled far. When exhaustion finally took him,

he drifted in the current, resting while she also dozed. He did this several times until he needed to exit the current. He swam through slower overland currents to his city.

Lucy asked a number of questions, which he answered as best he could.

Yes, the mer were good at avoiding detection. No, he did not know if the mer were descended from humans or sharks or whether they were extraterrestrials.

"Once, the mer moved easily between earth and ocean," he told her. "After a great war, about a thousand years ago, the mer withdrew from the air. You don't know of it?"

"We have a myth about Atlantis sinking, but nobody ever claimed the Atlanteans weren't human."

"We truly did disappear from your records," he reflected. "Once our females died out, only the brides of the sacred islands honored an ancient covenant to secretly provide our race with young fry. Now, you join their noble ranks."

"Now, me." She stroked the back of his neck. "God, I hope so."

He squeezed her.

They approached the border of Sireno's land.

Coral spires rose from the ocean floor, marking the beginning of the towering outer reefs. In the distance, glowing bulbs formed the floating city. The Sireno cave guardian warbled from his cave to the east.

"You really can hear those cave guardians," she said with a laugh. "This one sounds like a cat being strangled by a frog."

"Yes, he is a lonely male."

Torun slowed. Passing between the spires placed them in dangerous territory. They could be heard by warriors lying silent.

Lucy ignored this danger. "If he's lonely, why doesn't he go to meet a female? Mr. Huggles had no guy."

"Mating is dangerous for cave guardians. Sometimes one is not in the mood, and the other may get eaten."

She stilled. "That's not what happens when we mate, right?"

"No." He lowered his vibration. "We are not cannibals. Shh."

"Good," she whispered, "because I was so sure that you weren't really a merman that I left a lot of open ground. And I don't want to turn into some red-eyed, zombie-vampire squid."

"Yes, that would be quite unsettling. We are normal. It is fine."

Hmm. The guard towers above the spires were empty. No evidence of recent patrols marked the reef.

He approached the echo point, an intersection of currents. They had to be silent because while he could hear all echo points around them, anyone in those points could also hear him.

The water was clear and still. The tinkling chimes of the distant Life Tree, the peculiar song of Sireno, became amplified.

Something wasn't right...

She wiggled, clearly still anxious about his last revelation. "By n—"

"Shh!"

Their voices projected outward.

But still, the city was silent. Emptied, as though not even a single guard had been left home.

How very, very odd. The only time that could happen was during the death of the Life Tree.

Or an attack.

EIGHTEEN

Torun's movements were cautious and jerky. After shushing her, he was clearly on high alert.

Lucy clung to him. The closeness of pressing against his hard, muscular body was delicious, but if only her fins worked properly, she could help.

They passed a second echo point.

"There are many echo points around the city," he murmured. "And one current can take your voice to another city. Always a guard is stationed at that echo point. For the entire city to empty like this, something terrible must have happened."

Another mer floated on the far end of a ridged reef.

Torun froze. They drifted on their own, lower, current.

This merman was thinner than Torun, with red-and-black iridescent tattoos instead of gold. He carried a gold trident and stared up, the way they had come, transfixed. Like Torun, he was completely naked. Tattoos swirled around his impressive manhood.

With males like these, the future tribal dating site would not be hard to advertise.

Torun ghosted past.

They passed more tribesmen, all hot, all tattooed. Also, all kept glancing overhead, distracted and unwary, while Torun hugged the coral reef underneath them.

Much of the ocean floor was bare like a moonscape. Not the area around Torun's city. A great bubble of vibrant life exploded from its brilliant center, like a sun with a corona. Schools of deep-sea fish darted over the currents. The living reef spread out as a disc-shaped plateau teeming with a celestial glow.

Rising from the center of the disc, a city of shimmering bulbs floated in the middle of the ocean. Each bulb glowed with a subtly different shade of white. One with a dark chocolate- cinnamon tint attracted her. That must be Torun's castle.

These monolithic balloons, bull kelp grown to gigantic proportions, increased the song of the reef like a symphony director swelling to the crescendo.

Torun wove through the anchoring trunks to the central column. It looked thick enough to install an elevator. Scarred with age, it also glowed the brightest.

He swam up the column to the city. "We may swim near others soon. If any look at you, pretend that you are an injured male from another city."

Her hips and boobs hadn't exactly melted away in the transition. "Will that really work?"

"Most obey the council's restrictions from visiting the surface and have not seen a human since Prince Jolan's mother, decades ago. I will move at an average speed and try to avoid their interest."

"Fly casual," she murmured.

"Yes, exactly."

The central column widened and thickened to form a

dais. Torun flew above the lip. In the center, like the stamen of a gigantic lily, ruled the Life Tree.

Radiance shone outward with awe-inspiring grace, blotting out the rest of the ocean. Blessed silence fell upon her. She hadn't realized how loud the ocean's music was until now, when it had all been whited out.

Torun circled the dais. He was both reverent and watchful.

Little tinkles of sound cascaded through the bare branches and down the tree. Small pebbles exuded from the tree, fell from the upper branches, and piled around the trunk, like a white bonsai in a circular planter.

He swam closer.

Oh, wait. Those white objects were neither pebbles nor fruit. They were Sea Opals. The smallest was the size of her fist. Some were even larger than her head.

The pebbles were resin bleeding from the tree. These were the mating jewels? It seemed like the mermen had a symbiotic relationship. The Life Tree gave its own blood to draw new life to it. Each opal fell as a drop of hope for a mer to bring back his bride.

Torun seemed to read her thoughts. "When you and I unite, the Life Tree will sense our union and grow a blossom. The nectar inside will heal your body and transform you to live under the water permanently."

Wow. She gripped him closer. "How do we unite?"

"First, the commitment of honor. Second, the commitment of body. Finally, the commitment of soul. Are you ready?"

"I'm so ready."

He swam her to the edge of the dais. "We must cross onto the Life Tree platform together, as partners."

She disentangled from him and gripped his hand. The

dais glowed pure white like a holy church. She kicked her bare human feet to propel her across.

They landed in front of the tree.

"Now, follow my example." Torun knelt and bowed his head to its glistening white trunk. "I, Torun of Sireno, present Lucy as my chosen bride. Please shower your blessing and healing on our union and give us a young fry son."

He kissed the trunk and retreated.

This was her wedding ceremony. Her heart thumped. Fewer guests this time, and yet it was somehow even more meaningful.

Lucy walked in his footsteps. The Sea Opals shifted beneath her bare feet, warm and smooth.

She knelt. "I, Lucy of Newport, Oregon, present Torun as my chosen groom. Please shower your blessing and healing on our union and give us a young fry baby."

Torun could hope for all the sons he wanted, but she wouldn't specify. Any baby would fulfill her longest and most fiercely held dream.

She kissed the trunk.

Krish! Tinkling increased as though a new breeze shivered through the tree.

Huh.

Had Torun heard the same when he pressed his lips to the smooth bark? She rose to her feet and looked back at him.

His face was white, his mouth open. He looked up, over her head, to the top of the tree.

Uh-oh.

He focused on her, smiled, and held out his hand.

Maybe it was okay.

She pushed off the dais and floated to him. He linked

their fingers, sliding his warm digits between hers, and kissed the back of her hand. Sweet, tender.

The hunger in his gaze filled her belly with a sizzling promise. "Now, the physical commitment?" she asked.

"Soon."

"How soon?" She'd been pressed up against him forever. The shape of his body was imprinted on hers, and the dark chocolate-cinnamon scent pulsed in her blood. She wanted to consummate their marriage now.

His aquamarine eyes glowed. Did he sense her growing arousal? "Very soon."

Her stomach growled.

He blinked in surprise and then smiled. "Come, my queen-to-be. Let me feed you."

NINETEEN

Of all the timing!

Torun heard those funny words in his mind as clearly as if Lucy had spoken them aloud. Was it even a real communication? The foreign thought pushed into his mind, and then Lucy rubbed her stomach. It had to be from her. She was ravenous, and his castle was not far.

He tugged her through the city, swimming between the king's castle and council castles, and outward, to the periphery. They met no one, thankfully, on the approach to his domicile.

The city was empty. The border guards acted watchful, not warlike, meaning there was not a risk of attack. Perhaps the jack migrations had come early and the city emptied for a great hunt. Had the city been occupied, the entire community would have assembled at the Life Tree's single note, sounded when Lucy had kissed the trunk.

What did the note mean?

He had not heard any song from the Life Tree in

decades. Not since Prince Jolan's birth, the last presentation of a young fry.

Had the tree recognized Lucy's resonance? The note had tapered to a minor key. Did it hold a different, more sinister warning?

No. Impossible.

Lucy was his mate. He accepted no other woman as his queen.

But what if the Life Tree did not heal her?

The thought jarred him with shocking awareness.

He had intended to claim a bride. The brightest soul, whoever she was. But that was no longer true.

Now, he knew Lucy more deeply than any other. Even more deeply than his own warriors. He had met her friends and listened to her dreams. She was not his bride. She was *his Lucy*.

She resisted him. She threw herself at him. She spoke of transferring his attraction to another woman. She spoke of an incurable illness.

Madness. She would be healed by the Life Tree. She had to be. No other bride would ever satisfy him.

This odd, jarring note from the Life Tree was just its attempt to recognize and welcome her after so many years without a bride.

Yes.

Joining would sweep all doubts away.

Torun squeezed Lucy's hands and pulled her faster through the water. They approached his family's castle, and the entrance appeared as a pinprick in the center of the bulb.

"This is your castle?" she asked.

"Yes. Do you like it?"

"It's big."

His stomach churned. Everything she said and did took on extra significance as he evaluated whether her answers proved she was fit for this life or whether the Life Tree's note had been a warning of disaster. "Is that a problem?"

"No, it's just new." She looked way up. "A perfect sphere and one tiny entrance."

Although tiny in comparison to the overall size of the castle, the main entrance gaped wide enough for six mer warriors to enter, shoulder to shoulder. Thick walls dampened the music of the ocean to a quiet, fanlike hum of privacy.

They entered his castle. She craned her neck to look behind them. "No door?"

"If we are attacked, this passage will seal off the uninvited."

"That's handy."

They swam into the inner courtyard.

Windows of rooms dotted the inner walls. His family's castle was old, so the rooms had grown several layers thick. Soil was tilled in the inner courtyard, and gardens burst with overgrown food. Torun's ancestors had once housed large families of ten, fifteen, twenty grown mer and their young fry. Now, as in so many other emptied castles, he was the last of his line to survive.

In the center of the garden, one single column grew up and formed a living dais. It glowed with the pure white seed of the Life Tree.

She swam to the seed. "What's this? It looks like a big fava bean."

"It is our right and legacy. Every house pledges to protect and honor the Life Tree. In return, we are blessed with one seed. Should we fail in our duty, our seed is crushed, and we are cast out of the city."

She touched a notch in the dais. "Is this a decoration?"

"No."

Dread settled in the pit of his belly. Several more notches were near the first. Trident-points, dagger-marks. A battle had taken place here while he was on the surface, long enough ago that his castle had returned to relative normalcy, but recently enough to put him on guard.

"A rival tried to dishonor or destroy my house."

Her mouth opened. She looked at the entrance. "I thought you said it would close. Are we in danger?"

"The gate may be breached, but the house will defend itself from attack."

If the king had turned against him, the council would have mustered a large force, and his seed would be gone. *Good.* These marks were the act of a few disgruntled mer, not a concerted attack. He still had the chance to earn the king's goodwill with Lucy.

She studied the seed. "Will it ever grow?"

"Yes. The most honorable males choose a leader to found a new city. They plant his seed, and the others plant theirs around him. The leader's seed grows into a new Life Tree. Those around take on the power of its founding house."

"That's a heck of a down payment. It must be hard to move."

"We do not move."

She looked at him.

"We all"—he indicated himself—"form a life-blood connection to our Life Tree and remain where we are planted. Many feel angst about the young leader of Atlantis's wish to draw off males. That is another reason he has been imprisoned. Founding a new city bloods the old, and we cannot afford to lose more warriors. That is why you will stay with me and invigorate Sireno. Together, we will fill it with new hope and new life."

"Changing at home is the best place to start." She placed her hand over her heart. "I pledge...do I pledge?"

"It is not necessary," he said. "Brides usually do not. However, it is customary among close males, and I would be honored if you pledged to defend our seed."

"How do I do it?"

He told her the words, and she repeated them.

"I vow to defend this seed as I defend my home."

The dedication moved him. A lump formed in his throat, unexpected and tight. His queen-to-be pledged herself to their castle. It felt like she was vowing to join with him all over again.

"As it will defend you," he intoned, finishing the father-son recognition ritual. "Kiss the seed as you kissed the trunk."

Her hand hovered over the seed. "I can touch it?"

"Yes."

She picked it up. It filled her hand, oblong, striated, and white. Her lips touched its smooth surface. Sand wafted off.

How embarrassing. That was a result of his inattention. "Sorry for the mess."

"Not at all." She polished the seed and set it back in its place of honor. "This is a lot to take care of by yourself."

True. Since the passing of his uncle, only he remained to carry on the traditions and battle the upkeep.

First, he showed her the fruits and vegetables ready for harvesting.

"This one tastes like corn." She crunched a bumpy rhizome and bit into a succulent fruit. "This is like if an apple and a grape had a baby."

He repaired a basket and harvested a bounty, eating, as she did, while they worked.

"Do not lose all your hunger. There is still the physical commitment of the wedding feast."

"No problem. I feel like I haven't eaten in days!" She brightened. "Lead me to it."

"It is in the pantry."

He swam to the upper balconies and entered. The castle's passages wound and curled, making wonderful nooks and crannies. He had adored playing here as a young fry, hiding from his grandfather and bursting out to startle visiting warriors. Soon, their own young fry would fill these hallowed halls.

He swelled with purpose. The rest of the castle was a mess, but he cared for the pantry. He swam the last turn. At least here, his queen-to-be would see the glory of—

Disaster had struck in here too. Things had been pulled out of secure storage and thrown around. Empty shells and husks lay scattered across the floor and piled in the corners.

His heart sank.

He released her hand to sift through the devastation. "I did not realize I was absent for so long."

"Did the bad guys break in here too?"

"No. This assailant is still in the house."

His Lucy stiffened.

"Do not fear. You will see soon. Where is he?" Torun checked his locked cabinets. All emptied, some smashed. His vintage sea-fruit wines, all decanted. His private-reserve fish cakes. "Show yourself."

The culprit lurked in the shadows.

"Come out!"

Lucy peered into the small dark hole in the wall with concern. "What—"

The house guardian bolted from the hole and gripped Torun. His arms suctioned Torun's body, and his beak clacked furiously. His dark red skin turned bumpy with fury.

Torun protected his face. "Yes, yes. I am sorry. I expected to return sooner. I thought I left enough food."

His house guardian pinched Torun's forearm in his beak, hard.

"Ow! I am sorry!"

Lucy's laughter startled the house guardian. He released Torun and floated backward into his hole.

"Do not ink," Torun warned him. "She is the new mistress of this castle. Lucy, this is the guardian of the castle."

The house guardian regarded her with first one eye, then the other.

"What an adorable red octopus. He's skeptical of me," she said.

"He is hungry," Torun corrected, sweeping up the debris for unopened food to serve his new bride. "And he is a faithful guardian of the house and will not cause you any problems."

"You know, it's funny. I'd say he was large, but after seeing Mr. Huggles, yours seems like a mini pet."

"He is a dangerous pet, but only to those who would try to break in."

"I hope we're friends." Lucy offered a handful of crispy weeds from the courtyard garden.

The house guardian crept out and slunk along the wall. His skin changed colors, from green to white to speckled, and textures from ridged to smooth. He inspected the offering and then backed away again.

"I'm sure he's skeptical," Lucy said.

"He eats fish, not plants. And anyway, he is probably nervous. We have only just arrived, and he must have fended off one, if not two, attempts to desecrate my family seed."

Finally, Torun unearthed a case of fillet steak from a great hunt. This was a fitting first meal for a wedding night. Enclosed in its savory box, the meat had steeped in the aged wood's rich flavoring.

"He's like an attack dog," she said, understanding. "Are you, buddy? Are you a good guy?"

The house guardian rippled.

"He does not know dogs." Torun worked to open the aged seal. "And I do not know them well either. He is loyal to his family and faithful to his home and very, very hungry."

"That sounds like a dog to me." She approached the lurking house guardian again. "Shall I call you Lassie? Lassie was the smartest dog. Oh, but now that I think of it, Lassie was supposed to be a she."

"That does not matter."

"Really? Hmm. The dog who played Lassie on TV was a male, so I guess it's okay."

Torun offered her the first slice of the rare, savory meat. "We should eat in a grand room."

"This is fine for me." She tried a bite, chewed, and closed her eyes. "Mmm, mahi. Oh, I think this is the best tuna sashimi I've ever eaten. The meat is firm and melts in your mouth. Oh my God. It's so thick and flavorful."

Hearing her enjoy his food with such rapture made his blood hum. He would put the same expression of pleasure on her face later.

He cut off the rinds for the house guardian, served the

richest meat to her, and consumed enough protein himself to ensure he would have his strength.

The house guardian, Lassie, dragged the rinds back to his hole and ate them. He finished, crept out of his hole, and snuck close to the tasty meat.

Torun leveled the dagger at him. "Do not think any strange ideas. This food is for mer."

Lucy gasped. "He's missing his arms."

She was correct. Lassie had lost two full arms, and a third had been hacked off in the middle.

"What happened?" she asked the house guardian. "Did you lose those defending our house?"

He reacted to her tone, puffing up his sack. He loved her sympathy.

"This could have happened," Torun conceded. "He will fight to defend his territory. A formidable house guardian could fight off two or even three trained guards."

"And they respond by hacking off his arms? Monsters." She held out a piece of rich meat. "Here. Get your strength back."

The house guardian perked up.

"Lucy," Torun warned.

"Go ahead." She tossed the meat. "You deserve it."

The house guardian caught the rich meat and, with a sideways glance at Torun, scuttled back to his hole to consume the forbidden feast.

"That is the best meat," Torun protested. "For a special occasion, such as our wedding night."

"And Lassie is a member of our family," she said. "He lost two and a half arms defending our home."

"They will grow back."

"Faster, with the best food."

Lassie emerged from his hole. Torun gave the house

guardian a silent warning. Lucy cooed at him, and with a gaze to Torun that clearly told him where his loyalties lay, Lassie happily floated over to Lucy's side and accepted another chunk of her meat.

By the end of the meal, after performing all sorts of puffing and twirling, Lassie nestled in her lap, stuffing his beak full of the rare treat, one pleased arm curling around Lucy's wrist, gently tasting her. If the house guardian really were a dog, he would be licking her hand.

Lassie finished the final meat and puffed up, expanding arms out, and slowly twirled his appreciation. Lucy laughed.

Although a house guardian should not partake of rare foods when it could easily be satisfied by eating small parasites, the view of his beautiful queen-to-be befriending her castle's loyal guardian warmed his heart.

"You have an affinity for guardians," he noted.

"Octopodes are awesome." She watched Lassie float over to his hole and squeeze inside. "I always wanted one for a pet. It's not practical, so I had sea monkeys instead."

He tilted his head. "Primates of the sea?"

"Brine shrimp." She held her fingers close together to indicate the miniature size. "Teensy bit different. I got them on my tenth birthday. It was the first time I realized I could never really reach my dreams."

A shadow passed over her.

"And now you are here in a mer city surrounded by Sea Opals. You have reached a dream."

She glowed again. "And now I have. Because of you."

Her heat crackled across to him. It forced him to rise, as she did, as though they were linked by a powerful magnet. Her heart beat faster. Anticipation?

She licked her lips. Her gaze descended across his

powerful body. "Torun. I have another dream. Can you help me?"

"Yes. Anything, Lucy. What do you desire?"

A smile curled her lips. "Will you take me to our bedroom?"

Torun's blood heated with his queen-to-be's hungry words. He had fed her body, and the need she had now was for him to fill her soul.

"It is time for the commitment of the spirit." He held out his hand. "Come."

She linked hands and floated close.

He claimed her in a kiss.

Her lips teased his. Nibbling his lower lip, testing his firmness with her teeth. She cupped his rough jaw.

Her willing touch awakened all his desires. Hot blood flowed into his cock, and his arousal pounded.

"Hurry," she murmured, vibrating her desire in her chest while their mouths meshed and played. "I want you."

He broke off their kiss, nestled her within his arms, and dove down the winding passages to the shielded heart chamber of the castle. He wanted to wrap her in him until their bodies burned away and their souls melded into one.

Her pleased laughter warmed his heart. Yes, she affected him deeply. The knowledge made her soul burn brighter. And that was very good.

TWENTY

Torun held her close as he flew through the brilliantly green, organic passageways of her new home.

The plant-cell rooms flashed by. Sparkles traced their flight, as though the castle had stood empty and their heartbeats were bringing it back to life. Veins pulsed with energy, and gemstones gleamed in the breathing walls. They connected with her, energizing her. She resonated with Torun, and her new castle welcomed her just as Lassie had welcomed her. Here, she belonged.

She gripped her handsome husband's wide back. He flexed powerfully, darting through the narrow corridors. Eager. So wonderfully eager.

Lucy loved him.

Except...

He stopped in a dead end and touched the wall. "Put your hand beside mine."

She did.

The wall was cool and smooth as marble. It sparkled around their handprints, and then the marble flexed inward, opening to reveal a secret inner chamber. Soft cinnamon-gold light gleamed with promise like a treasure chest reflecting riches.

Torun carried her across the threshold. The door sealed behind them.

Her nerves jangled.

His fins retracted to human feet, and he held her gently in the still, soothing water. His tattoos matched the cinnamon gold, and everything softened in this private chamber. These inner walls were warm as a fluffy bed, yet smooth as the tile of a Turkish bath, and delightfully sensuous. The room itself seduced her.

She tangled her fingers in his silky black hair. "Thank you for bringing me here."

His eyes glowed with fierce aquamarine fire. "Your journey begins now."

Yes. This was the first night of their marriage. It began a new adventure, one that would change them both forever.

And she had never been more nervous.

He kissed down her jaw to her sensitive neck.

She clung to his broad shoulders. His muscles flexed. These muscles had carried her so safely to the city. She savored the dips and bulges.

Lovemaking was supposed to be easy and thought-free. How it used to be. Before the failures. Before everything went wrong.

Her heart clenched.

Don't think about the failures. Don't think about the past. Don't think about tomorrow. She closed her eyes and tried to recapture the delicious magic from moments before. *Lose yourself in Torun right now.*

His hands withdrew.

She opened her eyes. "Torun?"

Hurt scarred his face. "You do not wish to join."

What the heck? She jerked upright and covered her chest. "Yes, I do!"

"No, Lucy. You lie."

"But I do," she insisted. "We're kissing. I'm into it." And the sooner they got back to it, the easier it would be to push away the fears rising in her mind.

"Then why is your light dim? Now, of all times?" He gestured at her closed position.

Oh. Stupid light that only he could see. Her shoulders sagged. She covered her face. "I do. But…"

"But?"

"Well, I just keep thinking about how to make it work." She dropped her hands. "You're going to leave me if I can't have kids, and we haven't done anything to—"

"Hold." Torun gripped her biceps. "I will not leave you."

"But you—"

"You are mine." His aquamarine eyes gleamed with command. "I am yours. Our hearts connect. You will carry our young fry."

Okay. This again.

"Think only about us now."

"But I am thinking only about you!" She blazed at him. "Do we need to do a special position? Or eat fertility food? Complete a ritual?"

"No, Lucy. Mermen mate like human males."

"That tells me nothing!"

She'd read all the how-to-conceive books, the scientific literature, the case studies. Then the anecdotes. And after that, the old wives' tales. She was supposed to be relaxed and not think about it, but she hadn't been relaxed or stopped thinking about *making babies* in years. Clinical terms flew around her head at the most intimate moments, and there was nothing like instructing her body *now implant the ovum* to take the magic out of the moment.

And when it hadn't happened, and it hadn't happened repeatedly, not only had she felt bad, but she'd also leaned on Blake. She'd leaned on him until he'd broken.

What would happen when she broke Torun?

"You cannot break me," he said softly, swiping his large thumb across her cheek. Gentle. "I am strong."

"You say that now, but what about when nothing cures my problems?"

"Have faith."

"But—"

"If you truly are ill, then it is true, nothing we did today will cure you. You must drink the nectar of the Life Tree's blossom."

Oh.

Ohhh.

Disappointment warred with surprise, and then anger made her cheeks feel hot. She was done with this roller coaster. She'd stepped off, and she wasn't getting back on for anybody. Torun had gone and made her start to believe that maybe, just maybe, she actually could be healed by the magic tree. His others promises had come true, hadn't they? But now they were here, in his castle, about to make love, and she just felt...she just felt...

Lucy didn't want to start the hope-and-despair cycle all over again for nothing.

And Torun was looking at her like it was time to get busy. She wanted to get busy too. But if she couldn't get healed...?

She pushed back. "So what's even the point?"

He looked as though he were thinking, *Truly?* But he

answered her. "I wish to connect with you. Body. Heart. Soul. You are mine, Lucy, and I want to wrap you in me until you have nothing but me in your mind."

"That's all I want too." She sagged against him. He released her biceps to capture her body, and she curled her arms around his shoulders. She held on to that strength. He was steadfast. Like a rock. "I just don't want to disappoint you."

"That will never happen."

He didn't understand. She was part mermaid and partway through becoming his official wife, and she felt no different. Not deep down. The day he approached this chamber with trepidation, lay beside her staring at the ceiling, and looked away when he told her he loved her...that would be the day that the final brightness in her soul died.

She hid her face in his gorgeous shoulder. "I'm sorry. I'm freaking out. I really do want to join with you. I've had a bad time. You're probably not even interested anymore. Right?"

He slid his hands around the curve of her back and drew her against his powerful erection. It poked like an iron rod against her thigh. This serious talk did not frighten him. His desire was stronger than her fears.

He rumbled, "You want to have a young fry now."

"Yeah. I guess it's stupid."

"It is admirable." He stroked the curve of her derriere. "Your eagerness is as beautiful as the rest of your body."

She snorted. "Well, there's the problem, then."

He squeezed. Sizzling heat streaked to her center. Her channel clenched. "Lucy, you feel your body betrayed you. It did not give you a young fry when you tried so hard. But your body is strong. It listened to your soul light. And your soul light was waiting for me. For now. All those times you called upon it to give in and make young fry with another man, it did not give in. Honor your body's dedication. It is strong and beautiful. Just like you."

His words caressed her like a song. Her heart lifted. Tears burned in her eyes.

Torun said everything she needed to hear.

She swallowed the lump in her throat. "I don't think I can honor it. It's been too long, and I'm still too angry."

"That is okay." His wide palm moved down to her thigh, bent her knee, and possessively hooked her leg around his waist. "Until you can find forgiveness, I will honor your body for you."

His lips covered hers. His tongue stroked her mouth, slow and hot. This wasn't the rushed *let's-get-it-on strokes* of moments before. This was a promise. He was going to honor every single part of her. And he followed by kissing her cheeks, her forehead, her lashes, and her chin.

"So beautiful," he murmured.

Her skin heated.

He kissed down the column of her neck to her shoulder. She arched her back, opening herself to him. Here was her husband. Her *true* husband. Her body recognized him and opened, inviting in his complete possession.

He gripped her hips, stilling her. There was no rush. Only pleasure.

He sucked one hard nipple into his mouth and lashed it with his tongue. Her center throbbed. He moved to the other, palming the first in his hot hand. Had any other man completely focused on giving her pleasure?

He kissed down her thigh to her calf to her flat, human feet. Another symbol of her failure to transform. He kissed every stubby human toe. "Beautiful."

Her chest ached.

Torun's silken kisses rose to the back of her knee. Tingles shot out, and once more, her channel clenched. No man had ever kissed her there.

He smiled and massaged her thick thighs. "Strong."

She wanted to make a snide remark about size, but, weird as it sounded, she really did feel more beautiful. He healed a deep rift with his mouth and his tongue. With his kisses and his words. With *him*.

He kissed up her trembling inner thigh to her softly curved mons. One hand palmed the hot flesh of her pussy. Finally. The ache receded, and pleasure shot through her. She curved around him. "Torun!"

He parted her dark curls and lowered his mouth to worship her nub.

Her core throbbed with an incredible ache. Every stroke of his powerful tongue intensified it. His eyes latched on to hers, and she could almost feel his command. *Let go of thinking. Feel my devotion. Forgive yourself.*

Okay, she just had to force her mindset away from fertility. This time, sex didn't count. She could have him however she wanted. No prescriptions, no blame, no sadness.

She wanted him now. While her body was glowing inside and out. While she ached for his possession.

She yanked his dark head up and wrapped her legs around his taut waist. His long, hard cock probed her slick entrance.

His gold-rimmed eyes flared. "Lucy?"

She was ready. She was so ready. Lucy tightened her legs. His hot tip teased her.

His pounding heartbeat echoed in her ears.

She felt exactly the same way.

Lucy arched her hips to take him.

He groaned and pushed in, coating his hardness with

her slippery arousal. Oh, yes. This was the connection they both craved. It felt amazing. She lost and found herself in his first soul-searing thrust. *He* made this pleasure. *He* had kissed her and worshipped her and made her glow with aching need. It was all her husband. *Torun.*

In return, she gave him everything she had.

His buttocks tightened under her calves. He rocked his length all the way to her needy center.

Their connection locked together, hot, sweet, and eternal. He was hers. She was his. This was forever. No matter what.

She tangled her fingers in his hair. "Yes."

He eased out and thrust in, deeper, and again, deeper yet. His hard cock filled her completely, stroking her channel with sparkling tingles. He touched a place inside her that she didn't know still existed.

Her heart pounded. "Please. Oh, please."

"Lucy." His deep bass thrummed in her soul. "Lucy!"

She gripped his buttocks. He was so skilled at bringing her to the peak. This was his first time? It felt like her first time too, because she'd never had a connection so pure, so deep, so hot. His thick cock plunged in and out of her channel. The orgasm built, uncontrollable. She clenched her teeth on a scream.

He tightened in perfect sync and shouted with triumph. Her pleasure erupted. She saw the moon and the stars and the sky, the bottom of the ocean and the top of the universe. His male seed poured into her channel. Her soul flew, entangled with his.

And then her orgasm shattered, and she plummeted back to the castle, nestled safely in his trembling arms.

Her strong, beautiful, tattooed warrior held her so close. Emotion glimmered in his eyes as he stroked her.

She kissed his chiseled cheeks. "Hey. Are you okay?"

"Ah." He rested his forehead against hers. "It was more intense than I had imagined."

Hah. Her too. And she knew what to expect. "I saw a flash of light."

"You did. The castle accepted you as my bride."

"Oh. Ha-ha, it felt like more than that."

"Yes, like our souls took flight."

Funny how their thoughts seemed to mirror each other sometimes. "You did great."

"I will never forget this." He pressed his lips to hers, softly and firmly, sweetly. "Never."

Neither would she.

Because someday, she would look back on this moment and think...

At least we had one amazing night.

TWENTY-ONE

Torun awoke to his Lucy's soft hands caressing his abdomen. Her brown eyes focused on his hardening cock. Her gaze flew to his face. "I didn't mean to wake you."

This was his beautiful wife, in his arms, sharing herself with him. "It is an awakening I have waited for my whole life."

Her smile softened. "Me too."

"Then continue."

Her fingers curled around his hard cock. She stroked.

He slipped a hand between her sweet, succulent folds. She was slick for him. He pressed his fingers into her. Her eyes unfocused, and her lips parted. She moaned.

An invitation he could not refuse.

He fitted his cock to her pussy and entered her in one fluid stroke. She arched her hips and wrapped her legs around his buttocks. This was the way to greet every period of wakefulness. Husband to wife. He thrust, matching his rhythm to her moans. She gripped his buttocks. He felt her tip over the edge and explode with beautiful light, then unleashed his own release a thrust later. His seed poured deep into her womb. She held him so close.

He stroked her flowing brown hair as their heartbeats returned to normal. He provided her with a castle, with a house guardian, with anything her heart desired. Surely she would be happy here, like this, with him, forever.

Her stomach growled.

She laughed with embarrassment. "I guess I'm hungry."

He disentangled from her. "Let me feed you."

"Ooh, you know how to seduce a woman. You'll never get rid of me now." Her smile faded as soon as the words were out, and her eyes turned haunted.

She still feared the Life Tree would reject her. That Torun would reject her. He needed to ease her fears.

"We will collect the Life Tree blossom today," he said.

Her expression froze.

He took her hand reassuringly. "It will have blossomed, Lucy."

"Oh, I know." She tried and failed to laugh. "Breakfast first, then give me an orientation to this amazing castle. You can check later. Okay? That blossom's not going anywhere. Right?"

"Yes."

On the journey, he led his queen through her castle, spreading her light through the winding passages and chambers.

In the courtyard, they visited the house seed. Lucy approached reverently, as before, and caressed it. She glanced at him, blushed, and tilted away to whisper something for only the seed to hear. He heard it too, though.

"I hope your tree healed me. I want to stay."

His heart thumped hard. He leaned against the doorway, struggling to control his feelings.

She *would* stay. No one would take her from him.

By the time she bore his son, the council would be convinced that she was the future for their city. She chose this life of her own free will, and she would not leave him or their young fry.

"Of course I won't leave you." She left the seed on its small dais and bounced over, snuggled against him, and traced her fingers across the nearly healed white scars from Prince Jolan's and Malem's attacks on his wide abdomen. "Wherever we go, we'll travel together. Right? So, how about breakfast?"

She patted her rumbling stomach.

He followed her to the pantry, absently helping her tidy as they swam the canals and corridors in between. "Wherever we go? This is our home."

"Oh, sure. I just meant if you had to leave. You're fighting with your council, and that's hard. Plus, you seem like an explorer, and I'm a bit of a wanderer myself."

"I have been known to explore," he conceded. "More than once, when I could not argue effectively with my superiors, I embarked on a small quest to prove my point. And, yes, I have neglected my family castle for years longer than I had intended. But with you here to raise our young fry, I will stay and devote myself to rebuilding this place."

She cupped his cheek, a lopsided smile on her face. "Just so you know, you have options. Home is where we make it."

How odd. He clasped her hand. "Then we are home."

"Okay." She turned and approached the pantry.

The house guardian bolted from his hole and twirled around the chamber.

"Lassie!" She giggled at his antics.

The pleased house guardian spun. The entire room glimmered a deeper, healing green.

This was his family castle in the city of his blood. Torun had been an absent steward, but it was his responsibility. Lucy was right, however. With her, he could go anywhere. Onto her boat, or onto the land, or anywhere in between.

Lucy plopped her garden harvest in a cleared spot of the disheveled pantry.

The house guardian examined the greens with tentacle-curling skepticism and then pouted.

"Go do your job." Torun shooed Lassie from the eating area. "Catch parasites and spider crabs."

"You don't eat crabs?" she asked, crunching the vegetables.

"No more than you eat spiders."

"But crabs are delicious. Especially boiled and slathered in butter."

"I will take your word for it."

"No way! We'll go crabbing sometime, and I'll get some for you. Fresh is the best. Oh my God, you've never had anything so good. Lassie!"

The house guardian snatched a small crab hiding in the harvested greens and passed it into his beak.

"Hey, that was Torun's!"

The house guardian scurried away with what seemed like a smirk on his face. Lucy paddled after it on her human feet, demanding the crab be regurgitated.

Torun couldn't keep the smile from his face for the rest of the meal or the welling of deep satisfaction in his body.

The previous meal, their wedding feast, Torun had been nervous and eager.

This meal was more relaxed and filled with happiness. Perhaps it was the best meal of his life. Better even than the one he had shared with his father after completing his adult trials and earning his place with the city warriors. This meal was better because Lucy had made his castle a home.

His father had not lived to see him become a highly respected warlord. Now, he would never meet Lucy or see Torun's future young fry. But his father would have been proud to welcome her as queen.

After Lucy gave up chasing the house guardian, they finished their meal peacefully and embarked on a tour.

He showed her everything. The rooms and passages, the nooks and mementos. His castle responded to her inner glow. She resonated with the gardens and creatures that lived within the walls. The walls themselves bent to her presence, absorbing her radiance and gleaming.

Had a castle always responded to its queen like this? He could not remember the last bride. The celebration, vibrancy, and life had faded from his memory.

Lucy burned a new memory into his soul.

Bringing her had been right. Just. No matter what the council said.

The Life Tree tinkled in the distance. It called to him with an unstoppable siren.

Lucy stopped the tour to sort and dust his family's bent tridents, historic pieces deemed too useless to be confiscated after his last punishment. "Do you guys not wear armor? All I see are little wrist gauntlets. Ooh, this is like a Greco-Roman theme."

"I will go to the Life Tree," he told her. "Remain here until I return."

She dropped the gauntlets. "Don't I have to go with you?"

"No. I can collect the blossom and return."

Concern dampened her light. "You *do* think there might not be one?"

Ah.

He drew her to him. "Brighten your light, please. Now we are united. I feel your doubt as mine."

She gasped, and her light brightened. "I'm sorry. Are you okay?"

"That is better." He stroked her, taking comfort from her smooth skin. "Some emotions, like doubt and fear, dim your soul. Others, such as hope and anger, brighten it."

"Anger brightens my soul? I thought it would lead me to the dark side."

"You glow with energy to protect, seek justice, and make the world right. That is why it brightens your soul. Shame and powerlessness, anger you cannot channel, it only hurts."

"And then there's love." She stroked his broad shoulders and pressed her soft curves to his hard chest.

His desire pulsed. How soon until he could return and take her in the chamber, in their safe, protected place?

"Love makes you very bright," he said. "And you will be even brighter once you have drunk the nectar of the blossom."

"We really should go to the Life Tree together."

"It is safer here."

She let go and floated back to study him. "What's the game? What aren't you telling me?"

"I play no game," he said. "You think I have changed my mind and believe the Life Tree has not blossomed and that I intend for you to leave here without drinking the pure elixir. But the opposite is true. I am afraid someone may see you and force you away from me."

"But they wanted a bride. I'm here. I'm a bride."

"They fear any bride who is not of the sacred island. Some claim a modern woman could break the Life Tree and destroy us all."

"Break the Life Tree?" She gazed at the wall as though she could see through it to the giant, sturdy, eternal tree as old as the city itself. "I didn't exactly bring a chainsaw."

"Breaking the covenant with the sacred island brides could destroy us all. If the Life Tree fails, then we share its blood in our veins, and so we all die."

TWENTY-TWO

"Die?" Lucy repeated.

Torun's solemn gaze pierced her, and all her petty fears fled in the face of that terrible truth.

"If something happens to the Life Tree, you're all going to die?"

He nodded.

"Me too?"

"Perhaps not you."

He stroked her cheek. The tightness of his mouth promised that there was no *perhaps*. He meant, in fact, *never* her, and that he would raise the entire ocean and drop the entire sky before he would allow anything to happen to her.

"Not at first, anyway," he said. "The Life Tree is fading, and so are we. That is why I hope your presence will cause it to rally and grow strong with new life. And us as well."

Well, the tree was old. Those drops of Sea Opal resin hadn't piled up overnight. Could she breathe more life into it? She and their unborn child.

Please, please, let me breathe more life into it.

"That is why the others have tried so hard to stop me," Torun explained. "I believe they are wrong, and only you can prove which is true."

Only her. And whether she could carry his child.

No pressure or anything.

The rusty old tridents added a metallic tang to the water.

He twined his hand in hers. "See me to the gate."

"I still can't transform." She flexed helplessly. One toe accordioned outward, part flying squirrel.

"Practice while I am away." His powerful kicks propelled them effortlessly through the corridors to the open courtyard and to the entry passage.

She gripped his hand and kicked on her human feet. They reached the inner entrance and paused.

This was it. Blossom time.

Even though she'd promised herself on the cruise to Cancun that she would never allow herself to feel that anxious, helpless desire for a baby again, agonized hope squeezed her chest once more. It made her nauseated, cold, hot, and dizzy. She almost threw up her breakfast. Lucy wanted a baby so, so badly. The life she'd had with Blake was nothing. She wanted this life, here, now, under the sea, with Torun.

"I feel the same way." Torun stroked her cheek.

She heated under his touch. But the distance in his eyes reminded her that he was going out, and she needed to prepare.

"If someone comes while you're gone, what should I do?" she asked.

He tightened. "No one will come."

"But?"

"But if someone should come, go to the heart chamber.

We united our souls there. It is the safest room of the house. The house guardian will protect you. Not even the council can escape his wrath."

"Am I in danger from your council?"

"They would return you to the surface unharmed."

"Even though I know your secret?"

"They would never hurt a female. Not even if she told the world."

"I'd come back for you."

He smiled, crinkling the skin at the corners of his eyes. "And how would you do that?"

"By cave guardian song. It's as reliable as GPS."

His smile deepened, and he cupped her head. "I would work very hard to convince them you were not capable of such a feat."

"Okay. Hurry back." She lifted her lips for his kiss.

He softened and gave in to her demand, melding their mouths and filling her with delicious desire. The background music of the castle swelled, her heart lifted, and her soul melted into his.

Their kiss finished, and he drew back, wonderfully dazed.

"You truly are amazing." His aquamarine eyes glimmered. He released her reluctantly. "Stay within the house barriers. Lassie will protect you."

She nodded, not trusting her speech.

Torun swam down the long corridor of his castle, paused at the entrance to scan the water, and disappeared.

She furiously paddled after him on her skinny human feet, reached the entrance long after him, and peeked out. Torun was gone.

The other castles hung between her and the Life Tree. The Life Tree tinkled with melancholy promise.

Well, it wasn't far, so he should be back quickly. She leaned on the biological marble of the castle entrance. Nerves jangled in her belly. Just a little more time, and he'd return...

The wait was not long.

Movement flashed below the closest castle.

Huh?

Torun darted and dashed far below. Mer warriors were scattered around him, some in direct pursuit and others teaming up and attacking him on the sides.

Cold seeped into her chest.

What should she do? She flexed her empty fingers.

In the center of the mob, Torun moved fastest. But he had no weapon, and the others were armed with long, sharp tridents.

One stabbed at him.

No!

They missed. He wrestled the trident away and slashed the attacker, streaking the water red.

The attacker screamed and kicked away, holding his wounded shoulder.

The others backed off and formed a circle around Torun.

For a long moment, no one moved. Torun floated in the center of the circling warriors. He held a trident now, but he was badly outnumbered.

Fear eviscerated her.

This was horrible, and she couldn't do anything!

Torun twirled slowly around the circle, facing down his attackers. None dared to approach. He slashed the water, and they all heeded his deadly warning.

A small group of warriors flew around the nearest castle

at her height, carrying a giant hollow straw. They aimed for her castle entrance.

Oh, no.

Torun looked up and swam toward them.

The circled warriors overtook and blocked his path.

He fought them. Their tridents clashed and clattered. Torun smashed his attackers and kicked free of the mass. He peered up and locked eyes with her in the passage.

But he'd never reach her before the other warriors with the giant straw.

Snarling, Torun hefted his trident and launched it—not at the warriors, but at the castle itself. His trident burrowed deep into the living wall.

The castle shuddered. A loud shriek filled the passage-way, and the entrance aperture, where she was, started to close.

The warriors below threw a net over him.

She moved back.

Her last view of Torun was of him struggling as the net tightened.

She paddled through the shrinking passage as it closed around her, reached the inner courtyard, and looked back.

The entrance passage had closed around the massive straw.

From deep within the straw, fierce, strange eyes met hers.

Oh, no.

Lucy started for the heart chamber.

Wait, what about the seed? It was Torun's mark of citizenship. She wouldn't let his rivals steal it and destroy him.

Lassie streaked across the courtyard ahead of her. Thank goodness. Scars on his missing limbs showed just how hard the loyal octopus would fight.

She reached for the seed as the warriors burst in. They had tangled with something in the entrance and were hacking off angry vines. Three warriors stormed to her with a net.

Lassie attacked.

The warriors clashed. The house guardian lashed out, striking all and tangling one. Lassie bit down. The warrior screamed.

A fourth warrior stabbed Lassie with a trident.

The wily octopus shot out of its way and inked. A dense black cloud covered the courtyard, obscuring Lucy and the fight.

More warriors threw nets. The octopus whirled and darted. Nets cut off its escape and tightened, felling the small but mighty house guardian.

Lucy clutched the seed to her chest. In the confusion, she tried to crawl away from the fight.

"There!" someone shouted. "Another traitor is hiding. He must face judgment. Grab him!"

A net descended on her, and she too was dragged out.

TWENTY-THREE

They took Torun to the council gathering area in front of the Life Tree, ripped off the net, and bound him with seaweed bolas.

Tied so tightly, Torun could barely straighten to face his accusers. Ranged around him in a loose circle floated the warlords who had grown with him, the elders he had learned from, and the younger officers he had trained.

Lucy must have made it to the heart chamber. She would be safe.

"Torun, you were a warlord once respected by all of Sireno." The head of the council—his own grandfather—pointed a gold trident at Torun. The hollow ceremonial weapon trembled. "Now you are a traitor to the mer."

"I am the only one truly loyal," he snarled.

His grandfather clenched his trident. "Breaker of the ancient covenant and rejector of the sacred brides. You sought human company and attacked our people. You would destroy us by your rash actions."

"Rash action is needed! We are dying. Only I have the will to save us."

Another elder shook his head gravely. "You were a good warrior once. Now you are poisoned by the prison-crazed myth-maker of Atlantis."

"Kadir gives us hope!" Torun fought for his words to reach the others. The whole city had gathered. Some were swayed by his plea; he knew from his past conversations with sympathizers. "What hope have we here, resting on a covenant with an island that has been abandoned?"

Murmurs accompanied his words.

"I put my faith in the covenant," his grandfather intoned. "Brides have had missed years before. Always they returned."

"These are not missed years. These are missed decades." He struggled. Pins stabbed his hands as the ties cut off blood flow. "I put my faith in a *new* covenant. One drafted here, now, with modern humans. Where is our king?"

Silence greeted his rallying cry.

Prince Jolan's unit entered the circle carrying two more nets. Malem glared at Torun with special hatred and jerked his net harder than needed.

A tentacle curled out of it. Both nets emitted an inky black smoke.

So, the house guardian had been captured. His gut burned. Although he must lose his seed today, he prayed to the Life Tree that Lucy would remain safe.

"I wish to be judged by my king," Torun said again. "He is a friend. You are only his advisers. Where is he?"

"My father is dead." Prince Jolan's jaw tightened, his face pale and bruised. "You missed your friend by hours."

No.

The king's patience had stayed the council for years. Torun had fought beside him to defend their borders. The king had always liked him and his impassioned ideas, which, although possibly wrong, the king said had heart. He had been a friend. His loss wasn't just of a liege. The pain panged deep.

"May he sleep in still waters and hunt in the blacknight sea," Torun said.

Jolan nodded once. He was king now.

But without a son, he couldn't assume the throne. Only a mer who had raised a son could assume the responsibility.

Which meant the head of the council, the aged elder who had raised Torun's father and trained Torun, now was the king.

Torun's grandfather met his gaze. He straightened and tightly grasped his ceremonial trident. "Jolan's last act as prince was to request your forgiveness."

What?

Jolan lifted his chin and stared straight ahead, avoiding Torun's gaze.

How noble. Despite their fight, the injuries Torun had given him, and the dishonor he must have faced returning to Sireno empty-handed, Jolan had used his last favor to honor his father's friendship with Torun. He saved Torun's life this day. Someday, Torun would return the favor.

"In recognition of his dedication to uniting the city under the rightful law, I will grant his request on one condition." Torun's grandfather glared at Torun. "Recant your support of the insane warrior, Kadir. Rededicate yourself to the sacred brides of the covenant. Abandon your treasonous acts."

Please let Lucy be in the chamber.

"I cannot."

Jolan stiffened.

His grandfather smirked. "Then see your castle destroyed and you castrated."

Torun braced himself. He would retrieve her as soon as his injuries recovered enough for him to swim, and then he would take her away.

Jolan turned. Bitterness lined his lips. "My king. We did not collect the castle's seed."

"How is this possible?"

"It was not on its dais. However, we captured another traitor."

"The traitor will be judged also." His grandfather flicked his fingers.

Jolan and Malem shook the nets.

Lucy tumbled out.

Torun's heart descended from his chest. His body turned hot and cold. *No. Please. No.*

She spun. Ink drained from her mouth. She choked and arched her back.

"Which city has no honor markings?" Torun's grandfather asked. "I do not recognize this blankness."

"I do not know, my king." Jolan stopped Lucy mid-spin.

The seed flew out of her hand.

Torun's blood pumped. She had gone to save the seed. Curse it all.

Malem grabbed the seed. "It is Warlord Torun's."

"Malem, place it in the offering bowl to be destroyed. Then we will remove Torun's male essence. He will never sire young fry. Then we will judge his accomplice. Who is it?"

"I cannot tell." Jolan studied her. "Straighten like a warrior."

Lucy hunched away. "I'm not a warrior."

"What?"

Lucy curled in on herself

Jolan shook her.

She squeaked.

How dare they?

How dare they frighten her? Touch her? Even look at her with anything other than kindness in their eyes?

Fury tightened Torun's senses to high alert. Higher than when he outswam the jaws of the trench monkfish closing in on him with fangs and fury. Higher than his first battle with raiding warriors.

Torun would rip the young prince's throat out. "Take your hands off her!"

Jolan's frown lifted. His eyes widened, and he obeyed, releasing Lucy and retreating several strokes to a safe distance. "It is a human. His bride!"

TWENTY-FOUR

The world had been totally black a second ago, and then Lucy had been thrown out of a net and shaken. Her brain still felt scrambled, but when Torun snarled at the warrior, Jolan, to remove his hands the force of his rage calmed Lucy.

Torun was here. Everything would be okay.

Even though she was now floating in the middle of what felt like an arena full of angry, armed warriors who gaped with shock.

Her heart pounded. Her stomach squeezed. Her body trembled.

She tightened her hands into fists.

The purple-tattooed warrior, Malem, stared at her in awe. "A *bride*."

Many voices spoke at once. "A bride is here. A bride has come! Torun was right. We have a bride—"

"She is not a bride. She is *not* a bride!" The elderly council head's quavering voice carried over the rabble. "Torun. You have damned us all with your flagrant disregard for the health and happiness of Sireno."

"She is my queen," he said.

"*Queen*," the others whispered.

"Queen." Belief filled Malem's voice.

The old male shook with anger. "She is not a queen! She is an unaltered, untransformed human of the basest kind."

"She transformed," Torun insisted.

"She is no mer."

"Look at her! She spills no bubbles. She is able to see. She moves as one of us, without the bulky cages and lights and air."

The others agreed.

"Look at her hands." The council elder's lips pinched in frustration. "They are human hands."

Uh-oh. She spread her fingers. Were they supposed to be webbed or what?

"Look at her feet. If she were truly your queen, she would have fully taken our form. Instead, she hides in her own."

Lucy tried to flex her feet. "I had it once, sort of. I can do it. Just give me a second."

They gasped again. The warriors closest to her floated back, giving her a direct line of sight to Torun.

"She speaks." Torun burned with faith in her. "And she shines. She chose this of her own free will. You cannot be blind to her light."

They murmured.

Lassie crept free of his now unattended net.

"This is madness," the council leader said. "You cannot bind yourself to her. She is not from the sacred island. The covenant does not apply. You have brought a human to our city, and you must be punished for your blasphemy."

He ordered the closest warriors to grab Torun.

They refused.

"Malem," he shouted in frustration. "Take away that human!"

"She is another warrior's bride." Malem dropped Torun's house seed and kicked back. "I cannot touch another warrior's bride. Even if she did choose Warlord Torun."

The council leader shook his fist. "Obey my orders. I am king!"

Disagreeable mutterings followed his order.

Lucy paddled forward and grabbed the sinking seed.

"Listen, my warriors." The council leader regained pinched calm. "You are confused. But Torun's disgraceful actions threaten to destroy us. Even if we accepted this mainland female as a bride, we cannot accept Torun as her husband. The most honorable warrior always chooses his bride first. The last time a warrior chose a bride out of turn, Jolan's father was killed. It nearly destroyed us."

"What lie is this?" Torun demanded. "Jolan's father was killed in a duel."

"Yes, with the dishonorable warrior who stole his bride."

"But—"

"You were away. Jolan's mother rejected the worthy warrior who had earned her. Her arrogance caused his death."

"I do not believe you."

"Ask our former prince."

Torun swung to Jolan. "It is not true."

Jolan sighed heavily. "It is true, Warlord Torun. The king confessed it to me before passing into the blacknight sea. My intended father, who had earned the right to sire his son, was betrayed by his best friend, who stole my mother away. In the ensuing battle, both lives were lost. That is why I was raised by the king."

"How have I not heard of this?"

"The years were troubled. Many wished to forget the dishonor, and many others did not know the details."

"This tragedy happened because the bride chose," the council leader intoned. "*She* broke the sacred covenant. *She* caused the Life Tree to wither. *She* caused a male to raise the orphaned young fry. Now you bring another bride who chose you out of turn. *She* will be the death of the Life Tree!"

The others murmured. Warriors clenched their tridents. Their war noises overpowered the tinkling music of the Life Tree watching over them.

Fear curled in Lucy's belly.

"I won't," she promised. "I don't want to hurt anything."

The warriors ignored her.

"See, my fellow warriors?" The council leader crowed with victory. "The current Torun wants you to swim leads to madness. Cast him out."

"Wait." Torun's deep bass commanded attention. "There is another way to understand what occurred."

"Ignore his words. He has committed treason."

"Jolan's mother chose," he shouted. "Our warriors did not respect her! That is the lesson. The brides of the sacred island left us because *we* broke *their* covenant. They provided us with a bride. We denied her the male of her heart!"

Jolan's jaw dropped. He swayed back, hands out, eyes huge. "Could it be?"

His unit shifted uneasily.

"No." The elder pointed his trident at Lucy. "This false bride has led you astray."

"She is not a false bride. We shared everything." Torun flexed against his bindings. "She is the heart of my castle. She is my future."

"As you no longer possess a castle or a future, they are of no importance."

"You cannot deny our union. It is blessed by the Life Tree."

"Then you are the reason for its unnatural cry." His scowl grew. "You are the reason we ended the king's remembrance ceremony early and returned here. Your blasphemy is killing our Life Tree. It withdrew its protection and caused our king to die."

"No."

"Warlord Torun, you are hereby stripped of your honors and essence." He pointed his trident at Torun.

Warriors clamped their hands on him. The largest grabbed a long, wicked dagger. He slit Torun's bindings. The others forced his legs apart, exposing his genitals.

Torun fought them. "She is my queen!"

"Stop!" Lucy paddled for Torun. "Stop it!"

The council leader motioned for Jolan to arrest her.

Jolan did not move. His warriors remained with him.

She swam toward the violence. "Stop!"

Warriors loyal to the council barred her way with their sharp tridents. She pushed on the metal. They shoved her back with the broad side of the blades. Even so, the sharp edges sliced her skin.

"Ow!" she cried.

Torun bugled his rage. "Do not touch my queen!"

"She is no one's queen." The council leader stared right through her. "She is an air-breathing human from the mainland who cannot even transform. Do not covet this kind of bride, my kinsmen. She is unworthy."

Torun screamed insults at the council merman.

"Someone, silence him."

They brought another bola and tied it around his diaphragm, silencing the vibrations.

"What about her?" one of the warriors asked. "She knows of us."

"She does not matter. We will take her to the surface. She is broken and worthless."

"She is broken and worthless."

The words burned in her like acid.

"What good are you?" Blake had asked after the last failed fertility test. Her heart repeated those words with every slam to her self-worth.

Then Torun came and made her see the truth. His belief in her made her start to believe too.

Now some old fish stick, who didn't even know *her*, who just spouted whatever the heck he felt like, was going to call her worthless?

Well, fine. They noticed her shining, right? She'd give them all a better sense of her worth.

"Let him go," she said.

The warriors blocking her way frowned.

Not bright enough?

Torun said the more she channeled her anger, the brighter her soul shone. Those mermen threatened her love. The old fish stick called her worthless. She was stronger than that.

"Let him go!"

They eased back and glanced at the council leader. He ignored her.

"Let. Him." She grabbed their tridents and shook the metal. "Go!"

It worked. The two warriors dropped their tridents and shrank back.

The council leader shouted at the other warriors. "Carry on! Quickly, you must remove his essence!"

She paddled toward Torun, stupidly slow. Where were her fins? "Don't you dare hurt him!"

The warrior with the dagger grimaced at the council leader. Doubt warred with duty. "Proceed before the cauterizing is ready? The loss of blood will not stop. He could die."

"Now! Do it now!"

The warrior knelt and gripped Torun's ball sack. He positioned the knife to cut it off.

But they hadn't had a chance to try for a baby. They were supposed to save the city and his race. He needed to at least have the chance to try.

The warrior flexed to cut.

No. Not her love. Not her Torun.

Her scream ripped from the deepest part of her soul. "*Noooooooooooooo!*"

A supernova exploded in her chest.

In her hand, Torun's house seed cracked. Thick black lines crisscrossed its surface.

Her supernova flared outward, traveling in a blinding shock wave across the arena.

Warriors released Torun, shielded their eyes, and dove away.

The knife fell. It was clean. Nothing had been cut.

Oh, thank goodness—

Crash!

Beyond the arena, glass shattered. The horrifying sound went on and on and on. An entire glass skyscraper collapsed.

What was it?

The Life Tree shuddered. All its Sea Opals fell off. It split down the center and snapped off at the base.

Oh, no.

No, no, no.

She froze with horror.

The Life Tree of Sireno toppled from its dais and sank out of sight.

TWENTY-FIVE

The destruction of the Life Tree sliced a cord in Torun's heart. Pain spilled into his chest cavity.

But more importantly, the city warriors were distracted. They, like Lucy, stared at the fallen Life Tree with horror and grief.

He had already sworn to act after they unmanned him. Despite his disfigurement and pain, he would seize the moment to save Lucy and escape.

Instead, Lucy had saved him with her power. His manhood remained intact and unharmed. And now he was released.

He kicked free of his boneless captors, shifted to human feet, and caught the dagger. He sliced the bolas around his midsection, cutting his last bonds, and flew to Lucy. "Put your arms around me."

She blinked. His cracked house seed dropped from her fingers. "Torun. I killed it."

Lassie snatched the seed and bolted past the shocked mermen. The house guardian disappeared, swimming back to the castle to return the seed to its home.

"I *killed* it."

"Lucy!" He shook her. "We must leave."

His countrymen moaned and swam to the fallen tree.

"But it's true." Her voice in her chest thrummed with quiet grief. "I *am* the evil destroyer they warned against."

"No, Lucy." But she would not let go of this sadness soon. Neither would he. He secured her against his chest. "Come."

Torun flew from the judgment circle. The others would follow. He needed to put as much distance between them as possible.

She rested her head on his chest and cried.

He thanked her for her tears. She expressed his sadness, grieving for both of them, bidding farewell to his old life as an honored warlord of Sireno and farewell to the Life Tree that he had tried to save.

"We failed," she sobbed. "Now you're all going to die."

Like the dead king, he had striven to give hope. Lucy was that hope. She was not a destroyer.

Or, she was not *only* that.

They swam hard and far. His muscles ached from not enough rest, and his blood beat against his bones. He must not rest until he carried his queen to safety.

She sobbed herself to sleep nestled against him. The depths changed as he traversed the sea, rising and also crossing great gulfs. The ocean song wrapped around them, so ordinary and soothing. Despite their tragedy and the loss of his city, the world continued to turn.

When she awoke, calm replaced her grief. Her fingers traced the gold swirls on his pectorals. "You really don't blame me?"

"I do not."

She thrashed as though he had blamed her. In fact, she

blamed herself. "I couldn't let them hurt you! I didn't mean to break anything. Or shout so loudly. Only to stop them."

"You acted as a queen."

"I'm sorry."

"No." He risked slowing them by lifting his hand to stroke her sinuous back. "Never apologize for protecting our family."

She buried her face in his shoulder. "I don't even know how I did it."

"Females were said to have a great capacity for power. In the ancient tales, four queens once defended their city from attack. Their warriors were tricked into abandoning the city, and the attackers doubled back. The queens gathered their young fry around the Life Tree. They resonated with such force, no invader could approach. As a young male, I thought the story was a parable. Now I have seen your power. It is historical truth."

"They were defending their Life Tree. I destroyed it."

"You protected me."

"What will happen now?"

"Now..." He didn't wish to tell her. Not in this state.

"Tell me."

He sighed. "First, the empty dais will turn black and fall to the ocean floor. The castles will wither and follow. It will happen quickly, before we reach your boat."

"And then you'll die?" she whispered.

"We will disperse to other cities. Dragon Mar is closest. If their Life Tree accepts us, it will put forth blossoms. If their Life Tree is as sickly as ours, then it may not be able to put forth blossoms, and then yes, we will die."

Why hadn't he collapsed already?

The failure of Sireno's Life Tree ought to suck away his strength, turning his muscles to muck and his bones to glass.

Had his connection to Lucy given him this unnatural, almost normal level of strength?

She froze with horror and melted into sadness. "I should never have come."

"Only you could have come. No other would have resonated with my soul."

"I wish..." She closed off, but he heard the rest of the words. She wished she would have failed.

"Lucy, the Life Tree was old. It was also wise. It resonated with your soul and gave the last of its power to protect *us*. To protect *our* house. The Life Tree said *you* are a worthy mer, even more worthy than its own."

"Will the rest of your city see it that way?"

"I will not go back to Sireno."

"Right. Because I destroyed it. God!"

"No!" He twirled with her, breaking her from her spiral. "Because now I know the truth. I showed my city warriors a bride who breathes underwater and chooses us and is willing to stay. I showed them a bride who befriends a house guardian and defends a castle and eagerly joins with a mer. I showed them a bride who shines like a star and commands the resonance of the Life Tree! And what do they do?"

She swallowed.

"They criticized your fins!" He bit out his words, seething with the memory. "Ask me how many times we must practice shifting to human feet when we first go to land. Ask me!" He shook his head, changing their direction, and dove again to recapture the swift current. "Our kind are too covenant-bound and stupid to be saved."

"Perhaps if I became pregnant..."

"Not even then."

He must soon go to another city. Pledge himself to the

protection of another Life Tree. One to heal her, one where she could join him.

Her fingers stilled. "Hey, Torun?"

"Yes, my Lucy?"

"If I hadn't been able to stop the, uh, procedure, and I had been miraculously healed *and* pregnant, what would have happened?"

"I would have been exiled," he said. "Weaponless and injured, beyond the towers of the reef, I would have quickly succumbed to predators and died. You would have been cared for by another, probably the king, until you had your son."

She shuddered. "He was awful."

Oh, he kept forgetting that the king was not Jolan. "Yes. He was once my favorite elder. He always said running into battle was rash. Instead, now he freezes us all in place to death."

"So I would have raised our baby with him?"

"You would have borne our young fry. Then, you would have been returned to the surface, and he would have raised our son. It is the custom."

She clenched him tighter. "He would have killed you and stolen our baby."

This made her light shine brighter. The deep, protective love that she had apologized for and wished away, she now reaffirmed. He stroked her. "He is king and a father. He once raised a worthy son."

"By shafting the mom." She huffed. "Which 'worthy son' did this great guy raise?"

"My father. And after my father passed on, me."

Lucy's shock reverberated through the water. "You said he was your favorite elder."

"He was."

"Your own grandfather just tried to cut off his own genes."

"We have long stopped hunting from the same schools." He shrugged, interrupting their streamlined shape and changing their direction in the fast, rising currents. "He accepted a council position to leave our castle to me. The harder he advised the king away from Kadir's ideas, the more I fought his guidance. Perhaps he does now hate me. I no longer feel bound by him."

"I would have gone into exile with you."

"They would never have allowed that."

"Then I would have waited until I could make my escape, and then I would have found you."

"Lucy." He squeezed her. "It is too dangerous. In the open ocean, alone, there are many predators. We are only safe on known currents, which are guarded and protected."

"We could make it together."

"Everyone must sleep sometime. The mer city would imprison you to protect you. You chose this when you vowed before our Life Tree."

"Oh, no. I didn't choose your stupid city. I chose you."

A strange tingling moved through his body.

He had tried to convince her to join the mer, and his city, to gain the powers and riches of his undersea world. She had seen injustice and supported his idea to make their world better. Joining with any mer could prove the young lord of Atlantis right, and accomplish Torun's goal.

But she chose him. Not any mer. *Him.*

"Lucy." How to put his emotion into words? He struggled. "You would have stayed with me even if I had been sterilized?"

"Of course."

"Now the Life Tree has been destroyed, it cannot heal you."

"I know."

"It also cannot make you a mer permanently. Soon, you will try to make the change, and you will remain human."

"I got it." She shook off the heaviness of the conversation. "I'm sorry I'm going to lose these awesome powers. But I've been telling you from the beginning our relationship is doomed. You'll have to find another woman."

Why did she continue to push him to take another mate? Did she not feel their connection as deeply as he did? He would never consent for her to join with another warrior. The thought made his muscles clench for his trident.

"Don't look so frowny," she said.

"You speak as if separating were easy for you."

"I'm just telling you that I understand. You have to do what you have to do."

"I will not leave you."

"But when you do, I get it. Your species is dying."

He growled. "You are the one I want."

"God, don't you get it?" She smacked his chest. "I'm being noble over here. If you stay with me, you might as well have been castrated by your council. Okay? *I can't have kids.*"

That stopped his growl in his throat.

She had tried to make him face this possibility many times. He had always refused. But even so, Lucy had believed in him. Believed in his vision and been willing to try. Now, her face clenched with agony. She was unable to give him the one thing he needed for his race to survive. The knowledge killed her inside.

He never wanted to see that agony again. Never.

Torun held her close, burying her face in his shoulder, trying to physically transfer the burden of her agony to himself. "I will solve this."

"I already told you the easy solution."

"No other woman will replace you."

"You say that now." She turned away. "Give it a few years."

Curse the human male who had damaged her. Torun would not want a new woman in a few years. Lucy was his heart, his life, his soul. Without her, there was no him. They were one until death. Or beyond it.

"Lucy—"

"Hey." She stared up at the surface, shimmering finally, after all this time. "That's not our trawler."

He stopped before he could finish making his promise and examined the growing shape. Yes, it was larger and more elongated, had an unblemished underside, and the anchor chain was a different shape.

"How long exactly was I gone?" she asked.

"In human time? Almost two weeks."

She swore. "No way Gracie and Cash stayed. This must be someone else's yacht. Maybe one chartered by Elyssa." Her light dimmed. "You know, Elyssa can have kids. And she already believes you're a merman."

"I am not able to join with Elyssa. We do not resonate."

Her light brightened.

"I am glad that pleases you."

"I didn't say anything."

"Mm."

They broke the surface. Lucy smiled in the sunlight.

And started to choke.

He assisted her with the transition, emptying her lungs and relearning how to draw in air. This was, in many ways, the real test. She had adapted well to living underwater, but now she returned to air again. Would she remember her natural preference and refuse to descend with him again?

Lucy gasped, mouth open like a beached fish.

"Are you okay?" His voice sounded odd in the air. Higher pitched and tinny.

She nodded, red-faced and choking. "It's a...heck of a...kick."

"It will become easier." He helped her to the low rungs of the sleek white ladder bobbing on the surface. "Like clearing your snorkel."

She nodded, trusting him, and gripped the ladder. "Let's get out of here."

"Lucy." He stopped her. "You were willing to give up everything to be with me." He held her hand. "Thank you."

"I'm not that selfless." She tried to tug her hand free.

He was going to say something else, but her comment sidetracked him. "You promised to leave the air world behind and join me in the undersea kingdom."

"Yeah, but you were fighting with your council, and so there might be plenty of chances to surface and let every-one's heads cool. I was going to introduce you to my parents and stock up on whatever foods I craved, or even, you know, follow up your underwater wedding ceremony with the above-water version."

He couldn't follow her. The implications left him stunned. "You wished to marry me? According to the rites of your people?"

"You helped me recover my passion and reclaim my true self." She tilted her head. "Why are you so surprised? You said I was your mate, your queen, your forever partner. Is it so strange that I wanted the same thing? Our marriage would have been way better than my last one."

She spoke in the past, as though she were already grateful to be in the air again, and no longer wished to marry him now that he was an exile.

The fact that she had ever wished it made his chest tighten. He cleared his throat of pesky seawater, fighting the emotion. "We do not have a record of a bride bringing a warrior into her tribe. I will never forget this."

"Yeah. Sure." She hacked and spat. "Well, let's find the owner and get out of here before your city guards catch up."

They climbed the ladder. On the deck, she called out, "Hello?"

No one answered.

A low whistle of menace made Torun's hair stand on end. "There is something wrong on this vessel. Something out of place."

She picked up her expedition T-shirt. "You mean like this?"

"That is from your ship."

"Yes, exactly. And this yacht is way too big to have been rented by Elyssa or Mel."

She peered into the wheelhouse. A cup of coffee steamed beside the wheel, but the door was locked. "Someone's here."

How aggravating. In the water, he would sense what enemies stalked him from a great distance, but the air muffled his senses.

Movement was happening...

Humans?

No. The water around the yacht frothed.

Mer.

Torun shouted. "Lucy! Run."

The waters frothed with warriors from his city. They surged onto the boat. He swung his bare fists at a powerful male, but someone behind him knocked him to the deck.

Warlord Ailan, leader of Sireno's second unit, put the sharp trident blades to his throat. "Exile Torun. You have broken the covenant. Face your end with honor."

Two warriors started for Lucy.

Torun roared, "Do not touch my queen!"

They hesitated.

Ailan shoved the flat side into his throat, choking off his rage. "She is not your queen."

Torun struggled.

He had trained Ailan, just as he had many others. The male had always impressed him with his attention to accuracy. Ailan's methods were slow, careful, and exact as a judge. He held the rule book of the council in his heart and recited it with perfect correctness.

And now he judged Torun.

"What are you doing?" Lucy stormed up to Ailan. "Let him up. Now."

In the air, her brilliance dispersed. Ailan faced her wrath like a steel rod facing a tidal wave, unbent and unbowed. "He must face judgment for his blasphemy."

"What the heck are you talking about?"

Ailan's lieutenant reached out to pull her away.

She slapped at him. "Get your hands off me!"

The males retreated.

Ailan straightened. "Torun must face judgment before the council for—"

"We already faced your stupid council," Lucy screamed, frightening the other males awfully. "And Torun's still got his balls, so guess who came out ahead?"

Ailan lifted his chin even farther. "Torun broke the covenant."

"Yadda yadda sacred brides, secret existence." She waved him away. "What are you doing on this boat? Exposing yourselves to everyone?"

"Warlord Torun did it first."

"Oh, please. Nobody believes one crazy guy. You're a whole army of mermen."

Ailan's mouth pinched.

"It's a little late for secrecy." A new voice spoke from the wheelhouse doorway.

Lucy whitened. "Blake."

A thin man emerged onto the deck. "Hi, honey."

"What are you doing here?"

"Protecting my investments." His cold gaze flicked over the mermen. "Which means we have to talk."

TWENTY-SIX

When Blake emerged from the pristine, ginormous yacht—*with a helicopter pad*—in his crisp white suit, holding a sparkling glass of wine, Lucy was hit with the gut punch of shame.

He was still fit and strong. Healthy as the day they'd anchored here together, when she dove for what looked like a dropped flashlight and turned out to be a million-dollar Sea Opal. They had laughed and danced, screamed and planned. The future was amazingly bright, and they were a young couple who had just won it all.

His half had drained into leaky investments, while hers had paid off their student loans, credit card debt, and tanked businesses.

And yet, here they were, back in the same place a decade later. He looked exactly the same. Older, with less hair on top and longer sideburns to try to disguise it, but otherwise, he'd been lifted by their breakup.

She was the one dripping wet on his yacht, hungry and half drowned, with her new husband under arrest.

Blake's scorn said all that and more.

"That's a new look for you," he said, arching his brow.

She covered herself. In the ocean, her whole body changed and felt different. Even when she'd faced down the council leader fish stick, she'd never felt this exposed.

No way in hell did she want to reveal that she'd gained superpowers.

"I was reliving the old days," she said. "Back when clothes were optional."

He wrinkled his nose. "That option expired."

The insult stung.

Torun grunted and struggled beneath the blades of his captors. Oh, yeah. Her pain hurt him too. Lucy had to be strong for both of them.

She blazed back at her ex. "At least I can put on clothes. Naked or not, you're still a backstabbing asshole."

"Ooh, clever." He sneered at her and motioned to the mer. "Ailan, take them below."

Ailan and other warriors lofted Torun and carted him, struggling and grunting, down to the hold after Blake. Two reached out as if they were going to grab her. She glared. They hesitated.

"Why are you taking orders from a human?" she demanded.

One warrior grimaced. "He is your husband."

"God, for the last time! He's not my husband. He's my ex."

"Torun touched you. Your husband threatened to expose us. He is owed justice."

"First of all, your twisted 'mer logic' doesn't apply. In the air, the woman always chooses." She jerked her thumb at her chest. Their brows rose in shock. "Always. And second of all, Blake's the one who left me. Torun owes him nothing but a punch in the face."

The two warriors frowned at each other.

"Furthermore, the man you're helping right now is your worst enemy. The only thing he's going to do is steal your Sea Opals."

"No one can do that." The one warrior shook his head confidently. "They are beyond air-breathing humans."

"Except in the cave close to here, right? That has plenty."

"It cannot be entered by a non-mer."

"I entered it."

They regarded her blankly.

"Before I drank the elixir, I entered the cave."

"Lies." The closest warrior lowered his trident at her. "Go to your husband."

Crap.

"My husband is Torun," she insisted. But they didn't believe her. The look in their eyes was the same as the HR person calling her in for the conversation about her place in the company.

She paused to tug on clothes from the luggage Blake had stolen from her trawler and descended at trident-point to the hold.

The warriors had thrown Torun into a clear fiberglass cage reinforced with steel. Blake locked the door and pocketed the key. Beside it rested her equipment, Cash's surveying logs, and diving gear.

Her heart started beating. What had happened to her crew? Where was the Sea Opal she'd left with Gracie?

"I need days to deal with this home-wrecker," Blake told Ailan. "Weeks, actually."

"We return at sunrise," Ailan said. "You will not reveal our existence to the human world."

"I wouldn't dream of telling anyone else about you," Blake said with a smarmy tone to the warriors.

Of course he wouldn't. Announcing to the world that mermen existed would get in the way of him stealing their Sea Opals.

"This man is not my husband!" she shouted at the warriors.

Ailan paused.

The warrior who had pulled the trident on her murmured in Ailan's ear. "She claims this male left her."

"He left me for a size-one model. He divorced me because I couldn't have children!"

"Aw." Blake's tone dropped to deadly monotone. "That's not true."

That jerk.

Ailan narrowed his eyes. "Your argument is between humans. It is not our business." He strode to the doorway.

"Wait!"

They all disappeared up the stairwell. Distant splashes meant she was on her own.

Lucy bunched her fists and whipped to face her horrible ex. "You divorced me."

"I know." He sat in a metal chair. "Aya's a size five."

She started to snarl.

Wait.

Was that...?

On the table beside him rested a spear gun.

She crossed her arms over her chest. "What do you want?"

He picked up the gun and waved at a chair. "Why don't you sit down?"

TWENTY-SEVEN

The instant the man, Blake, turned his weapon on Lucy, Torun slammed his palms against the glass.

It rattled but did not shatter. Steel threads held it too tightly.

Blake jumped and swung the weapon on Torun. "Settle down in there."

He hated the man with the heat of a thousand undersea volcanoes. "Go on. Shoot me."

"Ha." Blake motioned for Lucy to sit again.

"No, thanks." She stood firm, arms crossed. "Let Torun out, give me back my crew, and I'll consider not prosecuting you."

"Prosecute!" Blake shook his head, his soul as black as the greasy engine. "Lucy, you're *dead*. They held your funeral last Tuesday. Do you know how long you've been gone?"

Her eyes widened, and her heart rate increased. Despite the syrupy, slow air and the thick glass, Torun sensed her feelings. She was worried about her parents and friends. Had she caused them to grieve?

"I could shoot the both of you, toss your bodies over the side, and people would be none the smarter."

"You mean 'none the wiser,'" Lucy said.

Blake tightened his grip on the spear weapon. "Wiser, smarter, you're not going to be anything but deader. So *sit*."

A tense beat passed.

Lucy looked at Torun, hardened, and scooted the deck chair next to the cage before she eased into the seat. She crossed her arms and legs, then faced their enemy. "What do you want?"

"Take me to the Sea Opals."

She raised a fierce brow. "I thought they were all in the Keys?"

"Oh, they are. But you've found a whole bowlful. Why fight success?"

"I'm sure your investors are wondering that too."

Blake's brows lowered. "Enough chitchat. Where are they?"

"Directly below us," she lied without missing a beat. "They're hidden in a reef. Let Torun go."

"Gracie swam over that reef. She went all around the atoll looking for you."

Lucy's light flickered. She must feel guilty for the young woman. How desperate Gracie must have become when her employer didn't surface, and it became clear she had been lost at sea.

"That's when she called me," the man continued. Lucy's soul darkened even more, this time in shock. "Surprised? Yes, I took out insurance. I heard you were going over our old hunting grounds, and there was no reason not to send in my own spies, who you eagerly hired."

She gritted her teeth. "So, you really did believe in me all along."

"Nah. I believe in taking precautions with my investments."

"If that were true, we'd both be millionaires. You wouldn't have lost all the money in stocks and gambling the first time."

He blackened. "If you hadn't been so afraid, I would have earned the money all back. It takes money to make money. You kept holding on to the capital when we needed to buy."

"Because you kept losing it!"

He cut her off. "The point is, the Sea Opals are in a cave. And if you want your fish man to keep breathing, you'll take me there."

"Keep breathing?" She looked at the cage. "What do you mean?"

"Want to see a neat trick?" Blake removed a black remote device from the metal drawer and pressed a button. "This cage was made for pressurized living specimens, but it can also do this."

The cage made a popping sound.

Torun pressed his hands against the glass. "Lucy?"

His voice echoed.

She stood and pressed her hands against his on the opposite side. "Torun!"

Her voice sounded farther away.

She glared at her ex. The light burning brighter. "Are you actually threatening us?"

Blake lifted the spear gun. "You just made the connection? Not the sharpest knife in the lightbulb store."

She stroked the glass. "The mer are coming. They expect him to be alive."

"Maybe I'll motor back to the Keys. I'd like to see them catch me."

She opened her mouth and closed it. Her eyes fixed on Torun. Could Blake outrun the mer?

His warriors could have caught her old trawler, but perhaps not a sleek, fast boat with a day's and night's head start. Not before the caged air ran out and he suffocated.

Searing heat boiled in his veins. Every muscle in his body clenched. His hands flexed for his trident.

They weren't beaten yet. This arrogant dark-souled male who had once damaged his Lucy thought he had won? He would soon know the meaning of pain.

"Show him." Torun forced the words through gritted teeth. "Take him to the church."

Her lips tightened. "He'll destroy it."

Torun shook his head. Lucy had made a special connection to pass the cave guardian without showing his Sea Opal. Anyone else would be destroyed. He trusted in Mr. Huggles. The cave guardian would protect Lucy and the sacred cave.

Blake raised his voice. "Let's move before I change my mind and use the more direct method."

Her eyes narrowed, and her light shone.

She whipped away from Torun to glare at her ex-husband. "That's murder."

"To harpoon a fish?" He cocked a darkly amused brow. "No law against it."

"He's no fish."

"He's no man either."

Lucy stalked to her ex. "What happened to you? We used to be satisfied with nothing but the open ocean and the next dive."

"Well, that's it." He looked down on her. "*You* were satisfied. I discovered there was more to life than beds infested with cockroaches and street cart tacos, and I deserved it. And so now I'm taking it. With or without you."

She stalked to the stairwell. "I need gear and tanks."

"They're on the bow under a tarp."

With one lingering look at Torun, begging him to stay alive until she kicked Blake's ass, Lucy left.

Blake changed into a skintight black suit, mask, and fins. He removed a small white packet from his pocket, spread a line of powder, and snorted it up his nose. His soul light went out entirely. He sniffed several times, tidied away the packet, licked his fingers, and stood. He stared at Torun.

"You will regret this," Torun growled.

A loose smile lay on Blake's lips, and he laughed with an edge. He crept to the cage and tapped the glass with two fingers. "Fishy, fishy, fish—"

Torun slammed against it with all his might.

The cage rattled.

Blake leaped back, fear jerking his limbs. He blinked and started to smile again. "Bad fishy. Stupid, dumb, idiot fishy who boinked my wife and deserves to die."

Perhaps death by enraged cave guardian was too slow.

"Open the door." Torun rested his fingers on the glass. "Go ahead. Try the harpoon."

"You know why you're really stupid?"

"Come in and tell me."

Blake stepped back, finally reacting to the deadly intent in Torun's echoing voice.

Yes. If the man opened this door, he would be made dead. Not sterilized, as was the custom of the mer. This human had deliberately dimmed Lucy's light and threatened her. Torun would make him dead.

"Your buddies told me you stole Lucy to have children."

Blake laughed. "You're so stupid. You stole the one person in Mexico who can't have kids."

"Not with *you*."

"Oh, believe me. We tried so many times. She didn't use to be fat." He leered at Torun. "Her baby-making meter is broken. You screwed up big-time."

Torun paced in front of Blake. The man with a black soul studied him with dead eyes, and his smile was empty.

Darkening a soul for too long injured the body. Blake's body was already beginning to fail. His heart lugged in his chest, and his teeth loosened in his head.

Torun's lip curled at this sick man. "Losing Lucy will become your greatest regret."

"No way!" Blake laughed. "Getting back together with her would be. Maybe if she lost fifty pounds. Oh hey, maybe when you're gone." His grin loosened. "Yeah, we'll hook out. I mean, hang up. You know what I mean."

His stomach roiled.

Lucy would never let this damaged man into her heart again.

But if this male dared to touch her?

Torun slammed the glass again. "You will not survive this journey."

Blake flinched, but continued smiling. "Why's that? Because some 'cave guardian' is going to stop me?"

"She will be your doom."

"Yeah. About that."

Blake reached into his pocket and held up Lucy's jewel. The one Torun had given her.

No.

His heart stuttered, stopped.

No!

The Sea Opal still radiated their linked energies, their

resonance. The man grinned wider, fed by Torun's realization and helplessness.

He tapped it against the glass. "See you after I spend a few quality hours with my old ball and chain. Don't breathe too hard. It would be tragic if you died before I got back. But hey, maybe I could sell your carcass to science."

Torun roared.

The glass vibrated.

But it did not break.

He seethed at Blake with deadly promise. "You are an enemy of the mer. You will meet your doom. I swear it."

Blake's eyes widened, and he backed up, laughing. "All right, freak. Here, enjoy some TV." He pocketed the jewel and the key, then clicked on the moving picture box. "Oh yeah, about that secrecy thing. Someone else already spilled the beans. See what the rest of the world thinks of the 'mer.'"

On the TV, pictures of the ocean were interspersed with photos of mermen.

They had been discovered! What? How?

Now what would happen?

"Have fun." Blake shouldered the gun and disappeared up the stairs after Lucy.

TWENTY-EIGHT

Leaving Torun was the hardest thing Lucy had ever done.

As she stood up on the deck of the yacht and shimmied into her old gear, minus her dive suit, rage at Blake burned in her chest.

Their relationship had ended painfully—for her—but she'd never once thought he was a criminal.

A jerk, yes. Cruel at the end. His increasingly chaotic moods hadn't just been from the stress and sadness of giving up the dream of parenthood. No, something was really wrong with him. Her love had been blind.

Torun's love had opened her eyes.

Blake ascended to the deck. This man was a complete stranger. That long-ago college grad with a dimpled smile and a cute butt had been eaten by a slick, smarmy investor. His gaze jerked, and his movements disjointed.

He set down his spear gun to check his gear.

Could she cross the deck and steal it from him? Low chance. On her old trawler, maybe, but the mega-yacht deck was wide and the gun remained within his arm's reach, and she didn't like the potential consequences.

No, she needed to face him where she had more of a chance.

In the water.

Blake brought her a tank. "I thought you wouldn't need this now that you were half fish."

"Do I look half fish?" She affixed the tank to the BCD. Shouldering it made her T-shirt bunch uncomfortably. "And anyway, there's no such thing. Did you actually see those guys with fins?"

He frowned, uncertain, and then insisted, "They found one off the coast of Indonesia. Caught on camera by tourists. Everyone's asking whether it's a hoax."

Her heart skipped.

She could get away from Blake in the water if he thought she was ordinary.

Lucy gave him her best scornful look. He always hated it when she knew more than he did. "Of course it's a hoax. What's wrong with you?"

"If it's not true, how come I could drop a mic in the water and make a couple announcements, and they came pouring out?"

"They're free divers with expanded lung capacity from a secretive island tribe," she lied. Stupid Ailan. "I've been staying with them. Their boat's on the other side of the atoll. This is a publicity stunt."

His eyes narrowed.

"You know what else? You can rent a merman to come to your party. A guy in a monofin sits in a tank. I'll tell your size-zero girlfriend to hire one for your birthday."

"Whatever. This doesn't matter. All that matters is a

cave full of Sea Opals, and you're about to make like a mule and carry them out for me." He lifted an oversize tank and motioned for her to grab on. "You'll carry my backup tank."

He zip-tied the tank to her wrist.

What the heck?

"Who carries zip ties on a yacht?" she demanded. "Were you planning to kidnap someone?"

"Shut up and dive."

This was bad. She'd planned to lead Blake to the cave, steal his cage key, and strand him while she rescued Torun.

"I'm going to tip upside down."

"I'll take off your dive weights." He didn't sound like he cared. "I don't want to run out of air halfway through the cave."

"What about me running out of air halfway through the cave?"

"Women don't use up as much oxygen."

"This is ridiculous."

"Breathe shallow." Blake cinched on two dive knives. He lifted the spear gun. "You get in the water first."

She hugged the extra tank and rolled in backward. Bubbles gurgled to the surface. The tank dragged her down. She reversed her descent with powerful strokes of her plastic fins, gripped the regulator in her teeth, and breathed in air normally. Through the water's surface, Blake shimmered, standing at the top of the yacht.

She inflated her BCD, broke the surface, and spit out her regulator. "Coming?"

He held her mask on his finger. "Forget something?"

Oops.

But he obviously didn't believe she was a mermaid who could see and swim underwater because he tossed the mask to her. While she put it on one-handed, he turned around and reverse-stepped in. His tank was weighted properly, and he descended.

She followed while plotting out her options. He only had one spear. She could probably whack him with the extra tank and then dodge his retaliation. Probably. He'd have to wind the spear back, and meanwhile, she could rush him, yank off his regulator, and grapple for the key to Torun's airless prison.

And get stabbed by one of his many knives.

Blake looked up at her and tapped his flashy dive watch.

She had neither timer nor altimeter nor plan. No. Something would come to her. Something would happen, and she would jump at the opportunity. She would get the key and not be stabbed.

Blake wrote on his tablet: *Don't be stupid. Air = low.* He drew a box around the word air so she would know he meant Torun.

She rolled her eyes and swam for the cave. With the tank, it was awkward. Even so, Blake struggled behind her. Was he out of shape? Funny, he didn't look it.

The cave's location thrummed in her chest cavity, and its familiar song grew louder as she approached. The ocean wove a musical tapestry. Threads of fish and reef animals sang and gleamed in the brilliant light ocean, and she easily followed the lines back to the origin.

There, the cave mouth glowed from within. The Sea Opals from the Life Tree called to her. She couldn't *not* hear it. Their song pulsed in her veins.

Mr. Huggles rose from the depths.

Her heart beat faster.

The mammoth octopus's warbling seagull song changed

with recognition. She stroked Lucy's cheek with her sucker, as she'd done last time. Lucy struggled not to greet the cave guardian back. Chest thrumming would sound strange to Blake and might tip him off.

The octopus's song darkened in warning. She curled between Lucy and Blake. Her arms waved in threat.

Blake aimed the spear gun at the octopus.

Oh, no.

The octopus bunched up, darkening further. Her skin changed to rippled red ridges, and her tentacles knotted into fists.

No.

He couldn't spear the gigantic octopus. Was he nuts? Lucy shook her head at him. Spearing Mr. Huggles was dumb, unnecessary, and cruel.

Blake took something from his pocket and held it out.

Her Sea Opal!

The octopus bunched up as if the Sea Opal were poison.

Blake waved it.

Mr. Huggles backed away, feinted as though she were going to hit him, and backed away again. The octopus knew something was wrong, but let him pass.

Blake paddled to the cave mouth.

As he passed, the octopus took one last swipe at him. The huge tentacle slammed into the outer wall.

He startled and dropped his spear gun. It fell onto rocks inside the cave.

Mr. Huggles disappeared into the depths, her song the melancholy minor key of a trash compactor.

Blake swept his flashlight over the uneven surface, missing the spear gun. The light played over the wrong rocks. The spear gun remained in shadow.

He'd lost the spear gun.

Now! Her chance!

Lucy kicked for it.

Something jerked her back. Her heart pounded in her throat. Hands closed around her mask. She rolled.

Blake clawed at her face. Water poured into her mask.

She elbowed Blake's regulator. It popped from his mouth. Bubbles cascaded for the cave roof, and he let go.

The tank dragged her down, but she kicked with it. There was the spear gun—

Blake grabbed her arm.

She struggled.

He tore her regulator from her mouth, bit it, and sucked in her air. His arm went around her throat. *No.* She clawed at his forearm, but she wasn't a fighter. Her muscles trembled and went weak. She didn't want to hurt anyone; she just wanted to save everyone. He squeezed.

No!

They floated in the water. Was he strangling her? *Oh, wait.* With his other hand, he captured his free-floating regulator, spit hers out, and put his own back in his mouth. He released her throat and shoved her regulator at her again.

Her arms stopped trembling. He wasn't trying to kill her. Okay.

Blake still didn't know about her abilities. He thought she needed the air.

Lucy took her regulator again and breathed the unnecessary air. Somehow, she had to use her secret against him.

He clipped his flashlight to his BCD and played it over the wrong rocks again.

She wasn't going to point out the right place.

He checked his clock and his air. Releasing her, Blake

unstrapped his thigh knife and twitched it at her. *Show me the way.*

If she had mastered transforming her fins, instead of napping on Torun all the time, she would be faster and better than Blake.

Lucy hugged the tank again and led him deeper into the cave. The way was actually very straight. How funny that her memories thought it was winding and confusing.

They arrived in the dry area of the cave and climbed out. The extra tank made her groan as she hauled it onto the rock. Blake took off his mask, unsnapped his diving equipment, and left everything in a pile, then moved his flashlight over the cave formations.

He saw her old dive gear and looked at her sharply.

"I had a backup," she said.

He checked his oxygen gauge and altimeter. "Take me to the Sea Opals."

She took off her new gear next to her old gear, then dragged the extra tank. It shrieked. "Take this off first."

He sliced the plastic zip tie. His knife nicked her wrist.

"Ow." She rubbed her wrist and sucked on the cut. It tasted metallic.

He shoved her forward. "Show me." His hands shook.

"Are you okay?"

He waved the blade at her. "Now."

Her heart sank. Why hadn't she already escaped? She led him straight to the Sea Opals.

He stood where, only days before, she also had, and he played his light over the vast pool. His flashlight flattened the Sea Opals' brilliance, a black light swallowed by a dark background. Was this how her flashlight had looked to Torun all those days ago?

Blake shoved a mesh bag at her. "Fill it."

She glared at him.

"The clock on your boyfriend is ticking."

She plunged her hand into the holy water and desecrated it.

The Sea Opals gleamed in her hands, responding to her resonance. Their energy glowed like the energy of the Life Tree. No wonder New Age practitioners noticed medicinal effects. Even before she had changed, the Sea Opal energy soothed like a balm on her soul.

Unlike Torun, she had no cultural heritage tied to this church. The desecration would hurt him and his people, while it caused her quiet agony.

But she needed to be strong and focused. To stop Blake, to get away, and to save herself and Torun.

Blake kept her under a sharp eye.

Lucy filled her bag until there were no gems left in the bowl.

He tied her two BCDs, old and new, to the bag and inflated them for cushioning and weight.

"How will I swim back?" she asked.

Before she could move, he clamped her wrists together and zip-tied them. He forced her down and zip-tied her ankles too. "You won't."

He was abandoning her in the cave.

"You're going to leave me?" She gaped at him. "For how long?"

He didn't reply.

"No one knows I'm here. I could die."

He still didn't look up from securing his bloody prize.

No... Seriously? But...

Shock flashed through her, along with another hot jolt of adrenaline.

No way!

She fought the ties. "Are you nuts? This is attempted murder!"

"Maybe one of your"—he made air quotes—"'free divers' will save you." He snorted.

So he actually believed in the mer. Oh well. She flexed her pinched wrists. "What about Torun?"

"The box isn't that big. He might already be dead."

No. Her heart told her he was still alive.

She refocused. "You can't hurt us. There are more. Thousands more Sea Opals. Torun knows where they are."

Blake glanced at her. "Oh yeah?"

"This is nothing. Torun can show you."

"He won't show me."

"He will if we're both alive."

Blake shouldered his BCD and the untouched tank of oxygen she'd carried for him. "With the equipment I can buy now, I'll find the rest on my own."

"You'll never find them. They've been hidden for centuries. They'll disappear, and you'll never find another opal."

He considered it. "Thanks for the info. I'll kidnap one of the yahoos that come for Torun's body. Just in case."

"Blake!"

He paused at the edge of the water. "Last confession? Want to apologize for being such a useless waste of my time?"

No. No, if these were her final words, then she sure did not.

She looked him up and down. "I'm disappointed in myself."

He snorted. "Yeah. No surprise."

"I fell in love and married a broke guy with a big heart.

Then you changed. I'm disappointed I made all the excuses for you to my parents, and I lied about how great you still were to my friends, and I lied to myself about how much we meant. I should have left you the moment you started skipping our commercial dives to gamble. You're the failure. Not me."

His ugly face turned white. "You can't even have kids."

"Thank God. You would have been a terrible father."

"You want to know what?" He leaned close to her. His breath smelled stale, like black seaweed moldering in the sun. "I never cared about kids. Your dad promised to sign over his charter business upon the birth of his first grandchild."

"You sick bastard," she hissed.

"Getting fat and weepy made the decision to close your loser investment easy." He stood and looked down on her. "Goodbye, loser."

She screamed at him as he disappeared into the water, dragging the BCDs with him.

Her cell phone was still attached to her old BCD. When it reached a shallower depth and connected to a signal, it would power on and transmit her videos to Facebook.

God, if only she'd gotten a video of him just now, threatening her. Gotten it and sent it straight to the police.

Lucy thrashed and wriggled.

The unevenly balanced rock beneath her butt shifted.

She slid into the water.

The ocean closed over her, muting her screams to *blub-blubs*. She sucked in seawater and choked. Panic shot through her.

I'm drowning!

She sank through the layers, writhing helplessly. Desecrating the sacred Sea Opals had stolen her powers. She was a human once more.

Blackness closed in.

She was human and dying.

TWENTY-NINE

How long since Torun's enemy had disappeared with Lucy?

Hours?

Torun paced in the glass cell. He stopped and put his palms against the glass. *Burst! By the almighty power of the Life Tree, shatter into a million fragments. Melt or bend and free me.*

It was not enough.

He paced again. Sweat poured off his swollen, trembling limbs.

He was a male, exhausted by two hard swims, without the powers of a female, and weaker in the air.

On the television screen, a young mer warrior appeared over and over. By his honor markings, he was a warm-water youth from Duyung. Bruises and cuts marred his body, and he swam off-kilter. A human hand grabbed his right fin and exposed his flat, scoop-like anomaly. He kicked free and disappeared in deeper water.

Many humans commented on this story. The images replayed over and over.

New images replaced the Duyung mer. Blurry images in black-and-white and sepia hinted at city shapes. More serious humans sat at desks and talked. Diagrams of the ocean meshed over drawings of human lungs and fish gills.

Then, finally, a picture of Lucy.

Torun stopped fighting the glass and watched the screen. Sad humans tossed flowers into the ocean. An older woman hugged a tearful man. Lucy's parents? A still picture showed her again.

She was below the sea. With that Blake.

He screamed and pounded the glass.

The videos changed to show Torun on the deck of her boat and in Cancun.

He quieted.

Her friend Mel spoke on the TV. Her eyes and nose were red. The family Torun had met in the restaurant ranged around her.

He held his breath. Mel's words barely penetrated the glass.

"Now that we know mermen actually exist, I think we're going to find her." She sniffed. "Lucy's coming home."

The newsroom anchors cut in with a sudden announcement.

"New videos have just been posted to the Facebook page of the missing, presumed-dead diver, Lucy Shaw. They are dated from two weeks ago, the date of her disappearance. I repeat, these videos have just been posted."

The videos were black. Perhaps there was muted audio? The news replayed them with different filters, and finally, the cave interior emerged from the gloom. At the sacred pool, underlit by her flashlight, Lucy cupped the diluted elixir and drank. A second video showed her kneeling beside the lip of the cave and fumbling with the phone, so it focused on the ceiling. The video skipped, and then feet walked past.

The anchors froze the end of the video, blew it up, and lightened it.

They were his feet.

And they transformed into fins as he pushed off the floor and leaped into the water.

"This brings up all-new questions about the final moments of Lucy Shaw," the news anchor announced. "We go now to an evolutionary biologist who will attempt to answer how, exactly, feet could be made to do what we've just seen."

The evolutionary biologist began to speak.

Torun slid down the glass wall and thumped on the ground.

The mer had been exposed.

Lucy's videos played over and over. Torun's still feet-to-fins transition was interlaced with the injured young mer.

There. It was done. They were exposed.

Torun had wished to find willing brides to join with mer warriors. He had not intended to ask the entire world. His action had led to this result.

When would Lucy return? Torun paced the cell. She must return. A dark-souled man would not defeat her. She would return, release him, and Torun would rip off Blake's arms.

A shadow moved on the stairs.

Torun faced the shadow. It was not Lucy's. "Show yourself."

Warlord Ailan stepped through the door.

"Release me." Torun slammed the locked, sealed door. "Now."

The warrior narrowed his eyes on Torun in fury. "I will not."

A trident prodded Ailan in the back. Ailan snarled at the male behind him: Prince Jolan.

Shock ricocheted through Torun, and then burgeoning hope.

Jolan still had bruises and cuts, but he wielded the weapon with grace. "Warlord Ailan. Apologize for your actions."

"Forgive me, Prince Jolan," Ailan spat the words. "I cannot humble myself before a traitor. And if all you have told me is true, why do I feel no grief for our Life Tree? It cannot be dead. You must be lying."

"You do not feel grief because the Life Tree has already reseeded itself."

Torun's chest lifted. Another miracle. He pressed against the glass. "Truly?"

Jolan nodded. "In Warlord Torun's castle."

Ailan shook. "Impossible!"

Jolan knelt, his trident still aimed at Ailan, and showed his respect to Torun. "What is your will, King Torun?"

Incredible. His feelings...that the Life Tree had selected *his* castle to bless with the new seed, that one had managed to be planted and take root despite his own being stolen in the attack...

He must return to Sireno at once. The mantle of leadership fell upon his shoulders like a boulder. He must defeat his grandfather and establish order. He and Lucy would never have the freedom to surface and take her people's marriage vows. He could no longer explore, and she could no longer wander.

Although it was a heavy burden, this was the will of the Life Tree.

He had no choice.

"Find Lucy," Torun ordered. "She left with the dark-souled criminal."

"The human male swims this direction. Loudly, and slowly."

"He is alone?"

The former prince nodded.

Lucy must have escaped. "Find her. She will want to watch the felling of her foe." He darkened. "My prey."

Jolan rose, called the order up the stairs, and received a response. He returned to Torun. "We must free you."

"I prefer to meet my would-be attacker in this place. Pierce only the glass."

Jolan pushed the incredulous Ailan out of his way and positioned his gleaming, sharp trident near the door lock.

"No, an inconspicuous place. Here, in the corner." Torun directed the deception. The glass broke with a sharp *pop*. "You, Ailan. Operate the cell phone camera."

"Camera? You would expose us all."

"We are already revealed to the world. Look!"

The others turned to the television screen. A scientist flexed a model of a human foot encased in a fin. The drawing of the injured mer youth showed in the background.

Ailan made a noise. "That is a loyal guard-in-training from Java. He has exposed us."

"He exposed the Duyung warriors," Jolan said. "You exposed Sireno."

"Torun exposed us when he stole another male's bride!"

"No, Ailan." Torun took the tone he had used many times when correcting Ailan and his other warrior trainees. "The dark-souled Blake saw these pictures and called to you. You exposed Sireno. Now he has desecrated our sacred church."

Ailan growled and shook his head violently. In his training, being wrong had always struck him harder than other males. "You lie! His soul is dark because his bride was taken by you. He is right to kill you."

"He is wrong to try." But Torun hoped he would. His trident would carve symbols of justice into Blake's unworthy hide. "You will record it."

Ailan tilted the cell phone. His curiosity about the device outweighed his judgment. He had always liked learning about new things.

"Can you not operate the cell phone?" Torun gestured. "Bring it here."

"Why do you know how?" Ailan put the phone up to the glass.

"My queen operates hers often. I have seen it many times." Torun made Ailan navigate to the square with the blue *F* symbol, press multiple "OK" buttons for things he did not understand, and finally pressed the red circle. Torun's image appeared moving on the screen. "Now, we record."

At the stairs, Jolan's voice dropped to a whisper. "My king. Your prey is coming."

Ailan held the cell phone uncertainly, then he hardened and growled.

"This is madness. The council declared you a traitor." Ailan placed the phone on the metal desk. "I will not obey."

Curse him. When Torun got out of here, Ailan would also feel the slice of his blades.

"Jolan, take the camera and point it at me," Torun ordered.

Jolan snatched up the cell phone and hid behind the

equipment pile. The camera appeared at the side, in shadow, pointed at Torun.

"Ailan, you are a worthless, frightened male. Hide and see how the human has acted with your aid."

Grumbling, Ailan at least moved to a hiding place.

Blake muttered as he slowly descended the stairs. Sea Opals crashed with every step. The other mer shifted angrily in their hiding places.

Torun slouched against the glass cage, feigning lowered consciousness. He moaned.

"Still alive, eh?" Blake dropped a black bag. Sea Opals clinked helplessly.

How dare he?

Blake opened the desk, sniffed more white powder, and ate a candy bar. He chewed with his mouth open.

Torun made his voice deliberately weak. "Where is Lucy?"

"What?"

He repeated himself, forcing the man to come closer to the cage. They needed to be in the same image.

"I left her zip-tied in the cave."

He would rip out the male's throat.

"You promised to release us," Torun said.

"I did no such thing." Blake grinned. "I promised not to harpoon you. And I'll keep that promise." He unlocked his desk, set the key on it, and removed a small black handgun. "I didn't say anything about shooting you and tossing your body overboard."

"Murderer." Torun tensed his body, forcing himself to be still.

Blake hesitated. He approached the fiberglass and put the key in the door, then stepped back without unlocking it. "Maybe I'll let you suffocate before I put a bullet in you."

Torun tried to look more helpless.

Blake must have sensed something was wrong. He backed away from the door. "Right. I've got all the time in the world. I'll shoot you off the Keys."

He started to leave. Their time was over.

Torun leaped to his feet and slammed his body against the cage wall. "Ailan!"

Blake startled badly and fell.

Ailan raced behind Blake, grabbed the bag, and leaped to the stairs. His actions showed his true values. He might not believe in Torun, but he must believe in his duty to protect their shared heritage.

Blake struggled to his feet and staggered up the stairs. "I'll kill you! I'll kill you all, you fish-blooded bastards!"

Jolan jumped from his hiding place, still recording, and unlocked the cage door.

Torun emerged and took the camera. His image loomed large as the live recording continued.

"Humans, hear me. We wish to be friends. Many have shown me kindness. Your female Lucy has accepted her role as our queen. But this man you have seen, Blake, tried to kill my Lucy for his greed. I do not know if he will face your justice. If she is harmed, he will first face mine."

Torun set the phone on the desk and started for the deck.

Oh. One more thing.

He went back to the desk, grabbed the phone, and spoke into it again. "We will gift our mating jewels, which you call Sea Opals, to women who will join our world in kindness and friendship, and love, and become our queens."

Jolan nodded.

Torun stopped the recording and set down the cell phone. "Where is Lucy?"

"We will find her, my king. What of our enemy?"

Shots erupted from the deck.

Torun took Ailan's trident. Now he would put down the man who had injured his Lucy and dimmed her soul. "Pray for him."

THIRTY

Lucy was drowning. The sea in her lungs was cold and heavy. Strength left her body. The world went black.

"Will you please stop screaming?" a man shouted.

She broke off and opened her eyes, then stared at the cave entrance.

"Thank you." Malem crossed the distance, his purple tattoos flashing. "It is difficult to enter with an alarmed cave guardian blocking the way."

"I thought I was drowning," she choked out. Her bubbles erupted for the surface.

"You know you are a mer queen? You will deafen all your enemies with that unnatural shriek." He severed the zip ties with his trident, and he was so skillful that the tip didn't even brush her skin. "Hurry and transform. We must go to King Torun before the other warriors attack."

"*King* Torun?" she repeated, stretching out her arms and legs. Her T-shirt floated up around her neck. She yanked it down.

"The new seed was planted in his inner courtyard. It took root and has begun to grow."

Oh yes. The seed had broken from her shout. Lassie escaped with it. Of course, the octopus had returned it to their castle.

Thank goodness.

Thank you, thank you, thank you.

Her eyes burned, and a lump threatened her water-filled throat.

A new Life Tree meant the city wouldn't wither. Sireno, and all the mer within it, would continue strong and healthy.

Including Torun, as soon as they released him from Blake's sick death trap.

"Transform," Malem said. "Come. Hurry. We must fly to King Torun's aid."

"It's not so easy." She flexed her feet. "I can't do it on command."

"You must." Malem darted to the bend and returned, impatient. "King Torun broke the covenant and dishonored our traditions. Because Prince Jolan has never fathered a young fry, the order of kings is broken. Many support King Torun's grandfather as ruler of both the council and the throne. Warriors are coming to ensure this unprecedented domination."

She forced her feet into awkward positions. "So now you're on Torun's side?"

"The Life Tree has selected his castle. However, his castle was also once his grandfather's, and King Torun broke many traditions."

"His grandfather is trying to murder him so *he* can break the rules unopposed. You people only care about 'traditions' when it's convenient."

"Why is that any surprise?" He frowned at her. "If you understand, please hurry. We must placate the cave guardian and escape."

"How did you get in? Did you steal a jewel too?"

"I did not." He held up a Sea Opal. Anger crossed his face. "A human was dropping them like pebbles from an overfilled net."

Blake.

Malem huffed. "Are you truly focusing?"

"How long did it take you to transform the first time?"

He avoided the answer. "Time is of the essence."

"Well, what do you expect me to do?"

"I expect you to summon the powers of the new Life Tree, defend King Torun, and destroy all his attackers in a brilliant flash."

She flushed hot and cold. A stranger who barely seemed to like her had complete faith that she was a badass.

Well, maybe she was worthy of his faith. Two weeks ago, she would have laughed him out of this cave. But today, thanks to Torun, she was changed. "Fine. Give me that."

He handed her the Sea Opal. It was small and pearlescent and, somehow in her hands, it "tasted" faintly of dark chocolate and cinnamon. Lucy paddled to the surface, clambered out of the water, and ran to the empty bowl. She dropped it in with a satisfying *plop.*

One mating jewel for one bride. Herself.

She put on her plastic magenta fins and dove past Malem's stunned disapproval. "I'll transform next time. Let's swim."

He flicked past her. Yep, he was faster. She'd work on that too.

At the mouth of the cave, a panicked giant octopus

poked a tentacle deep into the cave. Mr. Huggles! Her song gurgled, dark and worried, like the buzzing of bees.

Malem held back. "Where is the mating jewel?"

"I left it in the offering bowl."

His jaw dropped. "What?"

"We don't need it."

"Do you enjoy being squeezed to paste? To pass the cave guardian, you must show an offering."

"I've got your offering right here." Lucy snagged the dropped spear gun and swam directly into wildly curling arms of Mr. Huggles.

The giant octopus wrapped around her and dragged her out into the open ocean. Her grip squeezed Lucy with back-breaking strength. She clacked her beak.

An octopus's beak was dangerous, but as the last line of defense, it was also the octopus's most vulnerable place. Mr. Huggles was like a dog showing her exposed belly by letting Lucy see her vulnerable beak.

"I'm fine," she told Mr. Huggles. "And I've got a present for you. Check it out."

The octopus's song lightened from angry beehive to bedraggled seagull. She loosened her grip.

Lucy worked her arm free and shot the spear into the open ocean. The spear flew out and hit the end of its tether with a jerk. Lucy wound up the string again and remounted the spear. The giant octopus watched her carefully. Lucy shot the spear gun a few more times.

"Don't aim at anything important."

Mr. Huggles released her, collected the spear and gun, and descended with happy, horrible crooning.

Malem floated out of the cave. "You commanded a cave guardian with no mating jewel. You truly are a queen."

"Thanks."

Lucy rolled in the water and swam hard for the distant yacht. Other parties converged on it too. She pushed herself faster.

Malem swam ahead.

On one side of the yacht, the army sent by Torun's grasping grandfather faced off against the smaller unit that had turned her and Torun over to Blake.

Overhead, the water was pierced by a warrior. Ailan. He carried the bag of stolen Sea Opals.

Yes!

He swam hard, struggling for depth. Both armies surrounded him, momentarily united in protecting their Sea Opals. Ailan disappeared into their center.

The water was pierced again by *pops* and *hisses*. Gunfire! The warriors floated too close to the surface. Didn't they know about guns? Someone would get hurt.

"Run!" she shouted at them.

The warriors looked at her.

"Swim away!"

Malem, much farther ahead of her, took up her call. "Dive!"

Bullets slithered through the liquid, streaking deadly trails.

She focused. *Summon the power of the Life Tree.* A boiling white light curved like a dome over the warriors. The bullets hit it and skidded off wildly.

Some warriors startled and kicked away.

The leader of the large army snapped a sharp countermand. Those who had started to descend stopped and returned to their formation.

Crap. She struggled to swim faster.

A big, black-suited human crashed into the water.

Blake.

He paused on the surface, fully suited for scuba, and began to descend. He clutched a gun.

"Move!" she screamed and raised her hand. Her shock wave appeared a moment too late.

Blake squeezed the trigger.

The shot banged through the water, loud as a nail to the forehead, and the bullet zipped through the crowd. It smashed into one of the BCDs, deflating it. The Sea Opals inside shattered with a scream.

The warriors finally scattered.

Blake brought up his second hand and leveled the gun on the fleeing warriors.

Torun dove into the water, a trident held tight against his side.

Relief nearly made her weak. He had survived and emerged strong. She renewed her swimming to close the distance.

Torun slammed the trident base against Blake's hands.

Blake screamed.

Bubbles rippled for the surface. The gun dropped from Blake's hands and fell into the depths.

Blake yanked out his long, deadly dive knife.

Why couldn't she swim any faster? She was still half a football field away. The curse of being able to see endless distances was coupled with the frustration of not being able to zip across them like a mer. "Torun!"

Blake dove at Torun.

Torun dodged the blade and struck back. His trident sliced Blake's regulator line.

Bubbles poured from the hole.

Blake spit out the severed regulator and grabbed the loose hose. Oxygen poured uncontrollably from the tank. He drifted away from them, distracted and disabled.

Torun turned to face the mer warriors.

They re-formed into units and aimed their tridents at Torun in warning.

The army's noble leader floated forward. "Give up, traitors." He emitted a deep, commanding vibration. "Our forces are too uneven for an honorable fight."

Torun grinned broadly. "That is true. But I think you will find it is *you* who are outmatched."

The leader of the army growled.

Torun gestured to Lucy. "Make way for Sireno's queen."

The mermen of the army turned to look at her.

She waved, still a quarter of a football field away. "Hi!"

They turned back to Torun.

She paddled maniacally. It could have been an awesome entrance if she'd been remotely closer. In the air, she'd be gasping.

Meanwhile, Blake had found his emergency regulator. He kicked to Torun and lifted a dagger to bury in Torun's back.

"Behind you!" she cried.

Torun kicked forward. The dagger whooshed past his spine.

Blake cartwheeled.

Torun twisted and poked Blake's BCD with his trident. It popped. Bubbles released like caged doves, escaping to the surface. The emptying oxygen tank slipped free of the deflating vest.

Blake scrambled for his weight belt. Without the counterbalance of the inflated BCD, the weights dragged him to the sea floor. He yanked the release and kicked free. Murderous rage transfixed his face as he swam toward

Torun from beneath, knife out, single-minded in his suicidal fury.

Swimming up so quickly with a held breath was dangerous. "Blake, stop!"

Torun wheeled to bare his teeth at Blake. His trident sliced past Blake's throat.

Beyond reason, Blake kept coming.

Torun easily moved out of his path, rotated his trident, and bashed Blake in the face with the base. It struck Blake's mask and spiderwebbed.

Blake drifted. He put his hands out and kicked up, down, and sideways. Wait, was he disoriented? And only now realized he was out of breath and needed to breathe?

Lucy reached the last hundred feet. "No, Blake!"

He opened his mouth and sucked in water. But he was no mer.

Blake convulsed. He clawed at his throat as his body twitched.

She wished him dead, but not right in front of her. "Torun!"

Torun spoke to Malem. "Return Blake to his boat."

Malem's eyes widened. "My king?"

"He will face Lucy's human justice. She is right to punish her own, as we would punish our own. He attacked so incompetently under the water, no mer was injured here today."

"Of course." Malem bowed at Lucy, then grabbed the convulsing criminal and dragged him by the ankle to the surface.

Lucy finally reached Torun.

He opened his arms to accept her.

She barreled into Torun. He was alive! They tumbled

over and over in the water. The tightness in her chest eased. She wrapped her arms around his broad back and squeezed.

"I was so worried," she cried.

He held her.

But it wasn't over. The army of mer assembled around them to finish the fight.

"Lucy." Torun held his soft, curvy queen close to his chest. Her body felt whole in his arms. "You are well."

"But you're hurt." She stroked his bruised cheek. Her dark eyes shone with concern.

He bore many nicks from the short fight with Ailan's warriors. The salt water tingled as he healed.

Torun moved his hand under her waving clothes and squeezed her bare skin. "I will soon be well. And did you hear? The Life Tree was reborn. Our house seed responded to your power and has put down a root. Sireno will grow again."

She swallowed hard and withdrew. "I heard that makes you a king."

He needed her close. Torun drew her to his side again. "You are unhappy."

"I still can't have kids."

"The new Life Tree will heal you."

"But what if it doesn't?"

Her question contained all the sadness, all the longing,

all the tears she had shed. The evil Blake had made her feel less than a female because of her problem. The new Life Tree would certainly heal her in the future. But right now, she was the one who had been captured by her people and sterilized.

She would have stayed with him after he endured that punishment. In the reverse, he would stay with her. She needed to hear him say it.

"If the new Life Tree does not heal you, and you are never able to bear our son, I do not care."

"But Torun, your species is endangered. You have to—"

"Another will take my responsibility."

She shook her head on those doubts.

He held her gently. "Lucy, you are my queen. From the moment your soul shone onto mine, you earned my devotion. Every action since has only strengthened our bond. I love, honor, and desire only you."

"You love me?"

His heart swelled with the truth. "I love only you."

She covered his mouth with hers. Her sweet promise shimmered in the water. He held her close.

While their mouths meshed, he vibrated. "If you will agree, I would like to share the marriage vows of your people."

"Yes!"

"Even though it may be a long time before we can get away to do so. A very, very long time."

"I don't care. I can't wait!"

The army of warriors murmured.

Curse their interruption.

Torun calmed his excitement and drew back.

Lucy licked her lips, sharing his promise. He would claim her, and she would welcome him.

Torun faced the superior force.

Jolan had been captured and was surrounded by warriors, and Malem was on the deck, guarding Blake. No other help would come from any quarter. He and Lucy were on their own.

She was all Torun needed.

He ordered them imperiously, "Disperse now, before you are needlessly hurt."

Sulan, the warlord leading the army, faced him soberly. "Exile Torun. The council demands you return to face final justice."

Lucy turned in Torun's arms to face Sulan. "Torun's your king."

"He has broken our traditions."

"So you'll break them back?" She snorted. "You're hypocrites. All of you. It's disgusting, and you should be ashamed."

Sulan frowned uneasily. "It is for the council to decide."

He was an honorable, duty-bound warlord who had trained in the same age group as Torun. In their youth, multiple sacred brides had swum down to their city each time, and some warriors had fathered more than one young fry. Then the sacred islands had emptied, and where Torun had chafed under the increasing restrictions, Sulan had hardened himself to endure. He'd served faithfully year after year, knowing he would never receive the bride he deserved.

"Grow some balls," Lucy snapped. "You're going to need them if you expect to be a father."

Sulan's brows rose.

Ailan clenched the bag of stolen Sea Opals. "Address Warlord Sulan with respect."

"Ailan," Sulan growled.

"But she is a would-be bride who is already married, and she dishonors you and Warlord Tor—"

"I am a queen!"

Her proclamation rang through the ocean. A *shing*, like a chime striking a blade, flowed outward and surrounded her trio in a protective sphere.

Ailan's eyes widened. His unit darted behind him, tridents out. They hadn't witnessed her powers. Sulan's units moved back smartly, in formation, with a much better understanding of what they risked.

Torun stroked his beautiful queen's soft biceps. Her hair floated like kelp, tickling his face. She had never glowed so brightly. Truly, she was his queen.

She looked up at Torun, resting on his support. "They're all going to challenge you like this, aren't they?"

"You will win them over. It will take time."

"Even the old fish stick?"

"My grandfather? You will learn to work around his unkindness."

"I'm not really interested."

"We must both endure hardship to shoulder the responsibilities forced upon us. Do not grieve the loss of your passions. You will get used to ruling. We both will."

Sulan's warriors gripped their tridents and readied themselves for a fight. Torun also—

"Why?" Lucy asked.

He stilled. "Hmm?"

"Why do we have to give up what we love, wandering and exploring, to fight with a bunch of warriors who don't want to change?"

His mouth opened and closed, even though his words vibrated in his chest. "Because the Life Tree wills it."

"Does it?"

"My seed, planted in my castle, has sprouted into the new Life Tree. I am king."

"Maybe it was just rewarding you with choice." She rested against him. "You saw all the women in Cancun, but you chose me. I was done with marriage, but I choose you. Maybe the Life Tree seed sprouted not to force you to be king, but because it knew that we have a greater destiny, and we will choose it."

"Greater destiny?" His heart lifted. "Such as?"

"Your city desperately needs to solve the women problem. Nobody I saw was under the age of twenty-five. If you continue on like this, you really are going to die. Of course, the males of Sireno have to stop being such pigheaded jerks first."

"It is possible to change. Falling in love clears a clouded mind."

"Great. So let's leave somebody who has the patience to deal with your grandfather in charge, and after the rest of your city comes around, we'll have a big speed date with willing brides."

He cautioned her even though his heart thudded at what she offered. "You may change your mind once you see the Life Tree."

"When your council can promise I'll never, *ever* have to see you tied up with a knife in the town square, I'll visit."

"Are you certain?" he pushed. "An air-breathing queen who controls the Sea Opals would amass a great fortune among her people."

"I never wanted the money. I only wanted to find another Sea Opal to prove that I was right. So, I already have all the treasure I need."

Torun swelled with pride. She was not greedy or

warmongering like the council had said mainland women were, and she had proved it in front of all the warriors.

"We can form a club. An alliance of friendship with the mer." She tugged him toward the surface, seeming to forget the fact that they were still surrounded by a hostile army. "Mel and Elyssa will be our first members. We'll start organizing."

He resisted. "We must choose another warrior to rule."

"I'm okay with anyone but your grandfather."

"Agreed." Torun turned to his city's rightful ruler. "I give my castle to Prince Jolan."

Jolan pushed through the lax tridents of his stunned guards. "You cannot give up your city's rule. Sireno needs your voice, King Torun. We will wither and die without you."

"I have a higher destiny with my queen." Torun smiled at him. "Your task is more difficult. You must convince the warriors to break the ancient covenant and embrace a new tradition. But you will accomplish it. You have always been a loyal and careful prince." Torun caught himself. "Excuse my words. *King*."

Jolan swelled.

"Rule well," Lucy said. "Good luck."

King Jolan nodded to her and faced his new subjects.

The lower ranks straightened.

Sulan swam forward. "My orders came from the council. Exile Torun's words have no power."

"Think again," Lucy called. "If you let Torun's grandfather hold both positions without any balance, you're breaking traditions way worse than Torun ever did."

Sulan tilted his head as though he were considering the offer.

"Jolan was supposed to be king," Torun added. "It is

more stabilizing to leave my grandfather in the council, advising the new king, than to destroy both positions to make one."

Sulan straightened and pointed at Jolan. "Rally to your new king!"

The mer all bowed. They awaited their first orders from King Jolan.

King Jolan puffed out his chest. His turquoise tattoos, which Torun himself had helped to ink, shifted to a regal iridescence. "We return to Sireno."

"What of the mating jewels, my king?" Ailan held up the bags of Sea Opals; most were whole, but some had been reduced to shards. "Should we return them to the sacred cave?"

"No. These jewels belong to brides long departed. We will not bury them in a dusty place to be desecrated or hidden away. We will return them to the budding Life Tree for rejuvenation, so they will be ready to select new brides filled with our resonance."

The warriors straightened with the rightness of his words. Even Torun's chest expanded with hope. A ringing speech uplifted all who heard it; the pride and rightness traveled faster and stronger under the ocean. Yes. They had chosen wisely.

Sulan bowed to his new king, nodded to Torun and Lucy, and ordered his army to depart.

Well, awesome. They'd won!

Face down Lucy's ex? Check. Rout an army and install a new king? Double check.

Now it was time to hit the deck and stretch out for some well-earned tanning.

Actually, first, she had to get in touch with her parents. They thought they'd buried their only daughter at sea, and now she was about to emerge from the depths, reborn.

Ailan darted to Lucy. "Take this human cell phone." He cut the cord attaching her cell phone to her old BCD and pushed it at her.

No apologies? Well, whatever. She grabbed her phone. "Thanks."

He bowed stiffly and swam away.

Torun handed Jolan his trident. "Good wishes on your journey, my king. Some minds cannot be changed, but you have the patience to try."

Jolan clasped the trident. "By your honor, Warlord Torun, I will make this city into one you may return to with pride."

"We're looking forward to it," Lucy said. "Take good care of Lassie."

Jolan looked to Torun.

"The house guardian," he said.

"Lassie planted the seed," she said. "I guarantee it."

Jolan nodded. "I will venerate the house guardian as though he were my own son."

"Or daughter," Lucy said.

He blinked. "Ah. Yes."

They bid farewell to the new king and then ascended lazily to the yacht. "You guys and your 'I will only have a son' thing is getting old. You could have a daughter."

"A daughter would be an unfathomable blessing." Torun settled her arms around his neck and twirled them under the sun-dappled sea. "We do not remember because it has been so long. If a daughter were born, I believe she would change everything."

"When," she corrected.

He kissed her.

"Yes," he murmured, while their mouths remained connected. "When."

She heated. They'd been through so much together.

Lucy stroked his broad, strong body. How long had it been since she lost herself in his embrace in their castle?

He rumbled in agreement.

She twined her legs with his.

The water shook with the subtle slap of a warrior entering it. Torun tensed, but it was only Malem.

"A helicopter is descending," Malem said. "I placed the prisoner inside the glass cage."

"You removed the key?"

"I did."

Torun and Lucy swam to the ladder. He helped her out,

then wrapped his waist with a towel while heading to the bow.

She upchucked water over the side as her sopping-wet clothes slapped her body. Malem stood by, probably watching in disgust.

"Is it always this bad?" she asked, gasping and coughing out cold phlegm. Tears burned her eyes.

"Yes." Malem averted his gaze. "It becomes less awkward. Well, perhaps not for you."

"Gee, thanks." She wiped her mouth.

They joined Torun at the bow. Lucy tied the towel around Torun's trim hips and tucked the end in the waist. It wouldn't hold up in a hurricane, so she stood in front of him as the helicopter touched down on the bow, just in case.

"Go get the prisoner," Torun ordered Malem.

The purple-tattooed warrior disappeared.

The helicopter blades rotated more slowly. Inside the helicopter, Van Cartier Cosmetics' mercenaries in tactical gear and body armor leaped out with large, deadly black guns. Behind them stepped two women.

The first was Elyssa. She wore a faded T-shirt, green capris, and tennis shoes with mismatched orange and yellow socks.

The second was Aya.

Lucy's gut tightened.

Aya was a thin, dangerous woman in a sharp red business suit. Her icy-blonde hair was swept back in a severe bun. Her clothes hung off her angular body, and her white heels clicked on the deck. She snapped directions as she crossed the helicopter pad.

Elyssa tripped behind Aya. Literally. As in, Elyssa slipped in a puddle of water, slammed against the deck, and bounced to her feet again, rubbing her elbow. She barely winced and wasn't flustered, as though it happened all the time.

Aya, for her part, didn't glance behind her. She focused one hundred percent on Lucy and Torun.

Another betrayal? Lucy tensed.

Aya removed her sunglasses and fixed piercing blue eyes on the couple. "Torun. We observed your distressed message on Facebook. On behalf of the home office, I apologize for any inconvenience you suffered at the hands of a Van Cartier Cosmetics employee."

Not a betrayal. Lucy began to relax.

Elyssa suppressed her smile. Her eyes sparkled.

Aya continued, "Our former employee Blake Edwards acted well outside his authority."

The company-hired soldiers forced Lucy's trudging, shivering ex up the stairs.

Aya's red lips curled. "He was terminated several hours ago. As soon as we reach the shore, we will cooperate with the Mexican government to prosecute his actions to the fullest extent of the law."

"Mexico?" He coughed and struggled in the mercenaries' iron grips. His face was pale and sickly. "Aya, baby. I'm going to deliver."

"You had a unique opportunity to make first contact and negotiate a mutually beneficial trade agreement." Her disgust flashed. "You failed."

His jaw dropped. "Mutually beneficial? They're not even human! They—" He dissolved in a coughing fit. Nearly drowning was rough on the vocal cords.

"Yes, because of your senseless prejudice, the mer of Sireno now believe we are callous, greedy murderers with a flagrant disregard for life, caring neither for theirs nor our own."

"We can track them to their home," he protested weakly. "Take what we want! Strike—"

"No, Blake Edwards, we cannot." Aya studied him like the worm he was. "Winning an interspecies war underwater would be harder than a nuclear strike on the far side of Saturn. And there's no need to even consider it. Your inability to understand this, in addition to your criminal activities, is the reason for your termination."

"Aya!" He coughed as they dragged him away.

"Do they have hospitals in prison?" Lucy asked as they watched his rough loading into the helicopter. "He's at risk of pneumonia, and who knows what else."

Aya frowned coldly as though she didn't care.

Elyssa, the so-far silent partner, hurried to the helicopter and spoke to the crew.

Aya fixed her gaze on Lucy and held out her hand. "Lucy Shaw. Your exceptional videos brought light to a terrible crime."

Lucy shook Aya's hand. This was the woman Blake had supposedly left Lucy for. Now Lucy realized the truth. Aya was younger, harder, and more driven than Lucy would ever be. And Aya was smart. Smart enough to know Blake was all talk, smart enough to respect herself, and smart enough not to get taken in.

"So what now?" Lucy asked, pulling back her hand.

"I can offer you a flight back to the mainland."

"I don't fly."

"Or"—Aya glanced around—"you're welcome to take my yacht back to the harbor. You can relax from your ordeal. I'll leave a captain."

"Leave me." Elyssa returned from speaking with the

helicopter crew. Her tennis shoes only slipped a little on the deck. "I'll drive."

Aya turned slightly. "That's not wise. The report to my mother—"

"You turn it in."

"Lucy's your employee. You deserve the credit."

"I don't care about credit. Not this time." Elyssa's determination seemed to say, *not anymore*. "Auntie can think whatever she wants. I'm sailing with Lucy."

Aya pursed her lips.

Elyssa laughed and threw her arms around Lucy. "I'm so glad you're okay!"

Her fierce kindness filled Lucy with gratitude.

Had she really once imagined fixing Elyssa up with Torun? Torun had assured her he wasn't interested. Obviously, neither was Elyssa. Lucy had fabricated the interest because she didn't have confidence in herself or in his love.

Now she did.

"After you're rested, you have to tell me *everything*." Elyssa drew back. "What the city was like, and how you were, and how *they* were, and how you transform, and—"

"I'm not very good at transforming, and it's going to stop working soon."

"Your powers are permanent." Torun's deep voice resonated with comfort. He pulled Lucy firmly back into his arms. "You projected the power of the Life Tree to soothe the cave guardian and protect our warriors. Only mer queens can summon this power."

Elyssa's eyes glowed. "Cave guardian?"

"Giant octopus," Lucy explained.

"Really? This is kind of strange, but I always wanted an octopus as a pet."

"Me too!"

"My dad said I'd be better off with a pony."

Lucy laughed. "My dad didn't say *that*."

Elyssa clasped her hands. "I know this is sort of fangirly, but I *lived* for your Facebook posts. When they stopped, and we thought something happened to you, I was crushed. I mean, I was hopeful because I met Torun, but it was a small hope. Today, when we found out you were still alive and it was all true, was one of the happiest days of my life."

Lucy's eyes watered.

Elyssa had invested so much faith in her. She must have been horrified to lose touch, and yet her carefree, sparkling laughter now promised that she'd never truly given up hope.

And she never would either. No matter the situation, she had Lucy's back. Lucy knew this and would have hers too.

That was the kind of faith Elyssa inspired in people. She was a dreamer, a klutz, and irresistibly sunny. Her enthusiasm silenced even her icy cousin Aya.

Disaster had brought her friendship into Lucy's life, but Elyssa was the silver lining to the storm cloud.

Lucy cleared her throat. "I'm glad it all worked out."

"Me too! Oh, you have no idea—"

"Yes. We're all very glad Lucy is fine." Aya took a deep breath and smiled at Lucy. Her expression seemed colder after Elyssa's genuine, unguarded warmth. "So. Looking ahead..."

Elyssa quieted and stepped back into her cousin's shadow. Her enthusiasm was clearly on hold. She sparkled with barely repressed excitement and would surely erupt as soon as Aya finished.

"Lucy Shaw, we'd like you to come back to Van Cartier Cosmetics."

Ah. The very words she'd longed to hear. Firing her had been a mistake. Blake had been wrong. She'd been right.

"You and your associate, Torun."

"Speak to Lucy." Torun kept Lucy squarely between them. "I am an exile and in no position to negotiate."

Aya shifted her jaw. Clearly, she'd been hoping to move forward with a trade agreement for Sea Opals.

Elyssa's cell phone rang. She fumbled the device, then turned aside and spoke quietly into it.

Lucy focused on the past. "I lost everything," she told Aya.

"You can have it all back. Same house, same car."

"Same research vessel?"

"Anything you want."

As the daughter of the company president, Aya could grant those things. And despite Lucy's earlier anger, Aya hadn't really been the one to order Lucy fired. Someone in HR, about fifty jobs lower than her, had called Lucy in for "the conversation."

Lucy looked back at Torun. He rested his hand on the small of her back, supporting her fully without pushing her in any direction. His aquamarine eyes trusted her judgment.

Her judgment said not to rush in.

"I think I need a few days of vacation." She captured Torun's free hand and interwove their fingers. "Maybe a few weeks, actually."

Aya donned her sunglasses and focused on her cell phone. "I'll have HR contact you next Monday."

"Monday's too soon." Lucy leaned against Torun. "We need to think about our options."

Aya paused. "When can I schedule you?"

Lucy would need time to set up the dating site, speak with other women about the mer, and orient Torun to her air-breathing world. He could probably do fine now, but she wanted to be around, as in Cancun, to experience new things with him. Not back on the job Monday morning.

Elyssa returned with her phone in her hand, her eyes bright.

"I'll contact you," Lucy told Aya.

The businesswoman sharpened. "Are you entertaining another offer?"

"Of employment?"

"Because we would like you to strongly consider coming back to us," Aya said. "Van Cartier Cosmetics has been researching the medical benefits of Sea Opals for decades. We're uniquely positioned to turn these gems into health products for the betterment of mankind."

Lucy nodded. "Health Products For Betterment" was a company slogan, and Aya recited it without flinching. Aya and Elyssa both believed in it with clear eyes.

"As the only human who has successfully partnered and lived among the mer, you're in a unique position to assist us." At Lucy's continued silence, Aya added, "You will, of course, be properly compensated for your new duties."

"Oh yeah?" The exhaustion was beginning to drain her. "Hm."

"This yacht, for example. It could be yours."

Wow. Lucy straightened. "You'd give me this yacht?"

"Sign on the dotted line."

Oh. The yacht was worth way more than her old house and car. Wait, wait, wait. Aya was offering to give this to her? Right now?

No matter what, Lucy couldn't go back to her old life. Everything had changed.

With Torun beside her, she'd figure out a way to do everything. She'd pay off all her bills. She'd make the right choices. There was no need to rush.

"Thanks. I'll contact you when I'm ready to negotiate."

Aya stopped smiling. "We really need an answer—"

"Aya! Relax." Elyssa stepped on her cousin's white designer high-heeled shoe. She was playful but also pointed. "I'm sailing Lucy back. She can't get away."

Aya's frown deepened. "This will only take a few minutes."

"Great, but Lucy already said she wanted to do it later. If she or Torun have any questions about your offer, they can ask me."

"But—"

"They've been through a lot. The nice thing to do is *let them relax.*"

Aya's smile slowly returned. A business smile, plastic. "Yes. Thanks again for your service. Lucy, Torun."

Aya returned to the helicopter. The military men climbed aboard. The engine noise increased, the propeller turned, and they took off. Then only the three of them remained on the deck.

Lucy sagged against Torun. It was finally over.

"Sorry. She gets really focused. I'll get the engine started." Elyssa headed to the wheelhouse. Wasn't that nice? She was giving them space, kindly sensitive to their needs.

Malem appeared behind them and said, "I have spent these last minutes arguing with a man that I cannot sign away our Life Tree. The fact that I do not own it was the least of his concerns."

"Aya Van Cartier." Lucy stared after the helicopter, now just a black dot in the sky. "She's pretty awesome, right? She definitely takes no bull."

"Formidable," Malem said. "Do all these air-breathing women shine as Lucy and Aya do?"

"No." Torun softly stroked Lucy's hair. "Many darken when they approach the water. I have seen it. These women love the ocean, all of them."

That was true. And for all of Aya's tough business acumen, something had flashed in her expression as the helicopter lifted off. Something like longing. She was vice president of a large corporation, but that material achievement didn't soothe her cold heart.

The yacht engine rumbled beneath their feet.

Malem stepped back. "I must return to Sireno. I will convey what passed this day to Jolan."

"King Jolan," Lucy said.

Malem sucked in a breath. He'd been guarding Blake when the transfer of authority occurred. "King Jolan. Very fitting." To Torun, he said, "I forgive you for breaking the ancient covenant and finding a mainland bride."

"Thank you, Lieutenant. Someday, I will tell your son or daughter of this conversation."

"Daughter?" Malem snorted. "Perhaps you will. After the events of these past days, I believe almost anything." The purple-tattooed mer shook himself as if from the dream, nodded to the both of them, and slipped over the side of the yacht.

"Oh my gosh, was that another one?" Elyssa ran to the railing. She searched the empty waves. Her cell phone almost slipped out of her hands. "Whoops!" She grabbed it to her chest, finished her search, and turned in disappointment. "He's gone. All the mer are gone."

"Not quite," Lucy reminded her. "Torun's not going anywhere."

Elyssa brightened.

"Was there a reason you returned so swiftly?" Torun prodded. "Even before you saw Malem, you were running."

"Yes!" She smacked her forehead and pushed the phone on Lucy. "I can't believe I forgot. Mel's on the phone with your parents!"

THIRTY-THREE

At the mention of parents, Lucy went limp in Torun's arms.

Torun held his beloved queen until she recovered her strength and scrambled for Elyssa's phone.

Elyssa fumbled it again.

Lucy caught the device and held it to her ear. A huge smile lit her face. "Mom? Dad? Oh, it's both of you. Hey, I made it... Yep, totally fine. Except there's someone you'll have to meet... No, he's going to be a much better son-in-law, Dad. I promise... Oh my God, I was on TV? No way! What do you mean, they broadcast my Facebook?"

Lucy reassured them with laughter and giggles, in all the ways a child could reassure her parents.

Elyssa stood nearby, also smiling.

"Thank you for your patience," Torun said.

"Of course." Elyssa's gaze dipped down his half-covered body. She quickly averted her eyes. Her cheeks reddened. "I'd be doing exactly the same."

"Your parents are close to you."

"Yep."

This was, truly, his desire for his young fry. If Lucy healed enough to have a son—or daughter, as Lucy was always careful to emphasize—Torun might be blessed with any miracle.

King Jolan must convince the warriors of Sireno to accept the change. Anyone watching Lucy talk with both her parents would understand. How could the mer chase the old traditions once their young fry knew the love of both father and mother and became a full family? That was their future.

Elyssa edged away. "Are you hungry?"

"Very hungry." His belly grumbled, and his bones ached. He was starving.

"I'll start something."

"Lucy likes tuna and hot chocolate."

"I'm on it." Elyssa departed.

Lucy finished her conversation and skipped back to him. A huge smile beamed across her face. "You have to come home with me and meet my parents."

"I accept." He rested Elyssa's cell phone on a table and gathered up his queen. "Food is being prepared. How can I make you comfortable?"

"We're alone?" She twined her fingers in his hair. Her gorgeous eyes darkened to naughty. "I feel all salty. Want to take a bath?"

"Yes."

"Good. Come with me."

They descended the stairs, passing palatial rooms filled with pianos and white carpets and glass sculptures. Lucy opened every door.

"That bedroom must have been Blake's," she decided,

closing the door to the biggest, messiest suite with a shudder and tripped over to the untouched, second-largest suite. "This will be ours."

He liked the way she said that. *Ours.*

But there was still a hesitation in her voice and her manner and in the quick look she gave him. He tried to pull her close to reassure her that it was all over.

She avoided his gaze and tugged free. "Let me check on something."

Torun dropped his towel on the back of a chair and strolled around their new room.

A large bed piled high with fluffy pillows and a huge mirror reflected the nautical windows' soft golden lights. They would use this bed, perhaps, to rededicate their commitment to each other. Adjoining rooms beckoned off either side.

Lucy set out two thick white robes, towels, and fuzzy slippers. While the bath filled, she opened cabinets and revealed a cold-storage refrigerator. She squinted at a bottle's label.

"Champagne. Hmm. Something tells me this is worth more than my last car." She toyed with the silver foil. "I really shouldn't."

Anytime his queen spoke with that naughty look in her eyes and glanced at him sideways, daring him to stop her, he vowed that she *really should*. And he would help her.

He peeled back the foil, examined the top, and discovered how to pop it open while she found glasses.

She jumped in surprise and laughed. "Whew! That's fancy. Oooh."

Golden liquid foamed out. She thrust each glass under the fountain.

"And look what else." She bit into a strawberry coated in chocolate. "I found these in the freezer."

These were cold chocolates. "Elyssa is making you a hot chocolate."

"Yum. I could drink gallons." She sipped her champagne. Her eyes widened, and she drank more deeply. "Wow. I don't know if this is good or not, but it tastes great."

He also enjoyed the sharp, clear bite of the sweet, fizzy liquid. "It is great."

"We have to eat so it doesn't go to your head." She laughed nervously.

Hmm.

"I will do so." He ate from a small selection of creamy cheese spread upon crunchy crackers that Lucy placed out. "Will I need my head?"

"Yes." She trailed her gaze down his nude body with a heat that made his cock pulse with life. "And then some."

When she had also eaten and drunk, she led him into the calm bathroom. Soft lights reflected from the fixtures and mirrors around the vast tile. In the center of the room stood a large tub. She tested the water and turned off the tap. Bubbles floated on the surface.

He examined them curiously. The soapy bubbles tasted like a flower chemical. Vanilla, perhaps. Lilacs.

She noticed. "Is this your first bubble bath?"

"Yes."

"Let me take care of you."

He climbed into the tub. She divested herself of her wet T-shirt and shorts. Bending over to inspect her chipped toenail polish, she gave him a view from both the front and the reflection of the back. The mirror teased him with glimpses of pink promise. His cock pulsed again, a pleasant throb.

This was the woman he loved. His queen.

His wife.

She straightened and caught him looking. Her cheeks turned an adorable shade, and her smile grew. "Enjoying the view?"

"Very much."

She blinked. His honest answer had surprised her? Perhaps his ardor had. She was gorgeous, a goddess, radiant inside and out. He was attracted to her in every way.

"Come in the water."

"In a moment." She pranced around the tub, leaning closer and stepping away. Teasing him.

His cock responded. He gripped the thick shaft and stroked. It was very, very pleasant to be teased.

She made the mistake of leaning too close.

His hand leaped from the water. He caught her forearm. "Lucy. You are nervous."

"No. Well..."

He knew it. Torun melded their lips together.

She gasped in surprise and melted into his embrace. Whatever the reason for her nervousness, he would reassure her with his body.

He nibbled her soft lips. Her mouth opened, hungry and hot. She tasted of the champagne and chocolate, just like their first night. She intoxicated him.

"Okay." She licked her lips, her eyes dark with passion. "Scoot forward. I'm getting in."

That confidence was better. He obeyed.

She sat behind him in the bath and rubbed suds across his pectorals, down his abdomen, along his long arms and legs, and across his back. Her breasts nestled against his back. The hard pearls of her nipples, and her intense focus on treasuring his body, made his cock fill with heat.

"You have so many scars."

"I trained my warriors hard. They fought honorably."

"These are all from battles?"

"Yes, the recent ones. Those from hunts healed long ago."

She slid a finger over each one as though learning it. He warmed. She was studying his body more intimately. Soon, there would be no surprises left between them, only acceptance and love.

Lucy squeezed sweet-smelling shampoo into his thick hair. Her fingers dug into his scalp, causing little shivers down his spine. His Lucy was so powerful. He had never experienced such intense sensations before. He relaxed into her ministrations.

She rinsed off the suds and then paused.

He roused himself. Now to wash her hair and give her this new pleasure. "Come in front of me."

"Wait. I missed a spot." She slid her hands down his taut abdomen and curled her fingers around the base of his shaft.

Pleasure flooded him. He sucked in a breath and hummed. "Lucy."

Her small tongue licked his jaw. "Mmm?"

"You have me."

"Good." She tightened her grip and pumped. Pleasure danced along his shaft. Completeness filled him because she was his wife, his soul mate, his love. He thrust into her hands and groaned.

She nuzzled into his neck. "Don't let me go."

He rolled over, and the water sloshed, fresh and sudsy, as he covered her. "Never."

"I know you say that, but since the moment I pulled you onto my trawler, we've been going nonstop. Things are going to settle down. Everyday life isn't so interesting. We'll settle into a routine of eating, sleeping, more eating, more sleeping..."

"That sounds like a dream."

"I hope you won't get bored of me."

"Eating our wedding feast in my castle was the best meal of my life," he assured her. "And breakfast was better. Joining with you now is what I want more than anything. And I know that waking up beside you tomorrow will be better."

Her brows smoothed. "I want to believe you."

"Because we resonate, Lucy. Our souls glow brighter together. And every day, we increase our resonance. Our connection grows. And tomorrow, we will glow even brighter."

She squeezed him. Her chest glowed brilliantly. Happy tears glimmered in her eyes.

"Join with me, my soul mate."

She tipped her head, closed her eyes, and offered her lips.

He eased his hand under the back of her head to cushion her from the hard porcelain and aligned their mouths.

She moaned and opened herself to him.

Her complete trust made his chest swell. His tongue swept her secret depths, thrusting with the passion he wanted to give to her whole body.

She sucked in a breath and released his mouth. Her dark eyes were confused. She stroked his damp forehead. "You make me feel so safe. Like I could show you any side of me, even the ugly and scared sides because you think I'm fine just the way I am."

"You are beautiful."

Her full lips quirked to one side. "Well, maybe not the back side—"

"Every side." He lifted her upright and turned her to face away from him. "And the back."

She straddled his thighs so her derriere pressed into his lower abdomen. "Torun!"

"Relax." He pumped the liquid soap she had used on him, reached around, and cupped her breasts. "I am washing you."

Her breath hissed between her teeth. She arched her back, pressing her head into his shoulder. Her large globes filled his palms.

She was so beautiful. Her full form said female in every language. He spread slippery soap across her rounded abdomen and over her silken thighs. Her soft buttocks enveloped his pulsing erection. Her tapered waist tempted him to pull her closer. Lush breasts begged for his caress.

He brushed her sensitive pearls.

"There." She twisted and nipped his jaw. "That feels so good."

"I know." He listened to her body's desires so he could give her the pleasure she needed. Her curly softness enticed him. His hand moved up her inner thighs to the sweet, hot center.

She trusted him to care for her. He *was* worthy of her trust.

He caressed her soft, wet folds.

"Mmm." She shifted her hips, offering herself. "More."

He coated his fingers in her sweet wetness. His pores opened as though drinking her in. He would never need any other prize. Her pleasure filled his veins like a sweet drug.

She positioned her soft entrance against his hard tip.

And he existed only for fulfilling her desire. He pressed upward.

She arched. Taking in his shaft, she coated his full cock like a hot, tight sheath. She breathed out and looked at him over her shoulder. She was so beautiful. Sinuous. Powerful. Woman.

He gripped her feminine hips. They fit in his palms, just the right size.

She moved.

He rocked into her. His hard shaft pushed in and out of her feminine channel in a dance as old as the ocean tides.

She moaned and took him deeper. Good. He made her feel this powerful, this trusting, this beautiful. She released all her worries for the first time, and her whole body chemistry changed to pure liquid heat.

Her buttocks slapped his hard thighs. She tossed her head and gasped.

He would not release his seed until she had taken her full pleasure.

Her channel clenched him. "Torun!" She writhed in ecstasy.

Her release whipped through him with exaltation. He lost control, and his own release poured out, pulsing hot, into her wet, relaxed, ready body.

She shivered.

His body throbbed, wrapped in the warmth of his one true love, but his heart calmed. His lower face to the nose rested below the water. He had been so distracted by their joining that he hadn't noticed shifting to water breathing.

He lifted above the water and shifted back.

She glanced over her shoulder, grinned at him, and

brushed away the bubbles on his cheeks. In the twisting motion, her tight heat clenched his sensitive masculinity. It tickled, and he twitched.

"Oops." She leaned away to disentangle them. "Sorry."

"It is not an injury." He would take tickling from her any hour of the day so long as it meant they were joined in this way, but he lifted her off, helped her turn, and nestled her against his chest. "I am so very lucky you pulled me onto your boat."

"I thought I was rescuing you." She snorted at her naivete. "Rescuing a merman from drowning? That takes the cake."

"You did rescue me."

"What, in Sireno? That was terrifying." She traced his tattoos, the gold swirls of his identity. "I'm glad it turned out well. It's useful knowing I could fend off those warriors. Any mermaid can do that?"

"I believe only one who has claimed her power."

"Maybe someday we'll raise an army of women and save every merman who needs us. We'll be a Mer-Human Alliance. I bet Elyssa would do us proud. Mel is happily married, so she'll be our land support. Aya would make a fierce warrior."

He threaded their fingers together, his webbed, the skin reacting to the water. Hers didn't yet, but would, given time.

He would have her practice in the ocean far from the dangerous council, where it was safe. Where the two of them could be together.

"You also rescued me from my closed mind, a pointless exile, and ruling when I did not wish to," Torun said. "You have rescued me from so much. Someday, I swear I will do the same for you."

She held his gaze. Her eyes reflected belief, as simple and clear as the glow in her gentle, warm, powerful soul. She was now mer and human, united into one. A mermaid. His queen..

"Don't worry, Torun. I'm sure we'll rescue each other for the rest of our lives."

EPILOGUE: LUCY'S HONEYMOON SURPRISE

Crash!

Lucy bolted upright. The bed was empty. A body-shaped impression beside her showed where a large, sexy male had recently abandoned their warm sheets.

She swung her legs out and rested her feet on the familiar worn slats of her bedroom floor. "Torun?"

He didn't answer.

Ker-rash!

Had someone's fist bashed a cabinet full of glass? She pushed off the bed and hurried to the top of the steps. Below, the main floor of her parents' house was in shadow.

She raised her voice. "Torun?"

"Stay where you are, Lucy!" His deep bass reverberated in the old converted lighthouse. "Do not approach."

Crash! Crash, crash!

She clutched her white cotton nightdress to her neck. "Are you sure?"

"Return to bed this instant."

She hesitated. He needed help.

"Now," he demanded.

Lucy stopped at the bathroom on her way back, brushed her wild brown hair, and scrubbed her teeth of the previous night's champagne.

Crashity-crash!

Lucy took a deep breath. *Ignore the noises.* She returned to the bedroom, flopped onto the old wood-framed bed, and snuggled into the warm, fluffy blankets on Torun's side, burying her nose in his pillows and luxuriating in his scent. They held his warmth in the morning sunshine.

This was how her husband smelled, of sunshine and cinnamon. She breathed deeply.

Only a few days ago, she'd introduced Torun to her parents. Neither had quite known how to react to their new, tall, blue-tinged, covered-in-gold-tattoos son-in-law. Her mom had tried to flay Torun for disappearing with Lucy beneath the ocean for two weeks, but Lucy's dad kept interrupting. He'd get choked up and hide his face in his checkered flannel while they all pretended he wasn't crying.

Now, in their old family kitchen, she hoped Torun wasn't receiving the wooden-spoon beating her mother had practically threatened.

"The women in your family are fierce," he'd said after that first evening's dinner, straightening under her mother's lingering gaze.

Lucy had entwined her hands with his. "Stay good, and you'll be fine."

"I hope I am good."

She'd leaned into his ear and whispered, "Later, I hope we'll be naughty."

He'd kissed her forehead and made secret promises just

for them. Which included last night, when they'd been married.

Lucy rotated the simple wedding ring around her left finger. Strong wires encased a tiny Sea Opal. Torun had fashioned it himself from a shard lodged in her cell phone case.

She stroked the smooth white gemstone.

Lucy would never let it go.

The marriage ceremony had been Torun's idea. Their union was sacred under the water, but ever since she'd brought up marrying him human style, he'd been obsessed with having both. He wished for her to feel the same officialness from her home traditions that he felt because she'd performed his.

Of course, neither marriage ceremonies had been legal. Under the sea, he'd broken tradition by stealing her from outside of his city's abandoned sacred islands.

Above the water, their marriage was illegal because the United States and other countries still hadn't decided how to identify a male who spent most of his existence in the ocean—without a real central government, driver's license, or even pockets—and also transformed partly into a fish. Was he even human? Aya had promised Van Cartier Cosmetics would help the government work everything out.

So long as they could remain together and keep a low profile, it was good enough for Lucy.

Torun appeared in the hall.

She sat up and scooted to the center of the bed. "What have you got for me?"

"Many things." Her gorgeous warrior filled the bedroom doorway with his rippling, muscular physique, tapered waist, and powerful legs. He ducked under the casing.

Today, he wore long Bermuda shorts and an apron. His face and body were smeared with ingredients, and he was dusted with flour, muting his iridescent gold tattoos.

She'd bought the first Bermuda shorts because they were handy on the streets of Cancun. He'd latched on to the design and decked himself out like a surfer on their cross-country trip through places like Ohio and Idaho.

Everything inland interested him deeply. Torun's wild-eyed wonder had made the bus journey so much more fun. Lucy had enjoyed sharing the experience wrapped in his immutable love.

Now, he rested the tray on her knees. He'd placed a strip of bacon, a runny egg, and a slice of blackened toast on separate small dishes. The entrees were accompanied by a slab of what might be butter, a dollop of mayonnaise, and a scoop of shredded tuna fish.

"You cooked." She examined him for injuries. "With fire?"

He covered his hands, certainly hiding cuts and grease burns. "You cooked many times. This time, I will provide."

"You provided at your castle, underwater." A place where fire didn't exist, except when burning magma erupted from undersea volcanoes.

"We are not underwater now."

She poked the soggy bacon. "How did you know these are my favorites?"

"Your mother assisted. Only at first. She left before the tuna can, so I owe your family another knife."

"You opened the tuna can with a kitchen knife?" She chewed the watery shreds.

"Aged tuna was your favorite food at our castle. I wished for you to enjoy the same food here, in your family home, on your first morning as my wife."

She stopped chewing.

He gazed so clear, so steady. Words she tossed off and forgot about, he collected to his heart as treasures.

"Torun." She set aside the fork and placed her hands on his injured ones that he tried to hide. "This is a feast."

His chest lifted, and his smile mellowed.

She couldn't see the "brightness" he or the other mer saw in other people's chests, but she sensed her words had touched him. His efforts to give her the best food in a foreign environment, despite all his disadvantages, simply because he loved her, had not been in vain.

She squeezed his rough knuckles, and then she picked up the fork again and enjoyed her first breakfast as his wife, hardly tasting a thing.

"Where did my mom go?" she asked, munching the bacon. "Is she picking up a cake for the reception?"

"She said something about giving us privacy, then took your father out on their boat."

How considerate.

Actually, not counting the first emotional night, her parents had done great. They were so happy she'd emerged from being missing at sea for two weeks, and so shocked at the unconscionable actions of their former son-in-law, that facing a big, tattooed merman as Lucy's new husband barely caused a ripple. Everything else had already blown their minds.

Of course, it helped that Torun told them Lucy was special, the most powerful woman in recorded history, and recognized as a mer queen.

Every parent wanted their child to grow up, go out into the world, and be loved and treasured. That hadn't worked out with Lucy's first husband. Her second one more than burned away the dark wounds in her soul.

Even if Lucy still couldn't give him the children his endangered, male-only species needed to revive.

She rubbed the Sea Opal. Its inner light resonated with her soul and cast a healing balm on her heart.

Torun sat on the chair beside the bed and rested his elbows on his knees. "Should I summon your parents to return?"

"Huh?" She replayed the conversation. "Oh, no. I was just thinking it's too bad the original Life Tree was destroyed before it could heal me. I wonder if we'll ever get back to see the new one or if your council will still be out to get us when I'm old."

He stroked her cheek. "You will be welcomed as a queen. Someday."

"Someday," she repeated.

He watched her eat. His presence was peaceful and strong, and he seemed satisfied just being with her. Whether they were rich or poor, or whether they lived in the ocean or above it, he put her heart at ease. Everything would work out. Their souls had resonated. They were together.

But she still wished the Life Tree had healed whatever was wrong with her. Doctors had never identified the source of her infertility. She was functionally like any other woman, except she couldn't get pregnant. She'd wanted kids long before she met Torun. Having them now would be perfect.

Torun rubbed her idle hand between his wide, powerful palms. "I went out with your father yesterday. He took me to every confluence of current."

"You went in the water? That must have been cold."

He smiled. "Yes, Oregon is colder than Cancun, even in summer. But we found an echo point."

She stopped chewing. "Did you hear news of your city?"

He shook his head.

They both wanted to know how the new King Jolan was doing and whether Torun's obtuse grandfather on the council had tried to force anyone else into exile.

"But"—he patted her hand—"a large army composed of many different cities stormed the prison trench and freed Kadir, the young warlord who inspired my rebellion. He will lead the force to rebuild the city of Atlantis."

Her heart lifted.

More women like her would have an opportunity to drink the elixir, gain mermaid powers, and join with warriors who treasured them and their powers. The oceans would be filled with equals and not simply mermen who took on human surrogates and then kicked them out after they produced kids.

"Someday, Sireno will see you were right," she said. "Women who choose their destinies will change everything. Your oceans will thrive."

He smiled. "Perhaps your friend Elyssa will soon have her opportunity to meet Kadir."

"That's good." Lucy set aside her finished tray, texted the eager woman Torun's news, and turned off her phone. "She'll be their staunchest champion."

Torun picked up her tray and carried it downstairs.

The world was changing now that the mer had been discovered. The shock of learning just how much humans didn't know about the bottom of the ocean had been replaced by reactions from curiosity to xenophobia and everything in between.

For now, Lucy flopped back on the bed. Her parents

had replaced her childhood mattress with an adult-sized guest bunk, and it was just perfect for her and Torun.

Torun's footsteps sounded louder as he ascended the stairs.

She quickly rolled onto his side of the bed and wiggled in the fluffy comforter.

The floorboards creaked as he entered the bedroom. "You are resting on my side." His deep voice carried his amusement.

"It's the best side."

"You are welcome to trade."

"No way." She rolled over and teased him. "The fact that it's yours is what makes it good."

"I see." He unfolded his long body on top of her comforter, pretending to squish her beneath it. "Oh, I am becoming so tired. I guess I will go back to sleep. Is something wiggling on my side of the bed? No matter, I will sleep on it anyway."

She giggled.

He lifted up and rested his weight on his elbows on either side of her, hemming her in.

"Torun!"

"Oh, Lucy. I did not realize you were there."

"Mm-hmm."

Thank goodness he could joke with her so easily and carefree.

When they'd first met, he'd been desperately serious. His race was dying out, and he broke his laws to find and speak to her.

They still had very serious problems, uncertain futures, and, if left unchecked, his council would castrate and exile him if they caught him. But Torun could lie with her on a fluffy bed in her parents' house and laugh, smile, and tease? Yes. They'd come a long way.

His smile turned wicked. "What shall I do to you?"

Remembering what they risked to be together made her value their time together even more.

Her heart thumped. "I have a few ideas."

His nose nuzzled hers. "I am listening."

She reached up and kissed him.

Her lips touched his and started an engine fueled by liquid desire.

He opened to her. Their tongues tangled. He tasted deliciously familiar, and she could never get enough of him.

Her body rose to awareness. Her breasts swelled, and her nipples pearled with tingling aches. Her heart beat hard, flushing her body with warmth, and need twisted between her thighs with a pulsing, pounding hunger.

He threw the comforter out of the way and descended upon her with single-minded conquest.

His hands cupped her cheeks, and his tongue plumbed her mouth, filling her. His elbows held his weight on either side of her breasts, resting on the mattress. His hard pectorals pressed her down, and his tapered waist fit perfectly between her parted thighs.

She canted her hips and rubbed her pussy against his growing hardness.

He groaned. "Lucy."

"Now," she panted. "Please. Now."

He pulled up her soft white nightdress and trailed fiery kisses along its rising hem until his mouth found her inner seam. He spread her slick folds to feast on her need.

Pleasure throbbed in her center. She writhed. His delicious gift built her hunger and made her crave more. Her body tingled, rising on the welling tide of a powerful orgasm.

She tugged off his apron and forced down his Bermuda shorts. His passion-filled aquamarine eyes burned on her body. Although she still carried all the weight and scars, in his eyes, she felt a deeper acceptance of herself. He saw her true beauty.

And she saw it too.

He pulled her nightdress over her head, then took off his shirt.

Every muscle rippled in shiny perfection. Layered atop his skin, his gold tattoos glimmered, swirls and circles complementing his powerful body, iridescent. The colors trailed all the way down to his large arousal.

She gripped his hot shaft in her hands. The gold-swirled member pulsed.

"Lucy." He breathed hard and pressed his forehead to hers. "You are sexy."

It was a new word she'd taught him. Beautiful was good for most women, and gorgeous was perfect for a new haircut or outfit, but sexy was what his wife wanted to be called when she was naked and snuggled against him in bed.

Lucy rewarded his memory by wetting her hand and stroking his long shaft. He quivered. It was a reward for both of them. She loved the weight of his hard length in her hand.

He dropped his mouth to her rosy nipple. His hand massaged the other sensitive tip.

Need squeezed between her legs, and her body throbbed in readiness.

She positioned his smooth cock at her wet entrance.

He rested on his elbow and eased in, careful of his girth,

controlling his power, and thrust into her slippery channel, filling her to the brim.

She shifted her hips to take him to the place of rightness.

He bobbed his hard tip against her pleasure spot. She moaned. He could even hold himself perfectly still, and she'd eventually orgasm, coasting on an incoming tide that rose imperceptibly until it closed over her and shook her to fulfillment.

But she liked it a little faster and a little wilder.

She writhed against his body, rubbing her sensitive nipples against his chest while her pussy yielded to the thrusts of his cock. His aquamarine eyes burned and his teeth clenched. He fought to hold on to his control while she worked against him, pumping their bodies together.

"Lucy." A ragged edge to his delicious bass made her shiver.

She grabbed his flexing buttocks and squeezed.

He thrust harder. The pleasure tide rose, white water, higher. Tingles spread across her body, hot and unstoppable. She gasped.

He groaned and pounded into her sweet, glorious wonder.

She clung on, and then he lifted her bucking hips and poured himself into her, shouting with release. Pleasure grabbed her ankle and dragged her under.

The orgasm burst over her.

She gripped on to Torun, the pilot of her body. They both jerked and shuddered. Waves of pleasure slapped her, wringing her out with goodness.

When it was all over, and the last intoxicating wave passed out of her body, she threw her arms around him and held him close to her heart.

Their bodies eventually cooled, and their heartbeats returned to normal.

Lucy stroked the well-muscled back of her loving husband. He shifted his weight to her side, curving around her protectively.

"I want to go out in the water with you," she said. "The next time you go out."

"It will be cold for you."

"You swam in it."

"Yes, like jumping into an ice current. It is invigorating."

"I want to show my parents my transformation."

"The water is too thick and dark for them to see you. You would do better to shift on their ship."

Her transformations weren't going well. She could still only get half of one foot to flatten out like a fin. It wasn't the front half, but the right half, her pinky, second, and third toes. It looked like an ACME anchor had fallen on just the half, not impressive or mermaid-like at all.

"Still, you should enter the water. You will see through a bright-green lens. It is similar to a vast alpine meadow, like the ones we saw in your Rockies."

"I want to go."

He rose and stretched. "Then get dressed. Your parents will be ready as soon as we want to go out."

Lucy's stomach lurched. "What? Why didn't you say that sooner?"

"Because your mother told me to take my time." He smiled at her lazily. "I took my time."

"Oh, you..."

He enfolded her in his arms and dizzied her with his sweet, loving, satisfied kiss.

Then he patted her bare bottom. "Get dressed."

They met her parents down on the dock, at their sailboat. Her father greeted Torun gruffly. His salt-and-pepper hair blew in the late morning sun, the air cool enough to merit his patched red-and-black flannel.

Lucy's mother embraced her in a warm hug. Her dark eyes glimmered behind her familiar beaded glasses. "How was breakfast?"

"Delicious," Lucy said.

Torun beamed.

"Oh, well then, maybe you don't want this." She indicated the plain box of pastries she'd picked up from their favorite local bakery and two well-insulated hot chocolates.

Lucy snagged a crunchy bear claw. "Don't worry, I'm hungry again."

"Lucy-Boo!" Her dad called from the wheelhouse of their family daysailer. "Cast off!"

She assisted her dad, the pastry clenched in her teeth, and she also taught Torun the basics she knew by heart.

They were about halfway to the echo point, enjoying a beautiful day, when she suddenly got ill. She lost her pastry and hot cocoa over the railing.

"What did you put in those runny eggs, Torun?" she asked, only half joking.

Torun stroked her back. "The horizon can disorient even the mer."

"Mermen can get seasick?"

"On a rough sea. We do not linger near the surface."

"No kidding."

But her parents were both staring at her with wide, shocked eyes.

"Boo," her dad said, reverting to his childhood nickname for her. "You never get seasick. Are you sure it's not something else?"

"Maybe." She wiped her mouth and sent Torun to open

a soothing fizzy soda to wash the taste out of her mouth. "Actually, I think it's the flu. I've been feeling weird every morning this last week. I threw up on the bus ride here too."

"Only in the mornings?"

"Yeah. It wears off." Lucy shrugged. "Maybe I picked up salmonella at that one super-nasty roadside café. The one with the vending machines instead of food."

Torun nodded. "You felt ill immediately after eating that food."

"Yeah. It didn't really hit me until the next morning, though. And then, ever since, it goes away by midafternoon."

Lucy's father made a puffing noise of disbelief.

Her mother went to his side and put a calming hand on his arm. "What your father is trying to say is that we both noticed you seem to have an extra glow."

Lucy took Torun's hand. He had brought the glow of her soul back to life. Her parents had noticed.

"So maybe there's something you want to announce to us."

"Announce?"

Her father squared his shoulders. "I'm ready."

Lucy's mother patted his hand.

So much had happened in these last weeks. She'd met Torun, and they'd survived the disaster at Sireno. Lucy scratched the back of her head. "I got a job offer from Van Cartier Cosmetics. It's for way more money than they paid me before, but I think they might go even higher, so I'm thinking I should hire a lawyer to negotiate—"

"Lucy!" Her mother huffed. "We're wondering if you're pregnant."

The word fired like a gunshot.

Lucy twitched. "Pregnant? But I can't have kids. The doctors said."

"They said that because you *didn't* get pregnant when they did all the medical things to you. Not that you couldn't."

"Well, yeah. We tried everything."

"Honey, you come from a line of determined women. Your great-grandmother carried your grandma for an extra two months so she could be born in peace instead of wartime. And I was so worried about raising a baby alone that I didn't get pregnant with you until exactly nine months were left on your father's Coast Guard contract. We weren't trying to abstain. He left his retirement party to meet us at the hospital. Some part of you knew Blake was bad, so your body refused to become pregnant. Not until you met"—she drew breath and indicated Torun—"a better man."

This kind of talk had been excruciating when Lucy had been undergoing treatments. But now, her mother's complete acceptance of her new husband made Lucy all mushy inside.

She threw her arms around her mother. "Thank you so much."

"You're my daughter," she murmured, patting Lucy's back. "You're my kid."

"Well?" Her father turned red. "Then, are you?"

Her mother unwound herself to comfort Lucy's father again. "Hon, they don't know. And that's fine. We're fine not knowing."

Her father didn't look like he was fine.

Lucy turned to Torun. Could she actually be pregnant?

He looked right back at her, equally mystified. "Do you not know?"

"Why would I?"

He tilted his head.

Oh, jeez. He was a merman raised in an all-male society. As if *he* would know whether the Life Tree had healed her and she was carrying their child.

She rubbed her head. "Wow. I didn't even think it was possible. I mean, I just assumed I never would be. It's not like I have a test on me."

"You can perform a test?" Torun reached out and took her hand. His own was damp. He was excited, but trying not to seem so. "That is a useful invention."

"Tell me about it." She ran her free hand through her hair. Suddenly, she couldn't stand still. She wanted to jump into the freezing cold water with all her clothes on, swing off the mast like a monkey, or howl at the sun in the bright-blue sky. "Gosh. I wish I'd thought of this on the mainland."

"I can turn this boat around," her father said.

"Nah. I mean, most likely, I'm not. I don't want to get all excited for nothing."

All the times she'd gotten excited about nothing piled up against her memory like stones, trying to drag her spirit down. All the tests. All the disappointments.

Blake had only wanted a baby so that he could swindle her parents out of their charter company. Even so, Lucy had really wanted a baby. She wanted one even more now, shared with Torun.

"I can turn around," her father repeated, tapping his foot. He looked even more anxious and excited than she felt.

"No. No..."

Torun sensed her indecision. He wiggled his brows. "Maybe?"

She giggled and threw her arms around him. "Well...hmm."

"Well, if you're going to turn around anyway, then here." Her mother dragged a pregnancy test out of her reading bag and slapped the carton on the table.

They stared at her.

"Lilith," her father murmured.

"I didn't want to pressure her," her mother said, "but I thought it might come in handy. No reason to turn around and cut short a perfectly wonderful day of sailing."

Lucy's heart swelled.

Her mother understood too that if the results were negative, then Lucy could distract herself with a polar bear plunge and hide her tears in the dark, dense Pacific Northwest ocean with her husband, in private.

"You can do it if you want." Her mother leaned back on her seat cushion and pulled out the newest Nora Roberts. "If you don't, I don't want to know either. Call me in nine months."

"I think you'd know sooner than that." Lucy snatched the small box.

Her heart pounded in her throat. She went into the tiny shipboard bathroom and read all the instructions three times before she built up the guts to break the plastic.

Every kit was different, after all. It would be dumb to do this one wrong and receive an indecisive answer. Then she really would make her dad go back and ruin the afternoon, and they'd all miss out on sailing.

Her morning sickness was probably just a cold. It was probably nothing. It was nerves, or salmonella, or—

"Lucy? Hon?" Her mom tapped on the door. "I've got three more kits in my bag. If anything goes wrong, you just come on out and grab another one."

Tears leaped to her eyes. "Mom? How come you know exactly what I need to hear?"

"I'm guessing. But you're still, always and forever, my little girl."

Lucy sniffled.

"Come on out when you're ready."

"Okay."

Her mother's footsteps receded.

Lucy ripped open the plastic on the tube and took a deep breath.

Minutes later, she walked out of the tiny bathroom and approached her loving family. Her dad braced himself. Her mother looked up casually from the book, although it appeared she hadn't moved past the very first page. Torun simply rose and looked at her, the knowledge already burning in his tender gaze. Their connection would see them through anything. Any tragedy, any triumph, and any ordinary day in between.

"Mom." She swallowed. "Dad, Torun. You will never believe this. I'm—"

Her mother screamed and tossed the book over the railing. Her dad staggered and had to sit down. Torun smiled at her, steady and proud in his love.

Lucy's announcement rang out from that small boat. Her family raced to her and danced her around, hugging and crying. Then it crossed the entire ocean, all of the oceans, and changed the world.

———

DEAR READER,

Thanks so much for reading! The next book in the

series features Elyssa and the mysterious King Kadir in *Sacrificed to the Sea Lord*.

Would you like more mer shifter goodness? Join my newsletter and receive bonuses full of yummy mer warriors + the women who tame them. It's like the happy ending to the happy ending.

Subscribe here: http://smarturl.it/StarlaNewsletter

See you next time!

Sincerely,

Starla

ABOUT THE AUTHOR

USA Today bestselling author Starla Night was born on a hot July at midnight. She hikes, scuba dives, and swims naked in the ocean. She writes about smokin' hot dragons and tattooed mermen at StarlaNight.com.